BLIND
SPOT

Thanks Joan!

BLIND SPOT

A MIKE O'SHEA NOVEL

DESMOND P. RYAN

LEVEL
BEST BOOKS

First published by Level Best Books 2024

Copyright © 2024 by Desmond P Ryan

Author Photo Credit: Desmond Ryan

First edition

ISBN: 978-1-68512-629-2

Cover art by Level Best Designs

This book was professionally typeset on Reedsy.
Find out more at reedsy.com

To those who have the courage to become who they truly are.

Praise for Blind Spot

"A police procedural with heart! The fourth installment of the Mike O'Shea series finds the weary detective grappling with the retirement of a beloved partner, a new partner (a transgender cop handled with grace and flashes of humor), death of a potential love interest and the reappearance of the shadowy figure who may be responsible for the murder of his former partner. All told with wit, realism and a touch of melancholy. A must read! Ryan's Michael O'Shea is a remarkable creation—a flawed man whose integrity never waivers and whose dedication as a police detective has cost him dearly. His determination to track down the killer of his former partner takes its toll on his family, colleagues and above all, himself. Realistic dialogue and characters who feel like close friends make this a worthy addition to the series."—Blair Keetch, author, winner of *Best Emerging Crime Writer*, shortlisted for Crime Writers of Canada's *Award of Excellence*, contributor to numerous short-story publications

"Drawing from his experience on the Toronto force, Desmond P. Ryan delivers an immersive reading experience. Strap yourself in and ride shotgun with Detective O'Shea in this gritty police procedural as he navigates the city streets in search of a killer.

Blind Spot delves into the professional and personal life of Mike O'Shea during his investigation of a prostitute's horrific death. Haunted by the memory of his former partner's murder years ago as well as his own near-demise, and now dealing with his current partner's retirement, Mike adjusts to his new sidekick, Carla (formerly Karl). Tackling the issue of transphobia, bullying on the job, and mental health concerns, the author brings social issues to the forefront of Mike's work environment.

Fast-paced and well-written, with realistic cop banter and witty exchanges between characters, Blind Spot brings a touch of humor to the grim world of homicide. For lovers of hard-core crime fiction, Blind Spot delivers a real glimpse into the life of a city detective. Catch up with the rest of the series!"—Ivanka Fear, author of the Blue Water Mysteries

Chapter One

7:34 a.m., Monday, January 7, 2019

"Kinda surprised to see you here today," Mike O'Shea said, looking up briefly. He looked back at the screen in front of him and continued to type the synopsis for what felt like his millionth Fail to Appear charge.

"Where else would I be?" Ron replied sharply, taking off his trench coat and fedora. "I've got another four days to go before I hand in my badge."

He carefully arranged his coat on a hanger before setting the hanger on one of the arms of the coat rack in the corner of the grimy detective office. He then purposefully placed his hat on another arm that was much more precariously affixed to the rickety stand.

"I don't know. I kinda figured that you'd be just sort of making an appearance for the next few days."

"Really," Ron said.

"What are they going to do? Fire you?"

Ron sighed again and shook his head.

"You know, with all of the brains that developed this program, you'd think they'd have created an autosave." Mike pressed the SAVE button on his keyboard, then took a closer look at his partner. "And you're in a suit, no less."

"Uniform of the day for detectives, unless they've changed something since yesterday."

"Even with the fancy clothes, you look like shit," Mike said.

Of the two detectives, Mike likely looked worse. Between the nightmares he'd been having since 2005 and the painkillers he'd been taking since Mark Johnstone nearly beat him to death five months ago, Mike's sleep patterns were…what did the shrink they sent him to say…in an unhealthy rhythm that would be disruptive to his health in the long run. And it was starting to show.

Ron sank into the chair of his desk across from Mike's and took a deep breath.

"It was a long night. It's been a lot of long nights."

"I bet."

"They say she's not likely to…."

"You sure this is a good time for you to retire?" Mike asked, leaning in towards the screen to read what he'd just typed.

"Too late now. I've already put in my papers." Ron dragged the box that he'd scrounged from the photocopy room the day before out from under his desk.

"You could always pull them."

Ron didn't answer. Instead, he began piling years of memo books from the bottom of his desk drawer—items that should have been kept in the station's locked storage room—into the box.

"They'd pull them for you," Mike continued, tabbing and tapping as he filled out the checklist that would complete his disclosure package. "Extraordinary circumstances."

"Nothing extraordinary about death," Ron said, dropping a couple of books into the box.

"Unless it's your wife and it's aggressive cancer and—" Mike began, looking abruptly up at Ron, his hands still on the keyboard.

While the hair had gone gray and the grimace lines didn't ever go away now, Ron Roberts looked exactly the same as he had when Mike first met him more than a dozen years before. He had been a traffic cop and pulled Mike and Sal over while they were trying to keep obs on that hold house. If it wasn't for Ron—or maybe even Amanda Black—burning them, would

2

they have shut down that prostitution ring that weekend? And would Sal still be spitting sunflower seeds…?

"No. It's the right time."

"If you say so."

The two men continued working in silence, the only sounds being the tapping of Mike's fingers on his keyboard and the thump of the tiny books containing by-the-minute detailing of years of investigations being dropped into a cardboard box. Mike quickly looked over at Ron's hands—at the memo books he was packing up—and then back down at his screen, not allowing himself to wonder what he had written about that night in the burning warehouse. *If* he still had that particular memo book. Internal Affairs had seized everyone's right after the shooting. The content of Ron's memo book had been leaked to the press, but the media didn't pick up on it. Ron had done everything by the book. Even Janelle Austin wouldn't touch it. Which is why Ron was able to move on. The notes Mike gave to Internal Affairs were also clean, but he had another set at home that he kept adding to.

"Want to grab a coffee?" Ron finally said.

"Give me a second," Mike replied, pressing a key that sent the disclosure package off to the courthouse. "And sure. I'll grab the car keys. Meet you out front?"

"Car fire down by the lake. They're calling for a D," one of the uniformed officers said from the hallway before making his way to the back doors of the station to the parking lot. "Just giving you a heads-up. Got no details. Just going to the back for a smoke."

Despite the city by-law prohibiting smoking within thirty feet of a municipal building, most of the guys just ducked out the back for a smoke, especially when it looked like snow. Like it did this morning.

"Well, there goes that idea," Ron said.

"We could always grab one on the way," Mike pointed out, stretching as he got up from one of the better chairs in the office that made its rounds as required.

Superintendent Paul Landon poked his head into the office. "Ah, Detectives O'Shea and Roberts. Just the fellows I wanted to talk to. Our newest detective is waiting in my office. See you in about five minutes?" He inhaled, then stepped back out into the hallway. "And remind me to tell the cleaners that they need to give this place a wash on weekends, too. Or at least open the windows."

"Painted shut. Likely about three paint jobs ago," Ron said.

"I'll be glad when we get to the new station, then," said the unit commander.

"New station, same smell," Mike said. His head was beginning to pound. He reached into his pants pocket for the tin case that held the oxys the doctor said he shouldn't need anymore and gave it a little shake. Just knowing that they were there sometimes made him feel better.

"In five, gents."

"I think we'll be needed on the road, sir. Something about a car fire," Ron said.

"I'm sure the fire department can handle it until you get there. Five minutes."

"So much for coffee," Mike said from the doorway, watching as the unit commander walked up the hallway towards the front of the police station. "If they didn't beat it out of him in senior officer training, I bet Landon would whistle and skip around the station."

"I don't think they could beat it out of him," Ron said, continuing to shovel his memo books into the box.

"Someone from Homicide is likely going to want to talk to you about their investigation into Gregory Sanderson's death," Mike said, waiting for his partner. "If they don't hurry up, they'll be talking to a civilian."

"If that's the case, they can try to reach me at home, and I don't intend on opening the door to anyone," Ron said. "Regardless, Sanderson's death is suspicious at best. Given the number of kids he's done who knows what to, I doubt they'll ever figure out who killed him. He may have beat the system on your charges, but hell hath no fury like dozens of parents with a tremendous motive. In any event, not my case. Not my concern."

"I think he's tied to our human trafficking ring—"

"Your conspiracy theory, not mine," Ron said, smiling at the dates on one of the memo books before tossing it into the box.

"It's not a conspiracy theory. The consensus is that Sanderson was involved in that trafficking ring that's linked to Sal's murder and that Sanderson may have brought too much heat on the ring. It wasn't some vigilante parent group that killed him."

A gust of cold air came in from the back doors and wound into the detective office as that same officer brushed past Mike towards the front desk, thick with the smell of cigarette smoke. There was a woop-woop of a siren. An ambulance likely cutting through the alleyway that ran alongside the back lot. The cigarette smoke started to smell more like gunpowder. Mike looked down at the palm of his hands. No blood. He checked down the front of him, just to be sure. Nothing. He reached into his pocket and felt the smooth sides of the tin between his thumb and index finger.

"Did you hear me, Mike?" Ron asked, tossing the last of the books into the box.

"Huh?"

"I said: Who's included in this so-called consensus? You, yourself, and all of your imaginary friends?"

"You're kidding me, right?" Mike said, jerking his hand out of his pocket, leaving the tin and the softening of the edges its contents promised behind. "A cop gets killed, every other cop in the city shows up at the scene moments later, and the fucker still gets away. *And* he's got one hell of an obvious scar running up both sides of his face and yet…no one finds him. Thirteen years later. Yeah. I think there's a lot more to this than Malcolm Oakes being the luckiest fucker on the planet."

Mike and his team had been close—so close—to busting that sex trafficking ring wide open. Malcolm Oakes and his crew were right there, within arms' reach, so many times. And, each time, it went to shit. He slipped his hand back in his pocket and rubbed the tin again.

"And you think Sanderson was involved?"

Each time, Chelsea Hendricks, the teenage girl whose disappearance had led to the creation of the project, and all the other girls caught up in the ring were stolen away again, shoved onto another corner in another city for another group of johns to abuse them.

"I know it."

"Well, it would have been helpful if you had used your telepathic investigative skills a bit more while we were partners," Ron said, putting the lid on the box full of memo books.

"We're *still* partners," Mike pointed out.

"Until Thursday, yes. After that, you've got a new partner." Ron looked down at his wristwatch. "Shall we go see the boss and find out how Karl's sex change thing worked out?"

"No, I'll just stand here and keep six for you," Mike said, rolling his eyes. "And I believe it's called *gender reassignment surgery* now."

"I am definitely retiring at the right time."

* * *

"Gentlemen," Paul Landon said, standing beside the round table that had become synonymous with warm-and-fuzzy-talk time, "may I present Detective Carla Hageneur."

Carla looked up at her two colleagues. Her dyed black hair was cut into a bob, although patches of the male-pattern baldness she had before shone through. Her face, though square-jawed, seemed softer, perhaps due to the carefully applied makeup. She was wearing a tailored dark skirt suit that minimized her broad shoulders, the sleeves leading down to rather large hands with immaculately manicured and polished blood-red fingernails.

"You look good, Karl," Ron said.

There was an awkward silence.

"That's Carla with a C," she corrected, her voice sounding slightly higher and much softer than Mike remembered it having been when she was Karl.

Ron's face turned beet red.

"So, are you back on full duties, or…?" Mike began as he sat down in one of the chairs the superintendent offered.

"What do you mean?"

"You know. Can you go out on the road?" Mike asked, rubbing the back of his head. *Shoulda popped a couple of oxys.*

"Oh, absolutely. Just don't expect me to chase after anyone. Do you have any idea how uncomfortable these shoes are? I think I'm going to go back to flats once the thrill is gone."

"No worries. My last partner wasn't much of a runner either," Mike said, giving Ron the side-eye.

"But I was—am—one of the best shots in the country," Ron said.

Mike's mind flashed back to the warehouse. The heat. The smoke. The noise of the fire. Ron taking a single shot, saving Mike's life but killing an innocent girl. Letting Sal's killer get away, taking Chelsea Hendricks with him.

"Speaking of that, Paul," Carla said, "I need to have all of my requalification records updated with my new name."

"Already done!" the unit commander replied with a triumphant smile. "We take care of our people here."

"Excuse me, but is this a private meeting?" Julia Vendramini called from the open door.

"Didn't I relieve you about an hour ago?" Mike said to the only female detective in the division before today.

"Just in time to go see my boys at the bakery around the corner to pick up some fresh biscotti. If you think I'd leave without saying goodbye to Ron on his last day—"

"He's here until Thursday," Mike corrected.

"Well, I'm not. Keith and I are going to Cape Cod tomorrow morning. Unless this turns into a blizzard. Snows every year, and every year I tell Keith that January isn't the time to drive down the coast. I just hope we're able to get back for…."

Julia stopped speaking, slowly bringing her hand up to her mouth, her eyes welling up.

"*Sono una tale idiota!*"

"I have no idea what you just said, but it's okay," Ron said. "I was telling Mike earlier that it's just a matter of a few days now. Marie knows, and she seems to like talking about who she hopes will be at her funeral. You and

Keith go. Mike will call you when the time comes."

"You know, you're still a part of this family, Ron. If you need anything..."
Paul said.

"Thank you, sir. I'll keep that in mind."

"Well, let's enjoy these," Julia said, placing a tray of espressos and a bag of pastries in the middle of the table. As she stepped back, she looked down. "Oh my god, Carla, where did you get those shoes? Are those Jimmy Choos? I *love* them!"

"Thanks. I really like them, too, but, let me tell you, it wasn't easy to find them in size 12—I mean, women's 14!"

"While you ladies are talking high fashion, I'm going to help myself to one of these. Anyone else?" the unit commander said, reaching over to open the bag of pastries.

"It was never like this in Traffic," Ron said.

"No, we went for breakfast every morning after all the rush-hour fender benders," Carla said. "You didn't know I was a trafficma—in Traffic before leaving the Dark Side to become a real police officer, did you?"

"Before everyone gets too cozy," the unit commander'ssecretary hollered from her adjoining office, "I hear them calling for the detectives. Sounds like a car fire."

"Yes, we know. I'm sure they can wait a few minutes," Paul called back, gesturing to everyone to help themselves to the treats.

"Suit yourselves," she said, returning to her Google search for cheap lawn furniture. "And can I leave early today? Supposed to be a snowstorm coming in."

"Boss," the uniformed staff sergeant said as he appeared at the doorway, his gut hanging over his uniform pants, gasping to catch his breath after running up the flight of stairs. "I need my detectives. They found a body in the car."

"Should I go, too?" Carla asked.

"You heard the man, Detective Hageneur ," the superintendent said. "We need our detectives."

"Biscotti?" Julia offered Ron as he, Mike, and Carla got up from the table.

"Pardon?" Ron asked, looking quizzically back at her.

"With just a couple of days left, I don't think you—" Julia said.

"Yes. I still have a couple of days left."

"I would ask you to stay inside for the next few days, Ron," the unit commander began, helping himself to a biscotti as he stood up, "but that would be pointless. What I will ask is that you go as an observer only. The last thing I want is to complicate your life—and mine—with some ongoing investigation."

"I'll see what I can do," Ron said.

Chapter Two

9:13 a.m., Monday, January 7, 2019

Despite being unmarked, the dirty Ford Taurus could be identified as a cop car a mile away by anyone except law-abiding citizens, who, unfortunately, accounted for most of the drivers on the road at this hour of the day. As such, Mike, Ron, and Carla found themselves stuck in the same rush-hour traffic as everyone else on a Monday morning. Slapping the cherry on the rooftop would be pointless, given that there was really no urgency for their arrival: whatever had happened had already happened. And it would likely have been an exercise in futility anyway. There was nowhere for the other cars to go on these blocked streets, even if they wanted to move out of the way.

"If I'd have known that it would take us this long to get down to the beach, I would have walked," said Carla from the back seat, carefully putting the toque she'd pulled from her purse on.

"If I'd known that it would take us this long, I would have grabbed that biscotti to eat on the way," Ron said, pulling his gloves out of his coat pocket and putting them on.

"And if I'd have known that you two were going to be such whiny babies, I would have left you back at the station," Mike said with a good-natured smile as the wave of relief began to wash over him, having popped a couple of pills before getting into the car.

"Sorry, Dad," Carla said. "Would you mind moving your seat up a smidge,

Ron? I can't feel my legs anymore."

"Your legs?" Ron said as the seat slid forward. "I'm surprised you can still feel your feet with those shoes on."

"I agree. I think I'll switch to my flats tomorrow. I don't know how Amanda Black does it," she said.

"Years of practice, I'd assume," Mike said. "And she's only about five feet tall without them. I think she likes feeling taller."

"Boys, when will you ever learn that size does not matter," Carla sighed.

"Turn down here, Mike," Ron said, pointing to a side street. "It'll be faster. And you might want to wear boots tomorrow, Karl. Carla. No, here. Turn here, Mike."

"Trust a traffic man…" Mike said, winging the car down a tiny one-way street that looked more like an alley than a thoroughfare.

"If it was up to you divisional guys, we'd never get anywhere," Ron shot back as he pointed this way and that, directing Mike to turn again and again until he put them onto a street at the bottom of the district. From there, it was a straight run to their crime scene.

"I'm only going to say this once, boys, so, uh, listen up," Carla said, and then took a deep breath. "Thank you."

Mike parked the car without acknowledging her, his attention drawn to the crowd of uniforms standing around in a circle, billows of smoke rising from the center.

"Gang's all here," Ron said disapprovingly as he opened the door. He put on his fedora and adjusted it as he stood up.

"And he's off," Mike said, referring to Ron's habit of hopping out of the car before it had come to a complete stop.

"Where did that come from?" Carla asked. "I didn't see him with a hat."

"Have you ever seen him without it?" Mike said, turning off the engine and then reaching for a small accordion file that he'd jammed between his seat and the console. He got out of the car and walked around to the other side to hand it to Carla. "This is for you."

"What is it?"

"Don't tell me it's a Crime Fighting Kit!" Ron said as he turned back from the lake to avoid a bitter gust of wind. He gave a quick smile, recalling the identical-looking file he had given Mike on their first day working together.

"Maybe."

"No, seriously. What is it?" Carla asked.

"Okay. It's a Crime Fighting Kit," Mike said, handing it to Carla. She held it tight to prevent the wind from taking it down the beach.

"My legacy lives on," Ron said, his chin high in the air for a moment before he ducked down to keep the wind from grabbing his hat.

"Has property receipts, rubber gloves, a roll of police tape, some pens, and a couple of flash drives. One of them is loaded up with templates of all our forms."

"When I first came on the job…" Ron began.

"Jesus was in diapers," Mike cut in, rubbing his hands to warm them.

"You're not that far behind me, old man," Ron said. "Anyway, all I was trying to say is that I was told by one of the senior guys back then that no divisional guy ever had what he needed to do a proper investigation—"

"Well, this is just…swell!" Carla said, carefully opening the folder just enough to look inside.

"I don't recall *you* being that receptive when I gave you your Crime Fighting Kit," Ron said, looking at Mike.

"Yeah. Okay. Let's go see what we've got, shall we?"

* * *

The mostly empty parking lot was a familiar spot to all the officers in the district. They'd spent time there eating their lunches, having a coffee, or writing reports. By all appearances, it was in a deserted part of the beach at the foot of the district. In fact, other than being frequented by cops trying to get away from public view, it was occupied by dog walkers using the off-leash park nearby during the day, underaged drinkers later in the evening during the summer, and, after that, as a year-around haven for hookers and their tricks, as was evidenced by the numerous spent condoms stuck to the broken pavement.

This morning, the parking lot was occupied by a marked scout car, a pumper truck, and a lone vehicle that was blackened and still steaming. Two firefighters were by the truck, rolling up a hose. The remaining firefighters, along with two uniformed officers, were standing around the carnage, arms crossed, staring at what could have been mistaken for a torched sack of potatoes slumped in the front passenger's seat. Except for the clearly identifiable burned human skull on top. There was no doubt in anyone's mind that they were looking at the charred remains of a human body burned at a very high heat.

"Good morning, gentlemen," Mike said, walking a few steps ahead of his partners, oddly thankful for the heat from the scorched metal car frame.

The circle widened, with the officers, not taking their eyes off the charred remains, stepping aside to give Mike a better view. The firefighters looked back, but rather than returning their gaze to the scene, stared at Carla.

"Anyone here heard of a crime scene?" Ron said. "If so, I'm not seeing it."

"Yeah. We just, um, I mean, they just, um, got the fire out so—" Ricky Jergensen, the more senior of the two uniformed officers, began.

"So you better get your tape out and secure the scene, Officer," Ron said, looking over at Mike. Ron had a long history with Constable Jergensen that was not positive. Mike had a much briefer history with the constable, who had the dubious honor of being the only police officer Mike had ever knocked out cold.

"Right," Jergensen said, rubbing his thighs with his gloved hands to warm them. "Okay, guys. You heard what the detective said."

Jergensen's partner hustled over to the marked scout car along with Jergensen, but none of the firefighters moved. They all just stood there, staring at Carla. At 6 foot 4 without her heels, she was a very tall woman. Most of the women as tall as Carla in this part of the city were transgender sex trade workers, and there was no doubt in any of the firefighters' minds that Carla was a transgender woman. They held their gaze.

"You boys never seen a Coco Chanel suit before?" Carla said with a smile, and then looked down at the winter coat that covered her suit. "Although you could be forgiven for not noticing."

"Oh, we noticed you, Buttercup," one of the firefighters said. The others snickered.

"Gentlemen, this is my new partner, Detective Carla Hageneur," Mike said, setting his jaw. "Now, unless you want to spend several days on the stand in about five years' time explaining to a jury why you were in my crime scene, I'd suggest you go back to your truck. Now."

"I didn't know they were hiring he-shes," another firefighter said as they retreated to their truck, elbowing each other.

Mike opened his mouth to say something.

"Don't," Carla said. "They're not worth it."

Mike looked over at Carla, his lips and his fists tightening.

"And I can fight my own battles, Michael."

Mike hesitated, looking at the retreating firefighters, then at Carla, then back to the firefighters.

"Do you have any idea how much a heel to the head from this shoe would hurt?" she asked. "Especially a frozen one."

Mike dropped his head and smiled.

"Come on, partner" Carla said, giving Mike a poke in the side. "We've got some crime fightin' to do."

Ron, who had been examining the scene, said: "Except for this ring on what looks like the middle left finger, this is going to be a dental chart ID. Whatever the accelerant they used was, this fire burned hot."

"Hot enough to turn the body into a crispy critter, but not hot enough to melt a ring?" Mike asked.

"Yep. I say we step out of the area Jergensen will hopefully tape off sooner than later, give Homicide a call, and let Forensics work their magic."

"You're just saying that because you want to get back and have that espresso and biscotti," Carla said.

"No," Ron said abruptly, the lines on his forehead deepening even more.

Carla straightened her back as if she'd been stung by something.

"It's just his way," Mike said with a nod, blowing into his hands before rubbing them together. "Curmudgeon. That's why he's retiring."

"Do you want my help, or don't you?" Ron asked. "I can just as easily do nothing."

"See? Curmudgeon. Carry on, Ron," Mike said. "And as if you could do nothing."

"I'm looking around and not seeing any CCTV cameras. I doubt anyone is going to come forward as an eyewitness, and Homicide is going to take it over anyway, so I propose we make our calls from the car where it's warm and await further direction," Ron said.

"Works for me," Mike said, pulling the collar of his coat tight. "Let's go, team."

"Wait," Carla said. "May I say something?"

Mike and Ron looked at each other. The black waves from the lake were pounding the shoreline.

"In the absence of a road sergeant," she continued, pulling her toque down over her ears, "may I suggest we provide a little guidance to our uniform presence? They seem to be…lacking."

"That's one way of putting it," Ron said, glaring over at Jergensen, who was digging in the trunk of his scout car, presumably looking for yellow tape. "Have you got your Crime Fighting Kit handy, Detective? I think our divisional guys need some of that police tape."

Chapter Three

11:22 a.m., Monday, January 7, 2019

"What have you got for me this time, Crumply Pants?" Detective Sergeant Amanda Black asked as she passed Mike's unmarked car, her eyes on the smoldering heap fifty yards ahead of her. Mid-calf Sorels replaced the usual heals.

"You the only homicide detective in the city these days?" Mike asked, shutting off the engine before jumping out to join her.

"I wish. We're swamped. I'm just the lucky girl to be next on the board. And I stand corrected," she said, stopping to look Mike up and down. "You've certainly picked up your game since you and Bridget—"

"There is no me and Bridget," Mike corrected and then, motioning with his head, added, "We've got a crispy critter in the car over there. Likely murder."

"That's why I'm here. Homicide, remember? They don't often burn themselves, do they? And I thought you were gone," she said, seeing Ron get out of the passenger's seat.

"Not yet," Ron said sternly. "I've still got another few days."

"Good thing Carla's here to keep this guy in line once you go," Amanda said, looking at Mike as Carla came around the car. "Holy shit, you're tall! I never noticed before. How high are those heels? Of course, I'm wearing Sorels. Don't panic, detectives—I've got my shoes in the car. So?"

"Only two inches. The rest is all me."

"Well, there's not much of me, so I've definitely got to get higher heels.

And yes, boys, this is one of the only times where size matters. I didn't just say something offensive, did I? Who the hell knows these days. Okay, so who's the first officer on scene. I need to talk to him. Or her."

"Jergensen," Ron said, his mouth twisting in distaste. Everyone vividly recalled how, as an over-eager plainclothesman, Ricky Jergensen had almost single-handedly derailed one of Amanda's murder investigations.

"My day gets better and better," she said as she shook her head, not surprised to see him back in uniform—the standard punishment for up-and-comers who fuck up—but rather disappointed to find him at what was now her homicide scene. "You haven't punched him out yet, have you, Mike?"

"Not yet," Mike said, jamming his cold hands into his coat pockets.

"Good. I might need you to later, and I only have so many Get-Out-Of-Kangaroo-Court cards up my sleeve. I'm seeing by the footprints everywhere that the bucketheads have been here, and no one thought to…I don't know–tell them to get the fuck out of my crime scene?"

"Ron did," Mike said.

"I'm going to miss you, Ron," Amanda said, looking over at the burned-out car. She squinted as another gust of wind charged towards them. "Forensics on their way, I presume? Shit, it's cold down here."

"Yep."

"Road sergeant?" Amanda asked, walking towards the scene.

"None."

"Every case has sprinkles of shit in it. I get that. I accept that. But why is it that every goddamned case in this district is marinated in it?" she said, turning her back to the crime scene, the wind blowing her long thick hair around her face.

"I don't know," Mike said.

"I think that was a rhetorical question, Michael," Carla whispered.

"Thank god. Someone who understands subtlety. You and I are going to get along famously, sister. Now, is there anything that would ID the body?"

"Nope," Mike said.

"A ring," Ron piped up.

"Which is it, boys? I'm already not looking forward to the mess I know Jergensen has set me up for without you two adding to it."

"If I may say something?" Carla began, raising her hand.

"You're a D, Carla. You don't need to ask to speak. And never put your hand up, even if the knuckle-draggers from within try to say you ought to. You, of all people, should know this. Please tell me that didn't go with the…" Amanda looked below Carla's waist and then paused. "I'm treading on thin ice now, aren't I?"

"Four days," Ron muttered.

"I believe there was no road sergeant available because the call came in at shift change," Carla said as they all looked at the crime scene. "Which is not Ricky's fault. Having just come from uniform, I stepped in and helped him and his partner tape off the scene and told him to get the names of the firefighters who attended."

Amanda nodded approvingly.

"As Ron had suggested to Michael and me before you got here," Carla continued, pushing her shoulders back, "there don't appear to be any CCTV cameras, and the chances of an eyewitness are slim to none. Ron also noted that there appeared to be a ring on the deceased's finger which, and correct me if I'm wrong, Ron, is still on the finger?"

"Yes. I tried to see if I could slide it off with my pen—"

"For fuck sake," Mike said, screwing up his face. "That's disgusting!"

"And not a great idea, given that's what we pay Forensics to do," Amanda added. "You know better than that, Ron, or have you gone full-on Helpful Citizen already?"

"I was just trying to expedite things."

"Just trying to get a court card," Mike said.

"Hardly. At the four-dollars-a-day rate, I'd get as a civilian witness–"

"Gentlemen, please? I've got a homicide to solve. Continue, Carla."

"Well, all that is to say, we have very little to offer you."

"Thank you. I appreciate your candor. Translation for those of you with a lesser vocabulary: I don't have time for bullshit, especially since I don't have my partner today because he's in court. So, Jergensen. Where is he?"

Mike, Ron, and Carla looked around. The marked scout car was gone.

"I'd say he's back at the station," Mike said with a sigh.

"There goes my scene continuity unless I can consider you three high-paid help as securing the scene, which, apparently, you didn't do very well because you didn't notice the marked police car leaving. As I said, marinated in shit."

"Nobody entered the scene," Ron said firmly. "Nobody but us has been here."

"Okay. So get a uniformed car to sit here until Forensics tells them not to, which, judging by the scene, will only be a few hours. Once they take their photos, get the car and its contents towed to the coroner's office, and take a few more pics for posterity, the scene can be released."

"I'll call the front desk and speak to the Staff," Ron said. "The platoon's already short-handed, so he'll be glad to know his guys won't be tied up on this for too long."

"Are you with us for the duration, Carla, or just until...?" Amanda asked, watching Ron walk back to the Taurus.

"For the long haul, and very glad to be working with Michael," Carla said, smiling down at her new partner.

"About that—it's Mike. The only one who calls me Michael is my mother."

"Speaking of which, how is your mom?" Amanda asked. "I keep meaning to give her a call. I'm surprised she hasn't called me, to be perfectly honest."

"Sorry to interrupt, but our friends are arriving," Carla said, motioning towards an SUV with the local news station logos all over it pulling into the lot.

"That was quick," Amanda said.

"They must have heard Ron on their scanners updating the Staff," Mike said.

"Why would he use the radio? We do have cell phones, you know," Amanda said.

"Yes, I know. He doesn't," Mike said, and then, to Carla, added: "Curmudgeon."

The investigators all watched as Janelle Austin, the station's long-standing crime-beat reporter, got out of the SUV.

"I'll leave her for you to deal with, Mike. She's always had a soft spot for you, if I recall correctly," Amanda said, walking back to see Ron. "Oh, and can I have the car keys? I'm assuming you drove. Ron's probably freezing to death in there."

Mike tossed the keys to Amanda, while Carla looked at Mike, her eyebrows raised.

"No. It's not at all like that. I don't know how she still has a job, to be honest."

"Would it be wrong to say why I think she's still around?" Carla asked.

"Your guess is as good as mine," Mike said as he began walking towards the news reporter. Carla followed behind.

"Detective Sergeant O'Shea," Janelle called out, her hand, covered in a pink kid-leather glove, outstretched as she strode towards him. Her signature shapely legs were covered by a long Canada Goose coat that met the top of a pair of boots very similar to Amanda Black's.

"C'mon, Janelle. You know better," Mike said as she approached. "It's Detective."

Janelle took his bare hand in her soft, gloved hand, holding it for just a moment too long.

"Where's your partner?"

"This is my partner," Mike said, stepping aside. "Janelle Austin, Detective Carla Hageneur. Detective—"

"I believe," Janelle said, looking very closely at Carla, "we know each other. Your last name is very familiar, and you look—"

"Yes. We have known each other in the past," Carla said, dropping the unreceived hand she had extended to Janelle.

Mike glanced at Carla and cleared his throat.

"Not much to say on this one. Detective Sergeant Black is going to be the OIC," he said. "Might as well go back to your truck and stay warm. She'll let you know when she's got something to say."

Mike motioned to Carla, and the two detectives turned and began walking back to their car.

"Tara, get your camera ready," Janelle called over her shoulder. A very thin woman wearing layers of sweaters hoisted the video camera to her shoulder. "While we're waiting for Black to get her shit together, we've got another story. Get beside me. We're doing a walk-and-talk. Tell me when you're ready."

The reporter began walking in the direction of the two detectives. Tara hustled to get beside her.

"Go," she said, her camera focused on Janelle.

Janelle looked at the camera and then looked ahead of her just as a wind from the lake began to pick up again, causing Janelle's long hair to blow behind her. She looked back at the camera and began to speak.

"Being a cop is a tough job, and it takes a special kind of person to do it, whether you're a man or a woman. But what happens when you've been a woman trapped in a man's body, and you're a cop? At this homicide scene, I've got someone who can tell us. Detective Hageneur!"

Carla looked up over the unmarked car, just as she was reaching for the door handle. Mike, who had already sat down in the driver's seat, got back up out of the car. Seeing the camera, Carla dropped her hand from the door and turned away. She didn't want to get trapped inside the car. Mike quickly came around the car and stood just behind his partner.

"Shit!" she whispered.

"You don't have to say anything, you know," Mike said.

"Yeah. I do. I just didn't think I'd have to do it so soon."

Janelle had stopped about fifteen feet away, the car between her and her story.

"Want me to tell her to shut it off?" Mike asked.

"Yes," Carla said. "But don't. I can fight my own battles, remember?"

"Yeah, but—"

"This one, I think, is mine to take care of. Unless you want to talk about your lived experience as a trans cop?"

"Touché. But you don't have to talk today."

"Janelle," Amanda Black's voice cut through the air as she came up behind the reporter and her cameraperson, "I'm not quite ready to talk to you yet. If you want to take a few shots of the scene…well, you know the routine."

"Thanks, but that's not the story I'm doing right now," Janelle said, looking over her shoulder at Amanda. "Detective Hageneur—"

"Yes, it is," Amanda corrected, her voice firm. "And I don't have a story for you yet, so I would advise you to either take some shots of the scene and get back in your truck or just get back in your truck. Detectives, can I see you over here, please?"

"Excuse us," Mike said, walking purposefully around the car and past Janelle. "Duty calls. Detective?"

Carla took a deep breath and followed Mike.

"Jesus, can this day get any worse?" Amanda asked as she walked back to her car, the two detectives falling in behind like ducklings following their mother. "Don't answer that, Crumply Pants."

When they got to her car, Amanda turned and looked back at the reporter. "Listen, I need you two here as investigators. I know Janelle likes stroking your tender ego, Mike, but I need you to focus."

"It's not me—"

"See what you've got to look forward to, Carla? Subtlety's lost on these guys. Ixney on the Trans Cop Tory-sey. Unless that's what you want, Carla, in which case, not at my homicide scene."

"Trust me, Amanda, it is *not* what I want," Carla said, placing her hand on her chest as she took a few deep breaths.

"In which case, detectives, make yourselves useful. Go sit in your car and keep Ron company. I think he's trying to figure out a way to get that goddamned ring off of my deceased." Amanda looked over at Janelle, who was texting something while her cameraperson stood by, her window rolled down an inch or so. "I can see that you've got your footage," she called over. "I'll be ready to give you a sound bite in a couple of minutes. By your truck."

"I'd like to speak to Detec—"

"I'm the officer in charge of this investigation. If you have any questions, please direct them to me or my office. Detectives…?"

Chapter Four

10:34 p.m. Monday, January 7, 2019

"Look who the cat dragged in," Mike's mother called from the living room. "While yer at it, can ye let Wee Phil out? I'd do it meself, but, with me foot and all...."

The Jack Russell terrier bounced off Mary-Margaret's lap out the back door where Mike stood, exhausted from his long day.

"When is this dog going back?" Mike said as the dog skirted around his legs and ran into the laneway, tired of having his mother's neighbor's dog living at his house.

"When Sally-next-door calls for him."

"There is no Sally living next door to me, and this is the dog that caused your broken foot, so why is he still here?"

"Because I offered to take the dog for a while. And he never caused me broken foot: 'twas me own falling over him. And it's not ye who is keepin' the eye on me friend's dog, so stop interrogatin' yer mother. Now, I've got a plate made up for ye in the fridge. Pop it in the micro for—"

"I know how to heat up food, Mom."

"Look whose bein' narky and all with his old mam. Don't bleed on thems that didn't cut ye, lad."

"Sorry. Just a long day," Mike said, and then poked his head out the door. "Phil! C'mon, boy. Time to come inside."

"No, 'tis me who should be sorry. Ye have had a long day, and I should go easy on ye. Can I get ye a dram of whiskey to go with yer meal?" Mary-Margaret grabbed her crutches and hobbled towards the cabinet in the dining room that held the whiskey.

"Have a seat and tell yer mam yer troubles," she called to him.

"Ow!" Mike said, recoiling as he touched the hot plate in the microwave.

Mary-Margaret hustled back into the kitchen. She passed her crutches to Mike as she took the tea towel from the oven door handle.

"Here," she said. "Take these to the table there, and I'll bring ye yer supper."

"How will you be able to walk without—"

"Ach, the logic behind it is too complicated for me mind to unravel to ye in this moment, and it matters not, particularly if ye want a hot supper without burnin' yer hands. Now, sitcheedoon and tell me what's troublin' ye, me son."

Mike did as he was told, telling his mother about his new partner.

"So she's like Renée Richards, then."

"Who?"

Mike took two glasses and the bottle of whiskey down from the shelf.

"I don't have a problem with her having been a man—" Mike continued.

"And why would ye? Is it any business of yers? Sláinte."

"Sláinte. And no, it isn't. But I knew her before."

"Grand. So what I'm hearin' is that yer workin' with a friend. So what's the problem?"

Mike sighed.

"'Tis Ronnie retirin', isn't it? I know. I'll miss him, too."

Mike shook his head, looking at the glass of whiskey in front of him before emptying it with another gulp.

"Michael, I don't want to make a night out of this, so get to the point. What's the problem?"

"I'm afraid for her."

"Why?"

"I guess I just don't think the world is ready for a transgender detective," he said and then poured himself another shot.

"And since when were ye put in charge of what the world is ready for and what it's not?"

Mike looked at his mother.

"Listen closely, me son: God doesn't make mistakes, although I do wonder every now and again. Forgive me, Father," she said, looking up. "Regardless, every one of us was meant to be here, and every one of us was meant to do what it is we're doin'. Even the criminals. Without them, luv, ye'd be unemployed. So there's that."

"I hear what you're saying, Mom, and I agree, but—"

"Remember how ye felt about workin' with Ronnie back in the day? And did that change anythin' for ye?"

Mike fidgeted, recalling all the ribbing he took about working with a former traffic man.

"Was she a good cop when ye knew her before she became herself, Michael?"

"Yes."

"Is there any reason to believe that she won't be even better at her job now that she can be who she is?"

"No."

"And so, I ask, for the final time: what's the problem?"

"Thanks, Mom."

"Yer welcome. And shall I expect to see her at dinner this Sunday?"

"She's my partner, Mom. We're not dating."

"With the hours ye work, ye might as well be a couple," Mary-Margaret said, taking a sip of her whiskey. "And how was yer day otherwise?"

"We were at a homicide, so...." he said, letting the words trail off as he upended his whiskey glass.

"And I would know this how? Never mind. And, since ye haven't asked, Max, yer only child, is up in his room, likely watchin' somethin' inappropriate on YouTube. Be sure to go in and kiss him goodnight."

"I think he's a bit too old to have his father tuck him in."

"Is that so? Well, then, ye clearly have no idea that I used to give ye a kiss on the forehead every night after ye feel asleep when ye lived at home."

"I'm sure you did, Mom."

"And I've been doin' the same since I've been here. Now, eat up before yer supper gets cold."

Mary-Margaret finished off her whiskey. Mike reached for the bottle to pour himself another.

"If yer still takin' those tablets, Michael, I think ye might want to hold up on the whiskey," she said, giving him that all-too-familiar look. "I'm off to bed now, and I expect you'll be off shortly. Don't worry about the washin' up. Just rinse yer plate and leave it in the sink."

She gave him a kiss on the forehead before turning in for the night. He sat alone for a few minutes, looking at the bottle of Jameson, considering whether or not to pour himself another.

Shit.

Oct 31st, 2005. They were young, focused, and in a hurry to get shit done. Stupid. Robby Williams was the team lead, but Mike was the driving force. Or, at least, that's what he believed. Always in such a fucking hurry. Or was it because he was chasing Sal, trying to keep him out of trouble. Trouble? He was harmless. Just an eager young cop. It was Mike who was running too fast. And why wouldn't he? These were young girls. Children caught up in a sick Man's World. It mattered.

That afternoon. Just a door knock. That's all it was supposed to be. He and Sal and Julia and Hoagy had done it a million times. No forced entry. No foot pursuits. Just a door knock. Until Sal decided to chase after the guy that bolted from the apartment.

Fucking Sal.

Mike was too slow. He never caught up. At least, not in time.

Mike emptied his glass and took a deep breath. He could smell Julia's perfume. Armani. She never wore it again.

Did she ever get that coat back? Probably not. Probably in an evidence box waiting for them...someone...anyone, to arrest that fucker.

Without thinking, Mike poured himself another shot. And then another.

If I'd grabbed him before he jumped out the window....

Another mistake. They were supposed to stop the building from exploding, not get caught inside of it when it did.

*At least we got the girls out. Thanks Christ for Julia. Bucketheads would have
let me fry.*

He poured himself another.

*And Ron. Wonder if he sits alone like this. Probably not. Probably sleeps like a
baby. Weirdo.*

Mike looked at the empty glass and the near-empty bottle.

Might as well.

In his mind's eye, he saw Malcolm Oakes jump out the second-floor
window of the warehouse, pulling Chelsea Hendricks with him. He saw
them both disappear into the night. He remembered wondering what he
was going to tell her parents. How he was going to tell her parents. How he
told so many parents over the years.

You just do.

Both his glass and the bottle were empty. He stood up, waited a moment
to get his balance before taking his plate to the sink. On his way back, he
looked at the empty bottle on the dining room table.

Again.

He picked it up and put it back on the shelf before wobbling up the stairs
to bed.

Chapter Five

6:29 a.m. Tuesday, January 8, 2019

"Y ou can't sit there," Detective Russ McLean said as he looked over at Carla, the usually heavy bags under his eyes looking as if they'd been hyper-inflated overnight.

"Oh. Okay. Where should I sit?"

She glanced around the open-concept office as she picked her coat up from the back of the chair beside Russ's desk. The two sets of desks were arranged in groups of five, two facing two with one on the end. With only two or three detectives working at any particular time, barring shift overlap and overtime, there ought to have been lots of seating.

"She could sit beside Mike," Ron suggested, "but it would be a bit cozy with the three of us all at this cluster of desks. Why not—"

"Try over there. No one uses that desk." Russ returned his lizard-like gaze to the newspaper lying on his desk.

Carla looked over at the lone desk with the broken drawer in the corner by the coat rack. The bankers' boxes underneath and the piles of miscellaneous papers on top suggested that it was a relic from the past that was never picked up by workplace management when they delivered the replacement desks.

"But there's no computer on it."

"Not my problem if they're too cheap to give us the equipment we need to do our jobs," Russ said.

"In that case, you should have that desk, Russ," Ron said sharply.

"Fuck you, too, Roberts."

"Why don't you sit—" Ron began.

"I'm sure they'll give you Numb Nuts's desk when he finally gets the fuck out," Russ said, looking directly at Ron. "Shitty location, though."

"Why's that?" Carla asked, standing, coat over her arm, looking more like a lost tourist than a police detective.

"Because my back is to the idiot box," Ron said, pointing to the ancient TV sitting on a row of equally primordial filing cabinets behind him. "And, apparently, *some* people come to work to watch it all shift. Nice of you to show up, Detective O'Shea."

"Morning, fellow ace detectives. And Russ," Mike said, taking off his trench coat and tossing it on the empty desk beside him. "And, because you asked, Ron, I *was* here at 6, but got cornered by the staff at the front."

"What did he want?" Ron asked.

"He was asking about how things were going back he—" Mike cut himself off, trying not to glance over at Carla. He reached into his pocket for the tin. *Hangover or head injury? Hard to tell. Should be feeling better soon regardless.*

Carla straightened her back, adjusted her head, and plunked herself down at the desk near the coat rack.

"Is this one okay, *fellas*?" Carla asked, a plastic grin on her face.

Ron looked down at his pile of papers while Mike fired up his computer.

"Well, boys," Russ said, making a horking sound into his hand, "time for me to go. I got a couple hours and then off to court for some dip-shit sexual assault, if the fucking victim even turns up. Likely be there all day if she does. Anyone want to grab some breakfast with me?"

"Isn't it your responsibility to make sure she gets there?" Ron asked, his right eyebrow raised.

"Fuck that," Russ said, brushing his stained trench coat across Carla's back as he pulled it off the rack. "They're the ones complaining. Not me."

Russ pulled a package of cigarettes out of one of the coat pockets.

"You're not going to light that up in here, are you?" Carla asked.

Russ stopped, turned around, pulled a cigarette from the package, and put it in his mouth.

"What if I do?" he asked.

Carla raised her chin up even higher and cocked her head slightly, her lips tightening.

"Phfff. Fuckin'—" Russ began.

"You know," Ron said louder than necessary, "I'm not going to need this desk after this week, and the drawers are already empty, so if you have anything—paperwork, pens, you know—you can start leaving it here."

"Smell ya later," Russ said with a wave, shuffling out of the office with the unlit cigarette dangling from his mouth.

Ron stood up and removed a small key from the keychain in his pocket.

"I thought we weren't supposed to lock our desks anymore," Mike said.

"I keep my gun in the bottom drawer."

"I thought we weren't supposed to do that anymore either," Mike said with a laugh. "Are you sure you *chose* to retire, or has Internal Affairs finally caught up to you."

"I hardly think you're the one to ask," Ron said. "I can smell the booze—"

"Welcome to A Platoon," Mike said to Carla, shaking his head. "I can't believe they haven't fired him yet."

"Who? Russ? They'll never get rid of him," Ron said.

"Speaking of pots and lids!" Mike said.

"I'm a curmudgeon. He's..."

"A lazy prick," Mike concluded. "And the booze you smell is the booze I spilled on myself when I knocked a bottle...."

Mike stopped. He knew Ron wasn't buying it.

"And don't be putting your shit on my desk while you try to impress my new partner with your non-curmudgeonly behavior," he added.

"I'm putting *my shit* on Julia's desk," Ron said, taking the pile of files to the cleanest desk in the office. "By the time she gets back, I'll be long gone."

"You really like looking away from the TV, don't you?" Mike quipped, noting that the desk Ron had picked was behind his and faced the other way.

"No, although I don't have to look at you if I sit here," Ron said. "Which may also be why Julia chose this desk."

"You mean you're trying to wean yourself off of looking at my beautiful face every day," Mike corrected, relieved to have moved away from any discussion around his drinking. "And Julia likes the smell of my cologne, which is why she chose that desk as opposed to the one over there."

"Guys," Carla said as she draped her coat over the chair beside Ron's desk, "I'm not going to ask you this every day, but…how do I look?"

Mike and Ron stopped their banter and looked over at Carla.

"Not as good as some, but much better than most?" Ron offered.

"Yeah. I'd say you look okay. Why?" Mike asked.

She sighed.

"The Chief said this was a first for the service—"

"You spoke to the Chief?" Ron asked, scowling.

"He called me a couple of weeks ago. At home."

"As one would," Mike said, giving Ron a quick glance.

"He said it was a first for this organization, but it's also a first for me. And I'm scared shitless, truth be told."

Mike and Ron looked at each other.

"Oh."

"No. I mean…shitless." Carla repeated.

"I'm sure you've been through scarier shit," Mike said optimistically. "I mean, you've been on the job a long time, and you've had a life."

"And now I have a new life, and it's scary."

Mike looked back to Ron. Neither said anything. They both gave a shrug.

"I'm sorry," she said, dabbing her eyes with a tissue. "I seem to cry a lot now. They say it's the estrogen, and I'll get better at managing it. Right now, I feel like a pubescent girl."

Ron opened one of the drawers of Julia's desk, then closed it and opened another. Mike looked down at his keyboard, logging into his computer. Both studiously avoided engaging with Carla.

"Well," Ron finally said. "I imagine Amanda Black is going to have a group meeting at 9, after she briefs the boss."

"I don't think you have to worry about going," Mike said. "Do you want to come with me to grab a coffee, Carla?"

"I'd rather not," Carla said. "I mean, Ron might want to go, but I'm feeling—
"

"No. That's okay. I was just thinking…but no…I've got a ton of paperwork. It never stops. That's one of the things you'll have to get used to, Carla. It. Never. Stops," Mike said.

As if to confirm Mike's words, Ron began shuffling some paper.

"Good morning, detectives," Detective Sergeant Amanda Black said, charging into the office. She took one look at Carla and tapped on her own cheek.

"Oh. Right. Sorry. Mascara. I was just—" Carla began, taking her tissue out again to wipe her cheek.

"Talking about last night's game. Wow. Never saw that coming, did you, Ron?" Mike said.

"Cut the crap, Crumply Pants. I have to stop calling you that, don't I? No one gets it anymore. And put on more cologne or something, will you. You stink like last night's whiskey."

Shit.

"Oh, was that too close to home? Maybe we need to have a chat. Later. And I know that neither of you two faux athletes know anything about sports but I do know that Carla was crying so what the hell's going on here?"

Carla looked quickly up at Amanda.

"Honey, you're not the only one who has trouble keeping her face together once the waterworks start. That's why I don't wear mascara at work. The last thing you want to see is the officer in charge of your kid's murder with black streaks down her cheeks. The press would love it. Great photo op. But not very professional. Anyway, boys, stop making Carla cry. And get your shit together, Mike. And that's not why I came in here. All of you, in the Major Crime office at 9."

"Do they know you're having your meeting in their office?" Ron asked.

"*Their* office? Last I heard, this was a police station, and that room is a part of the building."

"I'll let the guys know," Mike said with a slight smile, slowly standing up.

"Guys? I thought they finally had a female officer in there," Amanda said.

32

"And don't tell me you're still taking those painkillers. Deadly combo, and nothing's worth it."

Mike sat down again.

"They do," Ron said, clearing his throat. "Have a female officer, that is. I mean did. And now she's on mat leave. I don't know if the two incidents are related."

"*Really*, Ron?" Amanda said. "And if there's something we need to talk about, Mike…."

The room suddenly felt very cold.

"I hear they may be looking for a detective to head up the unit," Amanda continued. "Might not be a bad career move, Carla."

"Oh, I don't think so," Carla stammered.

"There'll be enough people closing doors for you without you closing them yourself," Amanda said, strutting out of the office. "Nine o'clock. Across the hall. Don't be late."

Chapter Six

"Good morning, detectives," Amanda said, her eyes darting around the room, trying to match the posters on the walls—all of which varied in their levels of political incorrectness—with the MCU member likely responsible for it. "For those of you who don't know me, I'm Detective Sergeant Amanda Black from Homicide, and I am the lead investigator on the latest homicide to have occurred in your division."

As expected, there was no response from Ricky Jergensen, his partner, or any of the handful of bleary-eyed investigators, who, aside from Mike and Carla and one youthful-looking officer, looked as if they'd slept in their clothes for the past couple of nights. Given their roles as pseudo-undercover cops, the attire of the latter made sense. The 1990s dorm look of their office, complete with a beer fridge, which most supervisory officers were afraid to look into in the event that they'd be required to take some sort of disciplinary action, did not. And despite it being a smoke-free building, Amanda was sure there was an old hub cap, a la 1970s cop shop full of cigarette butts somewhere.

"Where's Ron?" she asked, looking around the crowded room.

"Unit Commander told him not to get involved in anything, remember?" Mike said.

"But I'm here if you need me," a voice from the hallway advised.

"You might as well come in and bring your chair with you. You'll be more comfortable," Amanda said without turning around.

"And less weird," a particularly burly Major Crime officer with a long beard known as Billy-Bob said.

"I heard that," Ron said, still seated on his chair as he pulled himself in by his heels.

"Gentlemen," Amanda said. "And Carla."

"You had it right the first time," Billy-Bob muttered.

"I'll speak with *you* later," Amanda said, looking directly at Billy-Bob. "And anyone else who interferes with my investigation, or anyone involved in it."

For several moments, a phone ringing out at the front desk was all that could be heard. The only thing moving were the officers' eyes as they looked from one to another. Carla looked down at her hands.

"Our deceased," Amanda said, finally cutting the tension, "has been positively identified as Lisa Clayton. She was known to police…."

Mike closed his eyes and didn't hear the rest. Instead, he thought of the last time he'd seen her alive. It was here at the front desk, right after Robby Williams's death a few months ago. And then he thought of her the first time he'd met her. She was a pretty young girl back in the day, newly scooped up by a pimp and too quickly swallowed up by the drugs. A series of arrests, releases, promises to turn on her pimp followed by months of being MIA. There were always reports of her getting cleaned up, followed by a series of chicken-shit arrests for prostitution, minor drug possession, assaults, and thefts. There had been a half a dozen or so calls from Family Services asking him to provide information for them to scoop every one of her babies up and away before she had a chance to hold them. And now this, just like so many of the others.

Fuck.

"I think she's talking to you, Michael," Carla said, nudging him gently.

Mike opened his eyes and saw that everyone in the room was looking at him.

"Sorry. What was that?"

"I'll be speaking to you after, as well," Amanda said, but in a much kinder voice than that used on Billy-Bob. "You and Detective Hageneur will be doing my background check on our victim—"

"Lisa," Mike said.

"Yes, Lisa," Amanda acquiesced. "I want to know everything about her: who she knew, how she made her money—"

"I think we already know that, don't we, Detective Sergeant?" Billy-Bob said, suppressing a smirk.

"Who her johns were, who her pimp was, and, given your background with…Lisa, I'd like you to be a part of the family liaison process. In the meantime, I want the rest of you," Amanda looked at the scraggly investigators, "to grab all of the video footage—"

"There won't be any," the young-looking officer piped up.

"For all of the routes leading to the crime scene," Amanda continued, looking directly at that officer. "I remember you from the last investigation I had here. You're a computer guy, aren't you?"

"I wouldn't exactly say—"

"Yeah, he is. Admit it, Nerdster. Yer a geek, and we love ya for it." Billy-Bob leaned over and gave the now-blushing thin man a huge bear hug.

"Yes. I recall that now. What's your name?"

"Theodore Weinstalk, ma'am," he said, shaking his partner off of him.

"Right. So you're in charge of going through all of those videos to pick out the license plates of the cars, Theodore, and to see if we can get clear shots of anyone on foot."

A hum of *ooooo*'s echoed through the room.

"Ya never learn, do ya, Nerdster? Keep yer fuckin' head down and yer mouth shut!" Billy-Bob laughed.

"I said 'in charge of.' I didn't say do it alone," Amanda said. "Get those plates, find out who they belong to, and contact the owners. Everyone here is going to help you. I want to know who these people are and why they were there. Same with the stills. If you can ID the faces, I want you to interview them."

"A lot of people use that beach for legitimate reasons," Jergensen advised.

"Yes, they do, and those will be the easy interviews. And there's a lot who don't. Those are likely the people I want to hear from, but you're going to get both. Theodore, you'll be in charge of figuring that all out. I want a daily report."

"My, uh, friends call me Ted," the young officer said.

"Junior man becomes the boss," Billy-Bob snickered.

"There is no rank in Homicide," Amanda said. "Except mine. Because someone has to put it all together, and that's me. And thank you for that information, Theodore. If we ever become friends, I'll keep that in mind. Now, where's my foot patrol sergeant?"

Everyone looked around the room.

"You see, Carla? Ever since you left, the place has gone to hell in a handbasket." Amanda waited a moment, as if the sergeant would magically appear.

"Maybe we can help you out, boss," Jergensen said.

"Oh. Right. I forgot about you," Amanda said. "Given how you managed the crime scene, I'd prefer you do nothing but, in the absence of a foot patrol, I'll have you and your partner canvas the corner where Lisa was known to work once we get that established."

Mike rubbed his forehead while sighing heavily.

"On second thought," Amanda said, glancing quickly at Mike, now vividly recalling how Jergensen almost sewered the last investigation they had together, "I suspect you and your partner are needed on the road. I'll wait until I can get some foot patrol officers. Thank you for your time, gentlemen."

"Suit yourself," Jergensen said, picking something out of his molar as he turned on his heels and sauntered out of the room, his partner in tow.

"Ron, since you were a traffic man back in the day—" Amanda continued.

"Still am," Ron said.

"You can take the man out of Traffic, but you can't take the Traffic out of the man," everyone in the room said in unison.

"Yes, well…" Amanda sighed, "given that you're so keen on joining us, can you spend the next day or so seeing if the intersections had red-light cameras and how long they keep the data—"

"Six months," Ron said. "And I can tell you every intersection in the division that has a red light camera right now if you'd like."

"By noon will be fine," Amanda said with a smile. "And you can give that information to Theodore…Ted. You've likely got a contact with the city for those as well?"

"Yes, I've got it right here," Ron said, reaching into the breast pocket of his jacket for a little black book.

"By noon to Ted is fine," Amanda repeated. "How many days left?"

"Three days and counting," Ron said.

* * *

"Got a minute?" Amanda asked.

"Sure. What's up?" Mike said, looking up from his computer screen.

"A couple of things. First off, how well did you know Lisa Clayton?"

"What do you mean?"

"How well, Mike?" Amanda repeated.

"We never had a thing, if that's what you're asking."

"Okay. Just checking."

"I never had a thing with any of them. We were the Good Guys, remember?"

"Not all of the Good Guys were good, Mike. You and I both know that."

Mike looked back at his screen.

"I need you to go talk to her parents," Amanda pressed.

"Sure," Mike said, continuing to peck away at the report he was working on.

"You know them, don't you?"

"Not really. I mean, I did back in the day, but…"

"When I did the notification, they mentioned you by name."

Mike didn't respond.

"Second thing: I think you should talk to somebody," Amanda said with a sigh.

"Yeah. OK. Whoever you want," he said, fingers still tapping away.

"I'm worried about you, Mike."

He looked up from the screen but didn't take his fingers off the keyboard.

"You smell like you just crawled out of a bottle of booze, and I know you're still taking those OxyContins. If you want to flush your life down the toilet, that's your business, except I like you. A lot. And I noticed how you zoned out when I was doing the briefing. Which fucks up my business. And I don't like that. At all. What the hell's going on?"

"What? A guy can't close his eyes for a couple of minutes?"

"Stop, Mike."

"Phfff."

"How long have we known each other?" Amanda asked.

"Okay. You've got me. Knowing you for twenty years would push anyone to drink, but I'm already seeing some shrink—"

"Not the right one, obviously. Landon is making arrangements for you to see—"

"Whoa whoa whoa!" Mike said, arching his back in a stretch and taking a deep breath. "No."

"Dr. Shimner-Lew—"

"They've already sent me to see the shrink I'm seeing now, and they sent me to see someone else after Sal got shot."

"Consider yourself lucky. We're sending you again. To Shimner-Lewis. She's good. Very good."

"Don't I need to consent or something?"

"No. Not this time."

"Involuntarily? Really? I have a couple of drinks on my own time, close my eyes for a couple of minutes during a briefing, and now I'm being ordered to see a shrink? I know you're fascinating to listen to, Amanda, but really? What gives?"

"Dr. Shimner-Lewis is the new psychologist from the Officer Wellness Program and she does the debriefs for all of my guys. I want you to go and talk to her and get yourself sorted out."

"Pffff."

"She specializes in post-traumatic stress disorder and addiction issues."

"Come on!" Mike said, raising his voice. "Really?"

"Yeah. Really."

39

"And what happens if I go and she decides that I'm bat-shit crazy?"

"PTSD isn't "bat-shit crazy," Mike. In fact, I'd think you were kinda bat-shit crazy if—"

"Fine, but I'm not an alcoholic. Or a drug addict."

"Sure, but if it becomes a diagnosis, remember that they're looking for someone to lead the Major Crime Unit."

Chapter Seven

11:04 a.m. Tuesday, January 8, 2019

"Grande with oat milk, Michael?" Carla asked, looking over her shoulder at Mike.

"What?"

"Your coffee. What do you want?"

"Americano," Mike said, now familiar with the language of baristas and still preferring a plain coffee.

"And for a snack—are you an oat bar kinda guy, or do you want a cake pop?"

"Just a coffee is fine," Mike said, feeling a heaviness come over him as he scanned the overpriced shop for a place to sit. He felt the tin in his pocket. *No. Not a drug addict.*

"I'm just leaving," a thin thirty-something man with a robust beard said, Mac Book Air in hand.

"Thanks," Mike replied. He sat down at a table too small for much, feeling very old. And tired.

"If it was up to me," Carla said, setting the coffees and something that looked suitable for a bird to peck at down in front of them, "I would live on double chocolate brownies, but the weight just clings to me now."

Mike looked down at his coffee, noticing a trash can by the door with the colorful logo of the coffee shop on it.

"Well, partner," Carla said, raising her latte, "here's to us."

"Sláinte," Mike said, half-heartedly raising his cup.

"Anything I need to know about you? Any weird quirks? Phobias? Got any hiders?"

Mike gave a half-smile. Getting a new partner was almost like an arranged marriage: you generally had little choice of whom you got and you had to make the best of it for the sake of the family. In both cases, things could become pretty disastrous if the arrangement didn't work out.

"No. No hiders," he said. "I have enough trouble with women that everybody knows about without getting involved in some side hustle."

"And who would those women be, Mike?" Carla asked.

Mike stared at her.

"If we're going to be partners...."

"It's not that exciting. My mother. My sisters. Amanda. Bridget—"

"Calloway? The crown? Really?" Carla cut in.

"Don't get excited. We've just known each other a long time," Mike said, looking at his coffee. "And now you."

"Okay. How about phobias and quirks? I don't think I have any phobias, but I really hate small rodents. Rats, mice, gerbils, hamsters. Even the cute ones like squirrels and chipmunks. My biggest fear is finding a rat in my bathroom, so maybe I do have a phobia."

"Who sees rats in their bathroom?"

"You should see some of the places I've been looking at. I want to live downtown, but my god, Michael, unless you're willing to sell a kidney for rent money, they're dumps."

"They can't all be that bad."

"Ones in my price range are," Carla said.

"But you've got money."

"Had money," she corrected. "Divorce costs, honey."

"You're telling me."

"And, to steal the words of Miss Dolly Parton, it costs a lot of money to look this cheap," she said, drawing her hand out in front herself. "Not to mention these. Do you have any idea how much it costs to get a good set of boobs?"

"Uh, no."

"And then there's the clothes. I've had to purchase an entire wardrobe. This suit alone, Michael, costs more than our annual clothing allowance. And I've had to start from nothing. Shoes, nylons, underwear…and then I have to get the things I wear off-duty."

"I never thought of that," Mike admitted, looking around and noticing that more than a few people were staring at them. At Carla. "Didn't you have any of that stuff before?"

"I did. But my soon-to-be ex-wife threw it all out while I was in Thailand having my surgeries."

"That's shitty."

"Yep. And it gets worse, like when my police brothers and sisters at Internal Affairs began investigating me."

"For what?" Mike asked.

"Being a prostitute."

"Were you?' Mike said with a smile.

"Michael, if I was a sex trade worker, do you think I'd be looking at places that had rats in the bathroom? I'd be high-end, my friend. Now," she said brightly. "it's your turn. Quirks, phobias, …?"

I drink too much; I cry before I fall asleep if I'm not almost pass-out drunk— hence issue one—I like the buzz oxys give me, I've become intimacy-avoidant, and I'm afraid my mother will live with me forever. And I believe that it's my fault that Sal's dead.

"I hate the rain," Mike said. "And sunflower seeds."

"Why?"

"Dunno. Maybe I can ask the shrink at HQ that they're forcing me to see."

"Might not be a bad thing, Michael. I mean, to go and at least hear what they have to say."

"You, too? I want Ron back. He accepted me as I was. Am. Am still being."

"I accept you, Michael, but think of all the career shit you've been through. You were partners with Brian Salvatore when he got his head blown off. That's got to leave a mark."

The wound heals, but the scar remains, he heard his mother's voice say.

"I suppose," he replied.

"And then D/S Williams did a header in front of you. He was your boss, wasn't he?"

"You know more about my career than I do," Mike laughed.

"*Everyone* knows about that stuff, Michael. Don't you ever google yourself?"

"No."

"Just as well, if you're this messed up already," Carla said, finishing her coffee.

"Wow. That was blunt."

"If this crap hasn't messed you up, then you're *really* messed up."

"You been talking to Amanda Black?" Mike said.

"It doesn't take a homicide investigator to figure this out, Michael. You've had every career disaster possible."

"Working with Ron *was* pretty bad…"

"Michael," Carla said, moving the empty coffee cups out of the way as she leaned across the table towards him. "When Brian got shot, did you get any counseling?"

Mike took a deep breath. *Shit. Here it comes. Again. The loop that plays itself over and over. Shit.*

"Yep," Mike replied, his chest tightening as if he was gasping for air, as if he was running after Sal, down that stairwell into the underground parking lot again. He shook his head. "I was out looking for that fucker the next day. Had him cornered, but then the building we were in blew up and if Julia hadn't pushed past everyone and pulled me away from the wall just as it collapsed…."

Mike's words trailed off, his jaw tightening, and sweat beads began to form on his forehead. He remembered following Sal, while Julia and Hoagy stayed back to clear the apartment. By the time Julia caught up with them, it was too late. Sal was dead, chunks of his brains splattered all over Mike.

"Yeah. You need to see the shrink. When you get an appointment set up, do you want me to drive you to HQ to see her or can you make it on your own?"

Mike looked at his half-empty coffee cup as Carla picked away at the seed snack.

"Come on," Mike finally said. "Let's go do some police work."

He tossed both of their cups into the trash can by the door and then paused before reaching into his pocket to pull out the small tin. He looked at it, rolling it over in his hand for a moment, and then tossed it in the trash can as well.

Chapter Eight

12:27 p.m. Tuesday, January 8, 2019

T he skinny woman wearing baggy jeans, a sweatshirt whose color had long been washed out, and Birkenstocks with wool socks opened the door, her severely cut mousy-brown hair not moving as she looked them up and down. Mike held out his badge, his eyes glancing at the notice by the side of the secure entrance: *No Men Allowed*. The woman pointed to the sign.

"I'm Det—"

"Maybe I can help," Carla said, stepping in front of her partner, fumbling in her purse before pulling out her badge.

"My name is Carla Hageneur. I'm a police detective, and I'm investigating the murder of Lisa Clayton. May I come in, please?"

The woman looked up at Carla, paused for a moment, and then stepped inside the doorway.

"Sure," she said, crossing her arms as she stood with her back against the wall. She looked Mike up and down. "*He* can wait outside, preferably off the property."

Carla looked over at Mike, who shrugged and nodded before taking a step back.

"It's nothing personal," the woman said, her eyes softening as she looked him up and down again. "A lot of the residents are triggered by men in their space."

Carla stepped inside. The woman closed the heavy metal door and clicked the lock shut. Carla followed the woman down a brightly colored hallway into the kitchen at the back.

"Do you mind?" the woman said to another woman who was sitting at the large kitchen table having a cup of coffee.

"Don't even think of having that thing share my room," she muttered as she walked away, taking her coffee cup.

"I'm sorry about that," the woman said. "Rachel can be a bit…difficult…at times. Coffee?"

"Thank you," Carla said. "That would be lovely."

"I'm Jo," she said, popping a pod in the Keurig. "I'm the house mom, for lack of a better title, and, as you probably know, that's exactly what most of the women here need. Sorry. This is likely the best of the bunch."

"But officially, you're…?" Carla asked, taking the chipped mug from Jo.

"A social worker. One of two on staff during the day. There's three more on staff. One for overnights, two as fill-ins for the three of us for weekends or if we call in sick. Milk of sugar? We have no cream, but we've got—"

"No, this is fine, thank you," Carla said, taking a sip of coffee and then pulling her mouth away quickly. "Ooo, hot. Are there social workers here all the time?"

"Yep. Most of the women who live here have experienced quite a bit of trauma. Deb and I—we're the weekday staff—work with them to help establish daily routines that will make them feel more secure so that they can benefit from the counseling and other services the government provides for them. Or, at least, that's the plan."

"So this is purely a residential facility?" Carla asked, setting the mug down on the table.

"Uh-huh. We have twenty-six beds that are always full. We don't take children here, which means that most of our residents have hit rock bottom because they've had their kids yanked from them by social services."

"Lovely. Is there much of a waiting list?"

"Oh yeah. About two years' long now and the thing of it is, most of the women on the list are very transient by design or default, and contacting them to advise that a bed is ready is next to impossible, which means that, a lot of times, a woman will be next on the list, but we can't find her, so we bump her to the bottom and move on to the next."

"How long can they stay?" Carla asked, pulling her steno pad out from her purse.

"Policy states six months," Jo said, eying the pad. She paused for a moment and then continued. "But there are women who have been here for a couple of years. Deb and I pretty much go case by case. It's against the rules, but if a woman times out without reaching the level of independence she'd need and has no place to, we can't just kick her out, you know?"

Carla nodded.

"You're not going to write that down, are you?" Jo asked, looking at the pad again.

"No," Carla said. "I'm here to talk about Lisa. How long was she here for?"

"Hmmm...I think she was coming up on the six-month mark."

"And was she likely to stay on or...?" Carla asked, jotting down some notes.

"Hey Jo," a large woman wearing Doc Martens, black jeans, a black long-sleeved shirt with the top three buttons undone said from the doorway, "may I speak to you for a moment, please?"

"Oh, hey, Deb. This is Carla—"

"Yeah. Can I speak to you for a moment?" she said, loud enough for her gravelly voice to fill the kitchen.

Jo looked apologetically at Carla.

"Go ahead," Carla said. "I'm good. Thanks for the coffee."

Jo got up and went over to the doorway.

"Why are *they* here?" Deb demanded in a stage whisper.

"*She's* with the police. And she's investigating Lisa's—"

"You know she's a man, right?" Deb said, running her hands through her long, greasy-looking hair.

"I figured she was trans, but—"

"No," Deb corrected, looking Carla up and down. "She's a man. And no men are allowed in here."

"I know how you feel about transgender women, Deb, but this is not the

48

time—" Jo insisted.

"And you know the policy on men inside the residence, Jo," Deb shot back. "I've got a floor full of women upstairs who are on the verge of hysteria because you let this…this…this man in a dress into their space."

"I'd hardly say—"

"Jo, he's gotta go."

Deb stared at Jo, who glanced over at Carla.

"She's a detective here to talk about—"

"He," Deb corrected.

"She," Jo persisted. "And she's here for Lisa. I'm pretty sure that, if you let the women upstairs know why she's here, they'll settle down."

"I'll see what they say," Deb finally said. "But don't hold your breath."

Deb's heavy footsteps could be heard going up the stairs.

"Sorry about that," Jo said, returning to the kitchen table.

"Thanks," Carla said with a sigh.

"I *am* sorry," Jo said a little softer. "Even though our policy allows for anyone who presents as trans or non-binary—"

"About Lisa," Carla said, steno pad in front of her. "You said she was coming up on the six-month mark."

"Yes," Jo said, making herself a coffee.

"And?"

"We were in the process of helping her find her own place," Jo said, taking her mug over to the fridge to add milk.

"What does that mean?"

"That means she wasn't using or associating with known criminals," Jo said, settling back down at the kitchen table, "had plugged into social services for financial support, and was actively looking for employment."

"What kind of employment?" Carla asked.

"Well, as you know," Jo said, taking a sip of her coffee. "Oh, that is hot. You'd think I'd know by now, wouldn't you? Anyway, because of her criminal record, Lisa couldn't do anything with money or vulnerable populations. So, with limited education, she had limited options. But her family—"

"Family?" Carla said, looking up. *Never show surprise.*

"Parents. They were very supportive. I bet they're taking this hard."

"I imagine so. Was there any concern that she might be going back to…." Carla deliberately let the words dangle. It was procedure for the police not to provide incriminating information about anyone—victims in particular— and Carla was all about following procedures, especially now.

"Prostitution? No," Jo said, blowing over her mug before attempting another sip. "Since she got clean, her need for quick money diminished, which isn't to say that she didn't need money, but she appeared, to everyone who monitored her at least, to be out of that cycle of selling sex to buy drugs to be able to sell sex."

"Hmmm," Carla said, putting an asterisk beside what she had just written down.

"Why do you ask?" Jo said, setting her mug down and glancing over at what Carla had written, unable to read any of it.

"I'm sure I wouldn't be speaking out of turn if I were to tell you how and where her body was found."

"No. I saw that on the news. It makes no sense to me, either," Jo said. She looked down at her mug and shook her head. "She was so close."

"And she was living here just prior to her death?"

"Oh yes. I can show you the room she shared if you'd like."

"That would be great," Carla said, stuffing the steno pad back in her purse before taking one last gulp of coffee.

"Excuse me, Jo?" Deb said from the doorway. "Your friend has to go now." Jo looked at Carla.

"Nothing personal," Deb continued. "It seems the issue is more that you're a cop than—"

"That's fine," Carla said as brightly as she could. "I completely understand. May I call you if I have any further questions?"

"Yes. I'm sure that would be fine," Jo said, getting up to walk Carla out.

* * *

"That was quick," Mike said, turning on the engine as Carla closed the car door. "Any luck?"

"She was clean and sober, no known association with her past life, and, by all accounts, on the road to recovery," Carla said as she pulled her seatbelt over her shoulder and locked it into place.

"I guess you didn't need any more time, then."

"Well, truth to be told, I did get asked to leave."

Mike looked over at her.

"They didn't like that I was a cop," Carla replied.

"Oh."

"Apparently, the residents weren't too impressed."

"Well," Mike said, looking over his shoulder before pulling away from the curb. "I have to say, I was."

"Really?"

"Yeah. Can you imagine how that would have gone if I was working with Ron?"

Carla almost snorted with laughter as Mike merged into traffic.

"Seriously. I think our working together is going to go well."

"Thank you, Michael," Carla said, consciously refraining from giving his knee a squeeze.

Chapter Nine

6:25 a.m. Wednesday, January 9, 2019

"What's this shit on my desk?" Mike asked, seeing the pile of folders as he walked into the detective office.

"Once you get your coat off, I'll go through them with you," Ron said, sniffing the air as Mike walked by him.

"I don't think I want to know," Mike said, hanging his coat up. "And I'm fine, if that's what you were wondering. Anyone in the cells? Should we grab a coffee first?"

"No one in the cells right now, but I think we should go through these before we do anything else. And I was just making sure. I don't want you falling into alcoholism on my watch. Anyway, here are the dummy files for all of my ongoing cases."

"Why do I want them?" he asked, ignoring Ron's concerns.

"You likely don't, but someone has to take them over. I suppose I could give them to your new partner, but I kind of want you to look after them for me."

"You're not going to get all teary-eyed on me, are you? I've already got one partner who's prone to crying. I don't need—" Mike said, still staring at the mound of files.

"No, I'm not going to get all teary-eyed. I just want to make sure they're handled correctly. I'm sure Carla is a fine officer, but she doesn't have much investigative experience."

"If I knew you thought that highly of me—"

"What makes you think I do? You're just my only option."

Mike wasn't sure if Ron was just winking or whether he was staving off a deeper emotion.

"Okay. What have you got?" Mike asked, settling into his chair.

"The ones in this pile are likely going to be guilty pleas, so you don't need to do much with them. The crown will be asking for more disclosure for the ones in this pile," he said, pointing to a larger pile. "These ones here just need to be taken downstairs for filing."

"Before we get too involved," Mike said, pulling the keyboard for his computer forward, "isn't everything we need for the active cases in the system?"

"Sure," Ron agreed. "But I wanted you to have the dummies, for when the crown loses the witness statements—"

And so it went, the two men nattering back and forth like an old married couple looking at what remained of their relationship, Ron pointing out things that Mike already knew, Mike giving Ron the odd jab. More than the end of a very short partnership, however, Mike was beginning to see that he was losing another direct link to Sal. And a shot at finding his killer, although Ron had had never bought into Mike's idea that Malcolm Oakes was being hidden away somewhere to protect the increasingly retired or deceased cadre of senior officers that he was sure were profiting from that prostitution ring.

"And these ones over here," Ron said, pulling out a pile of folders from his desk, "are the cases where the accused is still outstanding."

"I imagine Carla will be taking it," Mike said, looking at his computer screen, scrolling through the lines of crown requests for further disclosure on his own cases. "Speaking of which, have you seen her yet?"

"Second day and already late," Ron said, shaking his head. "You're going to miss me, you know."

"Doubtful," Mike said, looking around the overcrowded office for a place to stash all of these files that were already saved electronically. His eyes settled on the shredder.

"I'll miss *you*, my friend. We've been through a lot over the years."

"Yeah," Mike admitted. In fact, he couldn't remember a time when Ron *hadn't* been a part of his life. A time when Sal wasn't...dead.

Just as Mike was about to say something, he saw Carla, looking the worse for wear, come through the doorway.

"Sorry I'm late," she said breathlessly, straightening the collar on her otherwise disheveled blouse. No Chanel suit and heels today. It was dress pants, flats, and a plain maroon blouse. "It took me a bit longer to get ready this morning."

"What happened to you?" Mike asked.

"Oh? My hair? I didn't have time to do it."

"And where's your jacket? It's getting cold out."

"Is it?" she replied absently.

Mike and Ron looked at each other.

"Okay. Listen. I—I—I slept in my car in the parking lot out back last night, okay? There, I've said it. Now, do we have anyone in the cells or—"

"What?" Mike asked, not believing what he'd heard.

"What what? I'm sure I'm not the first person to spend the night in their car," Carla said, flopping herself down at the desk by the coatrack.

"Yeah, but—"

"The friend who said I could crash on her couch until I found my own place turned out to be a crazy bitch and changed her mind. Abruptly. Okay?" Carla said, pounding on the keyboard to sign into the computer. "I called my soon-to-be-ex, and she said I could come over. When I got there, she started screaming at me, and she basically...no, actually... kicked me to the curb. I had nowhere to go, so I ended up where I did."

"Oh my," Ron said, looking down as he moved the file folders from one end of Mike's desk to the other and back.

"Shoot!" Carla said, the computer rejecting her password.

"Wow," Mike said, looking back at her.

"It was pretty ugly," Carla said, biting her lip as she re-entered her password, this time a little more gently. "I knew it wasn't going to be easy, but I didn't think it would be like this."

"So what are you going to do?" Mike asked.

"I don't know. I just…don't know," Carla said, visibly trying to hold back tears.

"Why don't you just stay at a hotel until things cool down?" Ron suggested.

"Because all of my credit cards are in my dead name."

"Your what?" Ron asked, tilting his head to one side.

"Dead name: the name I had before," Carla said.

"Oh."

"Good morning, Dream Team," Amanda Black said, striding into the office. "And Ro—Holy shit, Carla, did you sleep in your car last night?"

Mike shot her a look.

"Excuse me," Carla said, wiping her eye as she rushed past Amanda. "I have to powder my nose."

"What," Amanda said, "just happened?"

"Clearly, your investigative skills are exceptional," Ron said.

"What do you mean?"

"She got kicked out and slept in her car in the back lot last night," Mike said.

"In this weather? Shit!"

"Yeah," Mike said.

"Does she have somewhere to stay tonight?" Amanda asked.

"Dunno. She just came in," Mike said.

"If not, what are you going to do?" Amanda asked.

"What am *I* going to do?" Mike replied.

"Yes, Crumply Pants. What are *you* going to do? She's your partner, remember?"

"She could always stay at your place. You've got a big house," Ron said blandly.

"What?" Mike said, his face puckering like he'd taken a bite out of a lemon.

"He's right. You've got—"

"My mother, living with me, remember?"

"Then there'll be no question of any hanky-panky," Ron said, winking at Amanda.

"No. Just…no."

The phone on Mike's desk rang.

"Thank Christ," he muttered. "Detective O'Shea. How may I help you?"

"I take it back. Yes, Mom," he said, rolling his eyes at Amanda and Ron.

When he looked away, Amanda looked at Ron and made a drinking motion with her hand. He shook his head.

"Why didn't you just get Max to text me on my cell?" Mike said into the receiver.

"Good," Amanda said softly.

"Yes. I mean no. I didn't take him out," Mike said.

"He's still going to see the psychologist," Amanda whispered to Ron.

"That's between him and his new keeper. I mean partner," Ron said.

Mike hung up the phone.

"And how is your mother?" Amanda asked.

"Aside from a broken foot, she's fine. And what's between me and my new partner?"

"When did that happen? I really must make the effort to call her more often," Amanda said.

"Dunno. A week or two ago? A dog ran into her at the park or something," Mike replied.

"Good thing you're more attentive at work, which is why I'm here. I think Lisa's parents aren't being entirely truthful with me and I need you to talk to them sooner rather than later."

"I bet they're taking it hard. Unless something has changed, they're good people."

"All of my next-of-kin are good people, Mike. They just have incredibly shitty things happen to their loved ones. I need you to do some digging. I think they're holding back on me, and I have far too much on my plate to try to pull it out of them. Speaking of which, the Johnstone matter is coming up on Friday. There was an opening in the judge's schedule, and the case was getting close to clocking out, so the trial coordinator took it. Shit," she said, reaching around to her waist in response to a ticking sound. "Is that me?"

She pulled the phone off the waist of her skirt, checking the number before answering, "Fucking thing was on vibrate. Detective Sergeant Black. Homicide." She looked at Mike. "And I need you to go see the parents. Today, preferably. No, I'm sorry. I was just speaking to one of my detectives. What's up?"

Mike collected the pile of Ron's folders that were to go downstairs and began to walk out of the office.

"Oh, wait," Amanda called after him, momentarily putting her phone to her shoulder. "Don't go anywhere. I want you—the three of you—on parade at seven."

Amanda turned away to continue her phone call.

"For what it's worth," Ron said to Mike, "I still think Carla should stay with you."

"What??"

The phone on Mike's desk rang again.

"Detective O'Shea. How may I help you?"

"Michael, 'tis yer mother."

Mike rolled his eyes.

"Is everything okay?" he asked.

"No, 't isn't. Are we out of tea, or are me old eyes just not seein' it?"

"You called me at work about some tea?"

"Because if we are out," she continued, "ye might have said somethin' and I could have ran out and got a box but, as 'tis now, I've nothin' to give Max with his toast and, with him feelin' so poorly, I'm hesitant to leave the house to fetch any."

"I'll pick some up on the way home. Will that work for you?"

"Barely, but here we are. I've got to go now, me hands full with a sick lad, a wee pup, and now, with no tea in the house…."

"I'll see you this evening, Mom. Tea in hand."

"Barry's. It's got to be Barry's. No use bringin' anythin' else home."

"I know. I will have a box of Barry's tea in my hand when I get home this evening. Bye, Mom."

Mike looked at the receiver before setting it back in its cradle.

"And," Ron continued, "it would give your mother something to do."

Chapter Ten

7:00 a.m. Wednesday, January 9, 2019

"Room!" an officer called as the parade sergeant, followed by Amanda, Mike, Ron, and Carla approached the door to the parade room. A shuffle of chairs could be heard as all of the officers stood, hats on head, memo books in one hand, issued smartphones in the other with the elbow held up to expose the sidearms and other use-of-force options on their duty belts.

"Return," the parading sergeant said, setting two clipboards down as she sat at the head of the two large tables positioned to accommodate everyone. The officers put their memo books and smartphones on the table in front of them and sat down. Amanda, Mike, Carla, and Ron made their way to the chairs on the periphery of the room.

"Before we get started this morning," the sergeant said, "I'd like to hand the floor over to Detective Sergeant Black. Given that this is our first day of dayshift, you may be unaware that there was a homicide here yesterday. D/S Black has some updates for you. Detective Sergeant?"

"Thank you, Sergeant," Amanda said, walking over to the table. All eyes in the room were on her. "For those of you who don't know me, I am Detective Sergeant Amanda Black and, as the sergeant said, I'm from Homicide. And either you're a very junior platoon, or I'm starting to age exponentially."

Amanda smiled and glanced back at Mike, Ron, and Carla. The officers around her remained silent.

"Given your lack of response, I'm going with junior platoon, which is wonderful because I can impress you with my rank."

Again, the room was silent.

"The 7 a.m. crowd is always a tough room. Okay, getting down to business," she said, walking around the room, all eyes still on her. "Yesterday morning, a body was found in a burning car in a parking lot at the south end of this division near the beach. We now know that the victim was one Lisa Clayton, a career street-level sex trade worker. I'll have a picture of her sent to your smartphones shortly. Some of you may have had contact with her as a witness to other crimes or may have arrested her for minor criminal charges."

The detective sergeant stopped and stood near where the parading sergeant was seated.

"I'm going to ask you," she said, still standing but leaning towards the officers as if she was confiding in them, "to take your mind back to those times and provide me with photocopies of your memo books or any other notations you may have involving her. I am also looking for associated individuals and vehicles, particularly if they were not arrested with the deceased."

Amanda stopped and stood up straight, taking a deep breath before continuing, the room still silent, no one moving.

"I say that because, if they had been, then we should, and I emphasize the word *should*, have details of associates on the records of arrest that I'll be having my illustrious investigative team," she said, looking over her shoulder at Mike, Ron, and Carla, "sorting through for me."

The officers' eyes shifted from Amanda to the detectives and then back to Amanda.

"Don't look at me," Ron said. "I'm retiring tomorrow. I'm just here for the ride."

"Contrary to what he's saying, constables, Detective Roberts is likely the hardest-working detective in this room," Amanda said. "Thanks for the info on the red-light cameras. I've got my analysts sorting through it now. I sure hope you're passing on all of your contacts to your successor."

Ron gave a vague smile and bowed his head slightly.

"And that's another thing, officers," Amanda said, looking down at each officer, stopping on a young man who was yawning while wiping the sleep out of his eyes. "Oh, look…it's Sleepy. Wake up. You're on the clock. The taxpayers clock. And this is where it all gets real."

The young officer blushed.

"Sergeant," Amanda said, turning to the woman by her side, "I hope you don't mind me commandeering your parade."

"Be my guest," she said, not bothering to suppress a smile.

"Thank you. I'll get off my soapbox now and talk about what I came up here to say," Amanda said, slowly circling the tables again. "We do not, and I repeat *do not* work in silos. If you look at the missteps in any investigation, most of them boil down to the non-sharing of information. If you know something, document it and make sure that document makes its way into my file, either electronically or, if you're like Crumply Pants over here—"

"Hey!" Mike good-naturedly objected.

"Print out your document and put it in the box that's now at the front desk."

"I only do that for important information that I don't want you to miss," Mike objected.

"Do you actually think I miss anything?" Amanda said, stopping abruptly to turn to him and then turn back to the platoon. "Speaking of which, and, again, Sergeant, I apologize for taking so much of your time this morning and suspect that you'll be going over this as well, Detective Hageneur, whom I'm sure many of you know, will be replacing—"

"Impossible," Ron said, smirking.

"I stand corrected. *Will be filling the void left by* Detective Roberts," she said, stopping behind the officer who had been yawning. "While I will be physically in the building for most of the next few days, if you have any questions or concerns regarding this homicide investigation, please direct them to her."

"What about me?" Mike asked.

"What's that old saying: the best man for the job is usually a woman?"

Amanda said, continuing her stroll back to the front of the room. "And now, unless you have any questions for me... No? Then I turn it over to you, Sergeant. Let's go, detectives."

"Thank you, Detective Sergeant Black," the parading sergeant said, picking up one of the clipboards on the desk in front of her.

"You didn't have to say that," Carla said, once they were out in the hall, hurrying to keep up with Amanda. The sound of the sergeant assigning details to the officers could be heard in the background along with the occasional groan of disappointment.

Amanda stopped abruptly once they reached the stairwell. Both Mike and Ron, oblivious to what Carla was referring to, almost bumped into her.

"Listen, Carla," Amanda said sharply. "I've been doing this female cop thing for a long time. Since you're the new girl on the block in so many ways, I'm going to give you the same advice that I give all new female cops: take every advantage you can, every hand up, every handout. If they're going to give you some opportunity because they think they have to, take it, even if they whine about political correctness. You know why? Because we are *not* one of the boys. And we will never *be* one of the boys. Not because we're not as good as the boys or can't play as hard as the boys, but because they don't want us in what they consider to be *their* little club."

Amanda continued her descent down the stairs to the first floor, through the glass doors, and down the hall to the detective office, Carla following closely, Mike and Ron lagging behind.

"I may be speaking out of turn, and I apologize if I am, but I suspect that you'll encounter challenges that very few women on the job have," Amanda continued, seeing that Mike and Ron weren't in the room yet. "I've said it before, and I'll say it again: enough people will tell you you can't, shouldn't, don't know how, aren't qualified, and don't belong without you ruling yourself out or not stepping into the moment."

"Rise up," Mike said, holding his arm up in solidarity as he strolled into the office, having caught the last of Amanda's words.

Amanda shook her head.

"Did I miss something?" he asked.

"I'm here to solve a murder. I need your help. I don't have the time or, for that matter, the patience for any undermining of my investigation or my people."

"Someone's on fire this morning," Ron said, seating himself at his old desk.

"Carla," Amanda said, ignoring his comment and pointing to his desk, "sit there. Ron, move."

"Isn't that what I suggested yesterday?" Ron said.

"Don't care," Amanda said. "For whatever reason, it didn't happen. I need you—both of you—sorry Ron, but—"

"No offense taken."

"To be on top of this investigation from the get-go. Mike—"

"One time I come in smelling of—"

"I sincerely doubt that yesterday was the beginning and end of your problems, but it's certainly not my problem today," she fired back, not missing a beat. "What I was going to say is that it might interest you to know that we think our victim was in contact with Malcolm Oakes."

If time could stop for Mike, it did in that moment. Aside from his own voice, it had been years since he'd heard anyone say Malcolm's name. And now one of, if not *the* most highly regarded, homicide investigators in the city was saying it. And linking it to this homicide, the victim of whom was linked to street-level prostitution, which was linked to human trafficking, which was linked to....

For a second, he was there. It all came back: the smell of the spent gunpowder, the ringing in his ears, the weight of Sal's body on his own, the taste of his partner's blood, Malcolm staring at him as they both realized the killer's gun had jammed. His own gun, still in its holster. *Coward. Incompetent. Fuck-up. Loser.* Everything he'd heard said or written about him came back to him. He reached into his pocket for that tiny tin.

Shit.

"...believe that Mr. and Mrs. Clayton may have unwittingly entertained him at their home," Amanda's voice broke through, "which is why they aren't being as forthright with me as they likely otherwise would be. I know this is loaded for you, Mike, but you're also my best bet in terms of relating to them, okay?"

"I don't think he heard you," Ron said from the desk by the coat rack.

"Then you tell him," Amanda said. "I've got a call with the Chief scheduled in three minutes." And with that, she left the room.

"Are you sure you're okay with this?" Carla asked.

"While I'd hate to call myself a feminist," Ron sighed, "I have to agree one hundred percent with Amanda. Take whatever you can get."

"But I don't want people to think—"

"They won't. Because they don't. Think, I mean. Where are you going?" Ron said as Mike rushed out of the room.

"He doesn't look well," Carla said.

Mike reached the unisex washroom and pushed the door open, quickly locking it behind him, before rushing over and crouching down in front of the toilet and vomiting. He leaned against the wall for a moment until the dizziness passed, and then, before he could talk himself out of it, he began to weep.

"Michael? Michael, it's me, Carla. Can I come in?"

"I'll be out in a minute," he called out, his voice cracking as he cleared his throat.

"It's okay, Michael. There's no one else around. Just me. Unlock the door."

"I said," Mike began, his voice more forceful, "I'll be out in a minute. There's lots of washrooms upstairs."

"I don't need a washroom, Michael. I'm worried about you."

"Give. Me. A. Minute."

Silence.

Mike wiped his eyes with the heel of the palm of his hand and then stood up. He looked at himself in the mirror. The years were showing. The booze was showing. All of his pain was showing. He cupped his hands and splashed some water on his face, rinsing his mouth as he did so. He looked again. Still showing.

"Michael, it's okay."

For fucks sake, leave me alone!

"I'm not leaving, Michael. I'll wait here as long as you need me to."

"I'm fine!" he hollered through the door, anger rising inside of him. He'd failed his own little brother, and then he let Sal, who was like a little brother, get his fucking head shot off. And now he was rinsing puke out his mouth, emotionally jonesing for oxys, and hoping he had some whiskey at home.

And they tell me there's a god.

"I don't see how you could be, Michael. Amanda dropped a lot—"

"You're not my fucking therapist, so leave me the fuck alone," he shouted, fumbling to unlock the washroom door.

"No, I'm not, And, if your–fucking–therapist was any good, Michael, the boss wouldn't be sending you to see Dr. Shimner-Lewis. When are we going, by the way?" she said through the door.

Mike took a deep breath. And then another. He turned and took another look in the mirror.

Maybe there is a god, but you're not seeing him because you're in Hell.

Mike smiled, looked at his face again, and then, realizing that what was staring back at him was unlikely to change, reached over and opened the washroom door.

"There. Was that so hard?" Carla asked. "And you have a bit of... something...on your tie.

"Must have been something I ate," Mike said, flicking it off as he brushed past her.

"You okay?" Ron said.

"Peachy," Mike said, sitting at his desk, logging into his computer.

"Michael," Carla said, standing beside him, placing her hand over his. "Should we go grab a coffee?"

"Amanda wants you to talk to Lisa's parents," Ron said. "The sooner the better."

"But it's not even—"

"I'm sure they're awake," Ron said.

"Just because you wake up early doesn't mean that all old people do."

"I'd get over there now, even if it meant waking them up," Ron said. "You and I can go for a coffee if you'd like, Karl. Carla."

Chapter Eleven

8:27 a.m., Wednesday, January 9, 2019

Mike considered parking on the street but, once he saw the width of the semi-circular driveway, realized that he wouldn't be blocking in either the Range Rover or the sporty little BMW parked closer to the house by pulling up. And so, he did.

He rubbed his aching head and took a deep breath as he stepped out of the car. While he'd told countless people that their loved one was dead, Mike hadn't spent much time with family members afterwards and, he had to admit, he wasn't sure what to expect.

A shot of courage would be good now.

He looked at his watch.

Not even 8:30. Shit. Maybe I do have a problem.

He took another deep breath and pushed his shoulders back.

Oh well. It's Showtime.

True to Ron's words, both of Lisa Clayton's parents were awake. The front door was opened, and they were both standing behind it before his shoe hit the first step of the porch.

"Good morning," Mike began, stopping on the step, suddenly very self-conscious about the spec of vomit on his tie. "My name is Detective Mike O—"

"We know who you are," said a gaunt woman. Even at her advanced age, and considering the circumstances, the magnificence of her high cheekbones, haunting blue eyes, and tight mouth almost made Mike gasp.

"Won't you please come in," she said, stepping back, the thick-bodied older man behind her stepping back with her, like a shadow.

"Thank you. I'm very sorry for your—"

"Would you like a cup of tea, or are you one of those coffee drinkers?" she offered, revealing a slight British accent as both she and her husband turned and walked into the living room.

"I'll have whatever's easiest," Mike said, following behind, noticing the expansiveness of the house, wiping his tie as he walked.

"I'm sure Renata will make whichever you prefer, won't you dear?" the woman said, stopping the procession to address an elderly Filipino woman who seemed to appear out of nowhere.

"Of course, Mrs. Clayton. Would you like something as well, Mr. Clayton? You haven't eaten—"

"A cookie. Do we have any of those chocolate cookies that I like?" the man asked.

"I'll check, Mr. Clayton. And you, sir? What would you like?"

"A coffee would be great. Milk, no sugar, if that works?"

"Certainly. And I'll bring your pills, Mrs. Clayton. The doctor says to take them with food, so shall I bring you some toast?"

"That would be fine," Mrs. Clayton stated, moving them forward again, directing Mike into the living room. She pointed to a chair, not unlike the ones in his living room. Any and all similarities between the two homes ended there. "Sit down, Detective."

"Here, put this pillow behind you, dear," Mr. Clayton said as his wife also sat down, taking a pillow from the corner of the couch and placing it behind her.

"Thank you, Edward," she said, looking up at him warmly before turning her attention back to Mike. "Too many hard landings on the soft snow."

"Pardon?" Mike said.

"Skiing. We used to ski quite a bit. Lisa and I. Edward never did, did you, dear? Do you ski, Detective?"

"No. I never—"

"Golf?" Mr. Clayton asked. "You look like a golfer to me."

"No."

"Shoot?" He persisted.

"I try not to."

"Ride at all?" Mrs. Clayton asked hopefully.

"Ride what?"

Mrs. Clayton smiled uncomfortably as Mr. Clayton cleared his throat. Mike glanced around the room. His eyes were immediately drawn to the large portrait of a semi-nude, much younger Mrs. Clayton. Below were several randomly framed photos of a woman with a girl of varying ages in assorted outdoor apparel whom Mike assumed were Mrs. Clayton and Lisa. There was a conspicuous absence of photos of Mr. Clayton, semi-nude or otherwise.

"Ah. Thank you, Renata," Mrs. Clayton said as the woman set down a tray on the coffee table in front of them. The woman nodded and left the room. Looking at the tray, Mrs. Clayton picked up two pills and the tiny glass of water before turning her attention to Mike. "She's not a trained maid. She came to us as a nanny for Lisa. Originally, the plan," she laughed, "was to have more children, but we changed our minds, didn't we, Edward?"

Edward nodded as she swallowed the pills.

"Which is to say, Edward had a slight indiscretion about that time, and I didn't want—"

"I don't think we need to get into that in front of—"

"He came to find out all of our secrets, didn't you, Detective?"

"Not necessarily," Mike began. "I just…" He pulled out his steno pad.

"I'm sure the detective is interested in more…recent events, am I correct?" Mr. Clayton said, raising what looked like a child's teacup in his fat fingers to his lips.

"I'm here to find out who killed your daughter," Mike blurted out.

"Ah," Mrs. Clayton said with a slight smile. "A prudent man. You don't want to hear what led up to Lisa's…chosen profession?"

"If you think it's relevant," Mike said. "I'm seeing you've taken some pills, Mrs. Clayton. Are those a recent prescription, or—?"

"What do you mean by 'recent'?"

"I think he's now asking about your dependency on painkillers, dear," Mr. Clayton stated.

"I am *not* dependent. And how cruel of you to suggest such a thing, Edward. Especially at a time like this," Mrs. Clayton said, looking as if she'd been slapped. "I am, however, taking OxyContin for my back."

"Oh," Mike said, rubbing his hand along the outside of his pants pocket where he used to feel the tin containing his stash of oxys. *Jesus. Pot. Lid.* He cleared his throat. "How long has that been going on for?"

"Too long," Mr. Clayton stated.

"Oh, Edward. You know Dr. Manny wouldn't prescribe anything that wasn't helpful."

"You mean Doctor Feel-Good."

"Shall we talk about your double-martini lunches, Edward?"

"If I may," Mike cut in, "take you back—"

"Indeed," Mrs. Clayton said. "Where are our manners? Coffee, Detective?" She gestured to the mug of coffee on the tray.

"When was the last time you saw your daughter?" Mike asked, reaching down to pick up the mug.

"Last Wednesday, wasn't it, Edward? For dinner?"

"Was that here or...?"

"Yes. Here. I wanted to go to the club, but Edward—"

"Lisa didn't want to go to the club," Mr. Clayton cut in.

"And why is that?"

"Edward was embarrassed—"

"Lisa had a prior commitment that evening that limited our time together," Edward stated.

"A prior commitment?"

"Oh, yes," Mrs. Clayton agreed. "She had a date with the gentleman she'd been seeing."

"Hrumph," Mr. Clayton said. "Hardly a gentleman."

"Why do you say that?" Mike asked.

"Edward never liked any of Lisa's boyfriends, did you, Edward?" When he

68

did not respond, Mrs. Clayton continued. "Although I have to agree, calling him a 'gentleman' is a bit of a stretch."

"Stretch? It's an outright lie," Mr. Clayton said. "Although she wasn't much of a catch herself."

"Edward!"

"Oh, come on, Jean. Tell me any of the eligible men we know would be interested in her. She was a drug addict, for god's sake."

Mrs. Clayton looked down.

"At least she comes by it honestly," Mr. Clayton muttered.

"Can you describe this man to me?" Mike asked, his mouth getting dry.

"Tall. About your height. Likely your age. Very short hair. Bit of a beard."

"Do you know his name?"

"Marty…? Michael…? Matthew…? I'm not sure," Mrs. Clayton said, suddenly looking very tired. "I'm sorry, Detective. You're going to have to excuse me. I'm feeling rather tired. All of this—"

"Of course," Mike said, setting his coffee cup down, preparing himself to leave.

"No, please. Stay. I'm sure you have more questions and I'm sure Edward can answer them, can't you, dear?" she said, rising up from the couch. "I'm sorry. Renata…?"

Both men watched Mrs. Clayton slowly walk out of the room on the arm of the maid.

Mike cleared his throat and took a sip of the strong coffee.

"Bloody shame, that," Mr. Clayton said.

"Pardon?"

"Jeannie. And Lisa, of course, but mostly Jeannie. She's as hooked on those so-called painkillers as any of the addicts you deal with on the street." Mr. Clayton looked up at the painting above the fireplace. "She was quite a looker in her day."

"Yes. I imagine so," Mike said, looking anywhere but up at the semi-nude portrait of the old man's wife.

The old man's gaze settled on the plate of cookies on the coffee table.

"About Lisa…?"

"Ah. Yes," he said, taking one of the cookies. "A difficult child. Didn't sleep well from the get-go. Couldn't settle. Couldn't sooth herself. Honestly, I'm not surprised that she turned to drugs."

Mike's eyebrows rose. The old man popped the cookie into his mouth.

"Not that I'd wish that upon her," he said as he chewed. "Or anybody else, but she was just so damned...flighty. I suppose now they'd say she had ADHD, but back then, the schools didn't know what to do with her, and god knows she went to enough of them."

"Not a scholar?"

"Scholar? I don't think she ever learned to read. Not past a certain level, anyway."

"That must have been difficult," Mike said, looking around a room that screamed achievement.

"I suppose. We later found out she was dyslexic. Nothing they could do back then."

"But she went to private schools, I'm assuming?"

"The best. And was discretely asked to leave all of them."

"Because...?"

"These schools aren't cheap, detective. And the parents who send their kids to them aren't stupid. They want some sort of guarantee if they're spending tens of thousands of dollars on their child's education. At least, that's what it was back then. Likely hundreds of thousands now. And said child had better be able to go to the best foreign colleges and universities once she graduates from these places."

"What if the kid doesn't have the marks?"

"Exactly. Which is why Lisa was...removed from every school we sent her to."

"I don't understand," Mike said.

"Simple math for marketing, detective. If something doesn't fit the equation, don't change the answer; remove the part that doesn't fit."

"So, what was the plan for Lisa?"

"Plan? Jeannie thought she'd get Lisa married off to some eligible young man who would take care of her for the rest of her life."

Mike's eyes narrowed.

"I know," the older man nodded. "*Beyond* magical thinking. Which is why, I believe, Jeannie was so eager to pawn Lisa off on the first guy that came to our door. Unfortunately, that guy happened to be a pimp. And so it began."

"So you knew…?"

"Not at the time, no. As Jeannie mentioned, I was in a double-martini-at-lunch phase, which is to say, the business was going full-tilt and, in my business, advertising, that means working all day and showcasing your talents in the evenings."

"So you weren't around much."

"No. I was not. Sadly."

"When did you know that Lisa…." Mike said with a gulp.

"When it was too late. Do I feel badly, you want to ask? Like hell. Was there anything I could have done? I tried. Sent her to rehabs, had her locked up in a mental ward, sent her off to Europe for a while, but all roads led back to…here."

"Yeah. I'm familiar with that."

"Yes, I'm sure you are, in your line of work. Lisa mentioned you a few times to Jeannie and me, believe it or not."

"But this last time. She was drying out. She was—"

"Right back in the same damned place she'd been a thousand times. Complete with a pimp in the wings."

"What do you mean?"

"This *gentleman caller* Jeannie spoke of—he was a pimp!"

"How do you know?"

"I recognized him," Mr. Clayton said.

"Sorry?"

"Well, I can't say I recognized him for sure, of course, but I think he's the man who murdered your partner."

Mike breathed out and was unable to breath in again for what felt like forever.

"What are you talking about?" Mike said, finally able to suck in some air.

"Lisa followed that case where your partner got killed as if she was the lead detective. She's got every newspaper clipping, taped every second of TV footage. She's got it all upstairs in her room."

A tsunami of thoughts, questions, and emotions ran through him, but all Mike could say was: "Why are you only mentioning this now?"

"Jeannie thinks I'm crazy. Told me I was mistaken, becoming a part of Lisa's obsession about this business, but I'm a details guy, Detective. And I've spent my whole career in advertising, making ugly things look pretty. This guy was a very ugly man trying to look pretty. And he looked a lot like an older version of the guy whose face is plastered all over my daughter's bedroom wall."

Mike's brain began to spin a million miles a minute but was numb at the same time. Everything and nothing rushed through his mind.

"Did he have any distinguishing features?" he was finally able to sputter.

"Jeannie says she didn't see it, but I saw what he was trying to cover up with that patchy beard. Looked like the guy in *A Clockwork Orange* underneath."

"A Glasgow smile," Mike whispered, making a line in the shape of a smile across his face with his index finger.

"I'd bet my house on it."

Chapter Twelve

7:30 a.m. Thursday, January 10, 2019

"Aren't we looking all casual this morning," Mike commented as Ron walked in the office wearing khaki pants and a golf shirt. He looked at his watch. "Oh, and nice of you to show up."

"I was here at six, but the boss wanted to see me upstairs, and then the staff sergeant wanted to talk to me, and then—"

"Wowza! It's a wonder you have time for us little people on your final day," Mike replied, continuing with his typing. "If you give me ten minutes or so, I'll have this paperwork wrapped up, and maybe we can grab one last coffee together."

"Actually, I was hoping you'd come with me to take my uniform and equipment back to Stores. Where's your sidekick? Don't tell me the car she's been sleeping in got towed."

Ron remained standing in front of his old desk.

"No," Mike laughed. "She's staying with a friend for a bit."

"Another...what did she call the last one?...crazy bitch?"

"I don't know. She just said with a friend. And she's just in the can. Make yourself useful before we head out," Mike said, motioning towards a pile of papers. "Can you photocopy these for me so that we can get this guy ready for court before the late wagon gets here?"

"'And what was your last official duty, Detective?'" Ron said. "'The same as my first—photocopying.'"

"The circle of life. Here."

Mike stretched as he stood up and handed Ron a pile of documents.

"Good morning, Ron," Carla said as she came into the office, looking much better than she had the previous morning. "Don't you look all I'm-so-retired this morning. I'm surprised that Paul didn't take you out for breakfast,"

"He offered, but—"

"One of the boys!" Mike interjected. "That's you."

"No, actually," Ron corrected, setting the papers down on his old desk. "I just have too many things to do today to be spending an hour or so having greasy eggs and bacon."

Carla stood uncomfortably by the desk. Her new desk.

"Like what? Drop a pile of shit off at Stores and then...?" Mike began, his fingers busy on the keyboard, nodding to Carla, who then moved around Ron to settle in at her desk.

"I may have to duck out early—" Ron began, shifting himself out of the way.

"What? Say it ain't so!" Mike exclaimed, stopping to look up at Ron. "I don't think you've ever—"

"I know. But Marie—" Ron said softly.

"Shit. Forgot. Sorry."

Mike looked down at his keyboard and began to type again, noticing Carla looking over her computer screen at him.

"I mean," Mike corrected, "I wasn't thinking."

"Oh, Michael," Carla said, shaking her head as she went back to typing. "Hey guys, if I press Send, will this send the entire folder or just my document?"

"Don't press anything," Ron said, coming around behind her. "Let me have a look at it first."

"Thanks, Ron. I'm certainly the new girl in the office, aren't I?"

Ron stood looking over her shoulder, his lips moving as he silently read what she had written.

"I'd just change 'should' to 'at the suggestion of the investigating officer'," Ron said, pointing to the screen. "Judges don't like to be told what to do."

"Right. Thanks," she replied, squinting at the screen and then at her keyboard as she typed out the new wording.

"And you might want to consider getting yourself some glasses," Ron said as he stepped back. "You'll go blind if you continue on like that."

"I know. I will," she said as she placed her finger underneath the amended wording, mumbling it to herself. "Does that look right?"

Ron took another look and nodded.

"Send?"

"Send."

She pressed the button and she and Ron smiled with as much satisfaction as if they'd just created a masterpiece.

"And yes to the glasses," Carla said with a sigh. "Once I get my name change documents done. Which reminds me: I need to change the address they're to be sent to. Don't want my ex-wife to burn them or something. I guess I'll use the station address."

"No. Don't do that," Mike said, looking over at Carla. "You don't want everyone knowing your business."

"Know my business?" Carla repeated with a slight laugh. "Have you looked at me lately, Michael?"

"I mean, any more than they need to," Mike said, clearing his throat. "Use my address."

"Really?" Carla asked, putting her hand to her heart. "That's so kind of you, Michael."

"Your bar is pretty low, isn't it?" Ron said with a sniff.

"Sadly, yes," she said, popping another screen up on her monitor.

The sound of high heels on linoleum was heard coming down the hallway.

"Good morning, Dream Team. And—" Amanda said.

"I know….'and Ron'. Don't worry: this will be the last time you'll have to see my face."

"I doubt that. We live around the corner from each other, remember? Anyway, Mike, what have you got for me?"

"Uh…." Mike stammered.

"Mr. and Mrs. Clayton? Lisa Clayton's parents? My murder victim's next of kin? McFly?" Amanda said, giving him a flick on the side of the head.

"I'm just finishing this, and then I'll write up—"

"For fuck's sake, Mike! You spoke to them yesterday, didn't you? Yesterday morning? What did you do for the rest of the day?"

"Well, I—-"

Carla looked over her shoulder at Amanda, curious to see the look on her face.

"Please tell me this man is not your investigative role model," Amanda said, looking sharply at Carla. "Listen, Mike, before you do anything else, I want you to get me a copy of your notes."

"Don't worry," Ron said. "Carla and I can finish the paperwork for the body in the cells."

Mike typed another couple of words, hit SAVE and opened the top right-hand drawer of his desk where the steno pad he was using yesterday was.

The phone on Ron's old desk rang. Out of habit, he picked it up.

"Detective Roberts speaking…oh…right…okay…I'll send her right up." He hung up the phone. "That was for you, Carla. They need a female detective at the front desk."

"Sit here, Ron. Use my computer. I won't log off," Mike said. "Just in case they've deactivated your access already."

"But I'm still…"

"In name only," Mike said.

* * *

Because she had no reason to do formal investigations in her previous role as a foot patrol sergeant, Carla was unaware of how dingy the interview room would be. The walls, painted years ago in what might once have been considered neutral tones, were now dreary and depressing. The upholstery on one of the three wheely chairs by the metal table looked as if at least one of its former occupants had soiled themselves while occupying it. Had she known, she would never have brought the woman sitting across the metal table from her here.

After sorting out the antiquated recording equipment that had been allowed to deteriorate and then reading all of the mandatory cautions, Carla looked across at the woman.

"Let's begin with your name, shall we?" Carla said, pen already poised to write on the steno pad she had in front of her.

"I ain't here to talk about me," the woman said, her eyes darting around the room like a hungry rat in a cage, periodically settling on the camera facing her.

"I realize that, but—"

"Don't I know you?"

"Perhaps, but I'm not here to talk about me, either," Carla said. "Now, you told me that you knew something about Lisa Clayton."

"Oh, yeah. Lisa. Nice girl." The woman began to gnaw on her well-chewed fingernails, spitting out whatever pieces remained.

"So I'm learning," Carla said with a slow, deep breath, trying not to recoil at the sight of the tiny projectiles. "And you said that you saw her recently?"

"Yeah. The other morning—"

"This would be…?"

"I dunno. I ain't got no smartphone to tell me what day it is. That day she got torched."

"So Monday morning," Carla said, noting it.

"Yeah. Sure," the woman said, looking a little closer at Carla. "You ain't always been a girl, have you?"

Carla knew this would come up, but she hadn't prepared a stock response yet. Instead, she looked back at the woman.

"Not like I fuckin' care. Not my business. And I got friends working the street who are trannys. Good people."

Carla remained silent.

"So yeah, I seen Lisa the other morning," the woman continued. "We was both on the same corner."

"I thought she was getting clean," Carla interrupted, and then silently chastised herself for doing so. *First rule of taking a statement…,* she could hear Amanda Black's voice saying.

"Me, too. I was happy for her. Gave her shit for bein' on the corner. What the fuck are you doin' here, I says to her."

The woman paused.

"And she replied…?" Carla asked, deciding that she'd forgo Amanda Black's rule in favor of eliciting information from this woman. And not giving her a chance to focus too closely on Carla.

"Said she had a regular that she wanted to meet up with. Fuck me. If I was that close to clean, I don't care how much he was payin'. I wouldn't be out there."

"Do you have any idea who he is?"

"Yeah. She told me his name was Jordy."

Carla knew it was pointless to ask about a last name.

"I seen him around. While Lisa was gettin' cleaned up. I tried to kinda help him out, if you know what I mean. Not like I'd take another girl's regular, but, you know, business is business, but he fuckin' flat out said no, and then I didn't see him until that day."

"If Lisa had been off the street for a while, how did he know she'd be out this particular morning?"

"Could smell her? I dunno. Maybe she called him."

"Do johns usually give their numbers out to the girls?"

"Girls like us, you mean?" the woman said with a self-deprecating laugh. "No, but maybe Lisa had plans on moving into the escort business. She kinda had the looks, when she wasn't fucked up."

"What was her drug of choice?"

"Of choice?" the woman said, almost snorting as she laughed. "Whatever the fuck she could get her hands on. Before goin' to get cleaned up that last time, I think she was usin' meth."

"That would have ruined her chances of moving off the street," Carla said.

"Suppose. Anyway, this Jordy guy wanted her and, as far as I know, only her."

"Can you describe him to me?"

"Pfff." The woman leaned back. "Like every other guy. White, middle-aged, kinda ponchy in that Dad-bod kinda way. I seen a ring on his finger…most of 'em have one. Streetlight picks up the glint when they're circling the block. Clean-cut kinda guy, you know?"

"You mentioned that he was looking for Lisa when she first got off the streets, then stopped?"

"Dunno if *stopped* is the right word, but he wasn't comin' around my corner any more."

"And then he reappeared Monday morning."

"Yeah."

"And Lisa was there specifically to meet him," Carla said.

"That's what I said. Yep."

"And then she ends up in a burned-out car by the water."

"Life's a bitch, ain't it?"

"Does that surprise you?" Carla asked.

"Lady, when you been in this business as long as me, nuthin' surprises you. I seen more girls get killed or go missin' than you guys know about. I seen guys do things to girls that you could never imagine. Shit, I done things I didn't even know my body could do. And I didn't always get paid for it, you know?" She snorted.

"Can you describe the car this Jordy was driving?"

"I dunno. It had wheels? Lisa and me always had this thing where we'd write down the license plate of a car the other one was gettin' into, but that morning, bein' close to the end of the month, I really needed to get as many tricks as I could, so I was payin' more attention to the guys drivin' by than to where Lisa was goin'. And we both sorta knew who he was, so I kinda figured she'd be okay, you know?"

"I understand," Carla said.

"I mean, if she was new to the stroll, or just pickin' up for the sake of makin' rent, like me, I'd-a been a little more vigilant, you know? But she knew this guy. I mean, I practically knew this guy; he was that familiar, you know?"

"Sure."

"But fuck, you never know, right? You just never fuckin' know."

Chapter Thirteen

12:40 p.m. Thursday, January 10, 2019

"Just like that cup of coffee, eh, Ron?" Amanda Black said as she popped her head into the detective office.

"Pardon?" Ron said, looking up at her from behind Mike's desk.

"Good to the last drop. Today's your last day, isn't it? I thought you'd be packed up and out of here by now. Where's your partner and his...partner?"

"*I'm* Mike's partner, and *I'm* right here," Ron said.

"In about four hours, I'll be referring to you as Mr. Roberts."

"Until such time, I think you'll be interested in what I've found out about our burned-out car," Ron said with a sniff.

"I'm all ears, Detective Roberts."

"Car is registered to a Jordan Hawthorne. I've got his home address here."

"How do we know?" Amanda asked.

"I called Ident—"

"FIS. They call themselves Forensic Investigations Services now. Actually, they have for about five years. And, from what I saw at the scene, the plates on that car were burned beyond recognition."

"There are more ways than one to find out who a car is registered to."

"Once a traffic man, always a traffic man," Amanda said with a slight twitch of her lip. "I'm assuming you have an address as well?"

"Yep," Ron said, handing Amanda a printout. "Jordan Hawthorne lives at—"

"I'll see who's around in the MCU office and have one of them—"

"Already did, and a couple of them are on the address now."

"Good thing you're retiring, or I'd be thinking you were after my job," Amanda said with a laugh.

"If I had wanted to be in Homicide, I would have been there before now," Ron replied.

"I don't imagine he'll be there," Amanda said, ignoring Ron's comment as she looked at the clock on the wall. "If he has a job."

"He does. He works for the city. But he's been off sick for the last two days—imagine that—so I'm thinking he's likely at home."

"Do I want to know how you figured that out?"

"I am, at least for another," Ron looked at his watch, "three hours and fifty-five minutes, a detective. And I know how to use a telephone."

"Any priors?"

"Nothing."

"So we have no photo of him. Damn!"

Without saying a word, Ron pressed the print button on his keyboard and the sporadically operational printer in the office chugged out five pages. Ron got up, retrieved them, and passed them to Amanda.

"Where are these from?" Amanda asked as she looked at the photos.

"The first one is the photo from his driver's license. The next is his city ID photo, and the other ones are from yesterday's CCTV cameras near his home address."

"You have been busy, haven't you?"

"It keeps my mind off of things," he said with a sigh.

"Right. Your wife. How is—"

"A matter of days, they tell us," Ron said.

"So what are you doing here?" Amanda asked.

"I don't know."

"You're a trooper, Ron. And a helluva good cop. I'm going to miss you. Truly."

"It has been a long time, hasn't it?"

"Yes, it has. We've been blessed to have front-row seats to the greatest show on earth. Speaking of which, where is Crumply Pants?"

"Oh darn it!" Carla said as she came into the office. "Michael called to ask if we wanted a coffee. I didn't know if you wanted one or not, Ron, so I assumed you did, but I had no idea you were here, Amanda. Shall I call him back?"

"God, no. I have no idea where he gets his coffee—"

"We all tried to bring him towards the light," Ron said with a sigh. "Especially Julia."

"I know," Amanda said. "That girl has connections. So no, thank you, Carla. Every time I have a coffee that Crumply Pants has brought in, I'm in the washroom for an hour. Speaking of which—Crumply Pants, not the washroom—why is he out getting coffee? And where were you?"

"I was downstairs interviewing a sex trade worker who knew Lisa, and Michael just needed to go for a drive."

"I hope to hell he gets his shit together. Is he getting worse, or is it just me?"

"No, he's getting worse," Ron said.

"Talking behind my back?" Mike said, waltzing in with a tray of coffees. "Uh-oh. The Boss-lady is here. Who's in shit?"

"You know," Amanda said, "there was a time when we all worked together so nicely. Ron and I were just talking about that."

"And then one of us had to go get herself promoted and moved into Homicide," Mike said, setting the tray of coffees down on his desk. "Not my fault you let our side down,"

"Our side? I would think that Ron's coming from Traffic would be—" Amanda began.

"Easy on Traffic," Ron said. "That's where all the good investigators come from."

"So the tender ducklings from Traffic tell us when they first arrive in Homicide," Amanda said. "Regardless, Ron has a name, address, and a team on the address of the registered owner of the car."

"Look at you," Mike said with a good-natured smile.

"Jordan Hawthorne is his name," Amanda continued, looking over at Mike,

"And I'm waiting to hear you trump that."

"That would fit the name my girl gave," Carla offered.

They all looked at her.

"She said Jordy was the name of the john who picked Lisa up before she ended up dead," Carla said, eying the coffee on Mike's desk.

"Great. So we're in agreement on that one. What have you got, Mike?" Amanda asked.

Mike dropped into the chair at his desk. His face went pale and he felt like he couldn't get enough air. His ears began to ring. The smell of stale coffee was replaced by a pleasant fragrance from a long time ago.

And then he was back.

"There's no way they couldn't find Malcolm Oakes. No. Way," he mumbled.

"Did you say something, Crumply Pants?" Amanda asked, looking closely at Mike. "Or are you stroking out on us?"

"No, I'm good," he said, taking a coffee from the holder.

That fucker has been somewhere, hiding under the radar. A cop killer doesn't just disappear. Unless he had help because he knew something that would rattle too many cages—cages in high places. And what could he know? That the underage sex trade ring he was running was tied to some high rollers who weren't going to be exposed. And they held their claws deep into some high-ranking cops.

And if Malcolm got arrested, he'd sing like a canary.

"Ground control to Major Tom," Amanda said. "You there, Mike?"

"Yeah, yeah," he said, twisting his lower lip with his thumb and index finger.

"And...?"

He looked at Amanda, wondering if, as Amanda got closer to that Senior Command trough, she was becoming a part of it. There's no way she couldn't be.

"I'm not getting any younger, Mike," Amanda said.

"Sorry," Mike said. "What were you asking?"

"I wasn't. I was reminding you that you'll likely be on the stand tomorrow for the Johnstone case."

"Oh. Right."

Too vested. If she blew the whistle, she'd be back in uniform in the basement of the Property Office before they could pick up her company car. But....

"I need you to stay sharp. And I need *you* to tell me about the interview you just did," Amanda said, motioning to Carla as she turned and walked out of the office, already on her cell phone.

"Of course," Carla said, quickly grabbing the steno pad off her desk before following the sound of Amanda's stilettos down the hallway.

"You okay?" Ron asked.

"Yeah. Fine," Mike said.

"You just looked a little...absent back there."

"I guess. Sure. You still want to retire and miss all of this bullshit?" Mike asked, passing Ron his coffee.

"Too late to pull my papers now," he said. "But you just reminded me: I have a box for you at my place."

"What box?"

"Remember when Christopher Williams came to pick up his father's property?"

"Not really, but okay," Mike said slowly.

"And left a box from Robby Williams's storage locker here for you? And I took it home because you didn't want to leave it lying around?"

"Oh, right. Yes, I do remember that. And I still don't want it lying around. How about I come by after work today before your party to pick it up?"

"I don't think we're going to have time, so why don't we pick a day after..."

Ron didn't need to finish the sentence. They both knew how Ron measured his time now.

"Sure," Mike said and then took a sip of his coffee. "Man, this is shit coffee. Sal always got shit coffee. Remember that?"

Chapter Fourteen

3:02 p.m. Thursday, January 10, 2019

What are the chances that there could be two men out there with a Glasgow smile traveling in the company of sex trade workers? Zero. If he was going to identify Lisa Clayton's boyfriend as Malcolm Oakes, Mike had to be one hundred percent sure—beyond any doubt, let alone a reasonable one. A photo would be great but, given that Mr. Clayton didn't even know this guy's first name, the chances of there being a picture lying around the Clayton house were slim-to-nil.

Prints. Foolproof. And, if he'd been to the house, there would be some in Lisa's bedroom.

"Well," Ron said with a heavy sigh, breaking Mike's train of thought. "I guess this is it."

"What are you, a half-jobber?" Mike said, looking up at the clock. "We've still got another hour!"

"The boss is sending me home. It's been the pleasure of a lifetime, Mike," Ron said, his arm extended.

Mike got up to shake his partner's hand, but the two men fell into an embrace.

"I'm gonna miss you, you weirdo," Mike said as he slapped Ron's back.

"You know where I live. Don't be a stranger," Ron said, his voice cracking.

"Sure do," Mike said, clearing his throat as he stepped away. "And I'll see you tonight anyway. Try not to make an ass of yourself, okay?"

"I don't think I'm the one we need to worry about," Ron said. "And that box. Don't forget about it. After…?"

"Yeah."

"And maybe have a beer together as well," Ron said.

"For sure."

Before things could get any more awkward, Ron walked the few steps to the coat rack, removed his coat from the hanger, and put it on. He then put the hanger back on the rack and removed his fedora from one of the pegs. He put it on and, giving it a slight tug to one side, took a deep breath and walked out of the detective office.

*　*　*

Mike waited a few minutes before grabbing his coat and ducking out into the same hallway. Instead of turning right, as Ron had, he turned left to the glass doors that led to the back parking lot, his cell phone in his pocket.

Being close to shift change, the tiny lot was quickly filling up with marked scout cars driven by road-tired uniformed officers, many of whom acknowledged Mike with a nod or short comment. Mike nodded back as he hurried into the alleyway that led to Dundas Street, trying not to slip on the overflowing trash from the dumpsters or step in the potholes full of almost-frozen water.

Once out of the alley, Mike made a right and sat on a bench that happened to be in front of a half-way house for violent sex offenders.

If the public only knew, he thought, glancing down the street at the community center just over the hill and then to the public school across the street from it. *If the public only knew.*

He pulled the cell phone out of his pocket.

"Forensics, Detective Stewart speaking. How may I help you?"

"Just the person I wanted to talk to. I need a favor, Amy," Mike said as a city bus stopped in front of him and two men got off. He watched them walk up the stairs to the halfway house.

"Hey, Mikey! For you, anything," she said, her already chipper voice picking up even more.

"I need you to go to an address for me and pull some prints from a room," he said, squinting his eyes as he considered whether or not a headache was coming on.

"Oh, sorry, buddy. No can do. I'm on light duties. Broke my wrist last week so I'm on the desk."

"Ouch. I hope you at least broke it on duty?" he asked, rubbing the back of his neck.

"Naw. I was playing baseball."

"At your age?"

"I seem to recall that you've got a few years on me, don't you, Mike? Shouldn't you be looking for a permanent desk job now?"

"Point taken. Sorry." *Smart ass.*

"But I can get someone else to do the prints. Give me the occurrence number."

"I don't have one," he said, looking across the street at the old toothless woman flopped out front of the filthy donut shop, her hand outstretched as a greasy middle-aged man brushed by her and went inside.

"Come on, Mikey. You know we can't—"

"Yeah. Forget it. Sorry. I hope your wrist heals," Mike said, abruptly clicking the phone off.

"Hey, Detective!" the toothless woman gummed as Mike stood up.

"Keeping well, Delores?" he called back.

"Got any change?" she called back.

"Sorry," he said, scraping something off the bottom of his shoe as he walked back into the alleyway that led to the back doors.

"Asshole!" she shouted at him. He did not want to imagine the amount of spittle that would have spewed out of her mouth with that one word.

What a fucking life.

* * *

"I take it Ron's gone now?" Carla asked as she watched Mike come into the office.

"Yeah," Mike said, clearing his throat. "He's gone. Likely having a nap before his party tonight."

"Oh, right. I forgot. Which means I've got some bad news for you."

"What?"

Mike meticulously hung his coat on the hanger before setting the hanger on one of the functional arms of the decrepit coat rack.

When did I become Ron?

"Amanda wants us to sit on Hawthorne's address."

"Shit," Mike said with a protracted sigh.

"I know."

"Does she want a door knock or…?"

"I think they're working on a warrant," Carla said.

"I hope they type fast," he said, yanking his coat from the hanger.

* * *

The house that corresponded with the address they were given was unspectacular: a non-descript 1970s-build semi, low hedge that ran across the bottom of the neighboring property as well, a car in the driveway. But for the brightly painted yellow front door, this house looked identical to all the other houses on the street.

"You'd never think a murderer lived here, would you?" Carla said.

"We all have our blind spots," Mike said, pulling the car over to the curb. He cracked his window a couple of inches so they could hear anything outside better.

"I suppose parking a few doors down on the street won't be too conspicuous," Carla commented sarcastically, looking at the empty street. "I'll give the front desk a call with the plate and see who it belongs to."

"Hopefully, we won't be here long," Mike said, turning off the engine while Carla made the call.

"It's a rental," she said. "So I guess we just wait now."

"Yep."

Mike rubbed the back of his neck. He had almost forgotten how much he disliked doing obs, especially in the winter. It would just be a matter of minutes before they'd start to feel the cold. And the damp.

"Want one? They're Werther's," Carla said, holding out a bag of candies that she'd pulled from her purse.

"Sure," Mike said, taking one. *A couple of oxys would be better.*

"Any kids?" she asked, taking one before putting the package back.

"One," he replied, looking straight ahead.

"Boy, girl, or gender fluid?"

Mike looked over at her.

"What?" she asked with a shrug.

"Boy," Mike said, looking straight ahead again. "His name is Max, and he's seventeen."

"Tricky age. I heard you're divorced. Do you see him often?" she asked, looking at the house.

"Why wouldn't I? He lives with me. And my mother, who seems to have taken up residence with me."

"I've heard about your mother," Carla said with a smile, looking over at Mike. "I understand she does a bang-up Sunday dinner."

"Yeah. I'll have you around the next time—"

"There," Carla said, noticing a minivan pulling into the driveway.

They watched as a woman who looked like she tried very hard not to age got out of the van, flicking her bottle-blonde hair as she talked on the cell phone she held in one hand while unclipping one child from a car seat and shepherding the other two out of the minivan with the other.

"Watch for ice," she called, moving her mouth away from the phone. "And don't leave your mitts in the van, Olivia."

"What're we having for dinner?" Olivia, who might have been nine or ten, responded.

"I gotta pee!" a boy who looked about six said.

"Help your little brother," the woman said to no child in particular while she set the one she'd been carrying down, still on the phone, digging into her purse for keys.

"I have to bring cookies for school tomorrow..."

"I really gotta pee!"

"Ms Zimmerman said if we can't..."

The conversations continued as the four of them flooded inside the house. The woman closed the door behind her.

"Busy household," Carla said.

"Yep."

"I have two children. Had. They don't talk to me now," she said, staring at the closed yellow door.

"That must be hard," Mike said.

"Very. I've cried myself to sleep more than a few times recently."

Mike didn't respond.

"Do you ever cry, Mike?" she asked, glancing over at him.

Boys don't cry. The words came at him as cold and cutting as they had back then.

"I never cried as an adult until I started to take estrogen. It's very cathartic," Carla continued, looking back at the door. "I've got it fairly under control now, but those first three months. Oh my god, Michael. If you looked at me sideways, I'd—"

He remembered watching his father's coffin being lowered into the ground, his mother's arms full of the other children, he left standing on his own.

"Of course, I still cry more than I thought I would. Seems to be my go-to emotion. Whenever I get angry, I cry. I watch a sad movie, I cry. I see a cute kitten video—"

Then he remembered the look on Sal's mother's face when he held out the velvet pillow with Sal's forage cap on it for her. They say there were over ten thousand people at that funeral. He only saw Janice Salvatore's face.

Boys don't cry.

Mike cleared his throat.

"Sorry. Was that TMI?" Carla asked.

"Hmmm?"

"The crying at kitten video part. Was that too much?"

"No," Mike said, looking over at Carla. "It's good to know there's someone

90

out there who cries more than Julia Vendramini."

"Didn't she get Police Officer of the Year once?"

"They tried to give it to her, but she refused. Said anyone else would have done the same thing."

"But they didn't. I heard everyone else at the scene just stood around and watched."

"Yep. Pretty much," Mike said, rubbing the back of his neck again.

Flakes of wet snow began to fall.

"I'm sorry," Carla said, wiping a tear from the corner of her eye. "I'm sure I'll get it under control once I get used to these damned hormones."

"Then maybe you can have a word with Julia."

The wet snow turned to a fairly steady rain as the two of them sat in silence for a while, watching the Hawthorne children run in and out of the living room, likely chasing something.

Mike wasn't sure what annoyed him more: that they let Malcolm Oakes get away, dragging Chelsea Hendricks behind him, or that they all stood watching the burning warehouse collapsing around him. If one cop could save him, a dozen or so should have been able to grab that cop killer.

Funny how things go.

Mike rubbed his hands together. The inside of the car was getting cold. He couldn't see his breath, but he felt the cold getting inside of him. Luckily, it was raining hard enough that the water was running off the windshield. If it had been snow…. He looked over at Carla. She had gloves on. And a hat. At some point, he'd turn on the ignition and jack the heat for a few minutes. Could only do that so many times before drawing attention. He brought his shoulders up and rubbed his arms.

His cell phone rang.

"Mike," Amanda said, "How are things there?"

"Tickity-boo," Mike said, taking the last suck of the hard candy he'd been rolling around in his mouth.

"Good. Is Hawthorne in the house?"

"No idea. There's a rental car out front and what I'm assuming are the rest of the family just arrived in a minivan."

"So no signs of him?"

"No, but he could already be home."

"Okay. I've been calling around, and there are no spin teams available."

"We can spin him if it comes to that," Mike said, looking over at Carla, who nodded in agreement.

"Yeah, about that," Amanda sighed. "You don't seem to have a lot of success spinning—"

"Come on," Mike said. "That was a long time ago, and, now that he's gone, there's no chance of Ron calling out for me on the radio, so think we're gold."

"I don't have any other choice, so okay. But be careful."

"You bet, Boss," Mike said, turning the key over in the ignition.

"I'll let you know as soon as I can get an actual team together. In the meantime, get comfortable. You might be there for a while. And don't call me Boss."

* * *

The conversation between Carla and Mike dwindled to the occasional comment about a squirrel running across the road or the slow temperature drop as the afternoon turned into evening and the rain turned back into wet snow that turned into a watery slush when it hit the road. A few cars came by, splashing the side of their car, and Mike had blasted the heat a few more times, but the warmth didn't last long. They both lamented the old days, when a car could be turned on without activating the running lights. Of course, had they had a proper UC car, those lights would have been disabled. But they didn't. Instead, they waited as long as they could, watching lights in the house a few doors up the street turn on, room by room, and then turn off, until the cold became too much, and then Mike would turn the car on again. The intervals between became shorter and shorter, despite their best efforts.

Looking at the target house, the only light still on was in the living room. Mike checked his watch before starting the car again. It was 10:30 p.m.

A car coming from behind them slowed before pulling up very close beside them.

We've been burned.

The passenger side window rolled down. Mike rolled his window down, his right hand moving over to rest on the butt of the Glock holstered on his belt. The driver of the other car looked over and then laughed.

"If it isn't Mr. Conspiracy Theory himself. Fuck. I thought they retired you on mental. I mean medical."

Mike slid his hand off the gun and put it back on his lap.

"And I thought one of your own guys would have killed you by now," Mike replied, recalling the old clothes officer from a few months back.

"Meow!" Carla said.

"Oh, sorry. I'm..." the old clothes detective began, noticing for the first time that there was someone in the seat beside Mike. He leaned over to take a closer look at Carla. "What the—"

"I'm Detective Carla Hageneur," Carla said, reaching her hand out across Mike. "Pleased to meet you, I'm sure."

"Detective Griffiths," he said hesitantly, slowly stretching his arm across the seat to shake her hand. "You must be new."

"New partner, yeah," Mike said. "So I'm assuming you're the spin team?"

"My guys are on their way. What have you got?"

Mike's briefing was short.

"I can sit here until my team arrives if you guys wanna fuck off," Griffiths said, taking a pack of cigarettes from the dash and pulling one out. He flicked an old-school Zippo to light it. He took a long drag from the cigarette with the look of satisfaction.

"So," he continued, "you fucking off or what?"

"Thanks," Carla called across the car. "I *so* have to pee."

"And we have a retirement party to get to," Mike added, sliding the window up as he dropped the car in gear and drove off.

Chapter Fifteen

11:47 p.m. Thursday, January 10, 2019

B y the time Mike and Carla arrived at the bar, Ron's retirement party was well into its second round of revelers, which is to say: those with family commitments or long commutes home had left, and those who intended to make a night of it or lived in the city had arrived. Most of the guys from their platoon who had come straight from work at 5 had gone home, fearing—rightfully so—that to do otherwise could result in a DUI arrest. The days of *informal memos* being passed recommending that traffic cops stay out of the areas where shift parties were being held were long gone. This change, as well as a perceived lack of social skills and aptitude for *real* policing, added to further fueled the enmity between traffic and divisional cops. Tonight, perhaps out of deference to Ron, the rivalry was kept to a low hum.

Mike ordered drinks for Carla, Ron, and himself.

"Not that he'll likely remember drinking it," Mike said as he motioned for the server to put the shot of whiskey in the line of shot glasses already formed in front of Ron.

"Y' may it!" Ron said, bleary-eyed, as the server pointed to Mike.

"Had to see it to believe it," Mike said.

"What…that he's drunk or that he's leaving?" Ricky Jergensen called out from the crowd around Ron.

"Both," Mike replied, raising his pint of beer. "Sláinte. When you get to it.

And to you, Carla."

"Is that what you're calling yourself these days?" an older guy with a crew cut and a handlebar mustache that taunted regulations called out. The chattering of the group stopped.

"Yes. Carla. With a C," she replied with a smile, looking directly at the off-duty officer.

Mike set his glass down and stepped back.

"It's okay," she said softly, placing her hand on Mike's arm before he could say anything. "I started in Traffic as a cadet. We used to work together."

"Cool," the Traffic man called back. "And good on ya. I mean, ya know…it takes guts to do what you're doin'. Here's to livin' yer best life!"

"Thank you," Carla replied, taking a deep breath as the conversations resumed. She turned to Mike. "I had forgotten that all men seem to think it's their God-given right to make comments on…everything. Sláinte."

"Hey, pardner," Ron called out. "Di' ya see my plaque?"

"See it? I ordered it for you," Mike said as everyone within earshot laughed. "How much *have* you had to drink tonight?"

"Enough to slink sev'al sips," Ron slurred.

"I'll get our server to bring him a pitcher of water," Carla said, making her way towards the bar.

By day, this was a family-style neighborhood restaurant, complete with six-seater booths against the walls. To avoid jacking menu prices too much, the owners had inserted free-standing tables and chairs wherever possible about seven years ago, nearly doubling capacity. And, while diners cleared out by ten most nights, the bar held its own until closing time, especially when the weather was bad. For some reason, people didn't like to drink alone on wet nights.

"How much?" a bearded forty-something man with very white teeth wearing a plaid shirt asked as Carla approached, hand up to try to catch the eye of the bartender.

"Pardon?" she said, squeezing between this man and a young woman whose back was to them both, her attentions focused on the older man sitting on the other side of her.

"How much for a blow job? If you're good, we can do it right here, under the bar," he said, taking a swig of his beer, close enough to her now to be able to almost whisper, but choosing not to. "Or we can go to the Men's. I'm sure you know where that is."

"I'm sorry. I don't—" Carla, eyes forward, raised her hand to block his face from view.

"Listen, buddy," the man said, looking her up and down while wiping the beer foam from his mustache, the dim light from the taps reflecting off his wedding ring. "You're a long way from home, aren't you? Did you just finish up and get dumped out front? This isn't your kind of bar, but you're here, so you might as well make some cash. Cab fare to get you back where you belong. I've slip you an easy twenty if you just get yourself down—"

"May I have a pitcher of water...no, make that two pitchers...for my friend over there," Carla called across the bar.

"The cops hired you? That's gotta be a first!" the man beside her said, looking over his shoulder to see the revelers in the corner.

"Sure," the middle-aged bartender said, his eye on the slowly filling glass beneath the Guinness tap as he pulled a pint of IPA from another. "I'll have your server bring it over."

"Thank you."

"So? Wadya say?" the man said.

"About what?" Carla said, looking him squarely in the face.

"Whadya mean 'about what'? About blowin' me." He leaned back slightly on his barstool and began to loosen his belt as if it was a done deal. "Right here'll do. Nobody's gonna see anything. Come on. Get down—"

"Here's the thing," Carla said with a smile, batting her eyelashes. "If I did that, I'd arrest you for a number of criminal offences, which would ruin my evening with my colleagues over there, who are, as you've noted, cops. Just like me. And then I'd have to cart your sorry little soul off to jail, and you'd likely hire a lawyer that you couldn't afford, and we'd have to go to court because you'd probably want to tell the judge that I seduced you. Or that you were just too drunk and stupid to know what you were doing. But the judge wouldn't buy it because, as gorgeous as I am, you're not my type and I'd be more than willing to say that under oath. And you're not that drunk and, hopefully, not that stupid, and you'd get convicted and," Carla said, pausing to look down at his left hand, "your wife would leave you and, assuming you have a job, you'd get fired. But do you know what the worst thing of all would be?"

The man, whose jaw was almost to his chest, eyes like dark saucers against the sickly pallor of his face, slumped down, dropping his elbows on the bar.

"The worst thing of all would be that I've never given anyone a blow job, so it probably wouldn't be that good."

"You pumping the water from the well yourself over there?" Mike hollered over to Carla.

"Enjoy your evening. Asshat," Carla said before turning to go back to the party.

"What was that all about?" Mike asked, noticing the drunk at the bar with his belt undone.

"Just a lonely guy looking for love," she said.

"A quick ginger ale, and I'm out, boys," Amanda Black said with a laugh as she rushed over to the group. "I had to come and say goodbye, but I don't want to be any part of what I know is going to happen."

"Y' made it!" Ron slurred.

"Hopefully, before you black out and forget this night ever happened," Amanda said as she pushed through the crowd and gave him a hug. "Congratulations, Ron."

"Thank you," he said softly in her ear.

"Keep me posted, okay?"

"I will."

"And I'll buy you a drink," she said louder as she stepped back from him, "another time. I don't think you'll be able to drink the table-full in front of you before closing time—"

"Closing time's for amateurs!" someone from the group hollered out.

"Even *our* closing time," Amanda said with a smile. "I have to get back to work. I'm still on the clock."

The server came over with two pitchers of water and several plastic cups on a tray.

"Whoever ordered this: good call," Amanda said. "The old man is going to need it."

"Ol' man?" Ron said. "I'm in my pime. Pine. Prime!"

"Prime-*ed*," someone called out, and the group erupted in laughter.

"And don't you have any more to drink, either," Amanda said to Mike.

"You've been talking to my mother, haven't you?" he said with a smile.

"No. But you're driving Ron home at the end of the night. The roads are getting icy, and we've got Johnstone up in court tomorrow morning. I won't be there, obviously. I left a message for Calloway, so she's likely going to looking to you to help her out." She looked over at Ron. "Make sure he gets inside his house. And up to bed. And put a pot or something close by. I would not want to be him tomorrow morning."

She reached down to her waist and pulled her cell phone up.

"Shit. I gotta go. No rest for the wicked. Okay. Remember: take Ron home and let me know how it goes in court tomorrow, Crumply Pants." She looked over at Ron, who was in the type of deep conversation reserved for drunks and fools. Amanda turned to leave but stopped. "Oh, by the way, you look great, Carla."

"If you're propositioning me, get in line," she replied as Amanda disappeared out of the bar.

"That asshole propositioned you?" Mike said, looking at the man at the bar.

"It doesn't matter, Michael. He couldn't afford me anyway," she said with a smile. "Would you like me to pour you a glass of water, since you've been cut off?"

Chapter Sixteen

10:00 a.m. Friday, January 11, 2019

"All rise," the court clerk called out to the near-empty room. The twelve people in the jury box stood up, as did Bridget Calloway, Mark Johnstone, and his lawyer. Mike shuffled to his feet, his head a bit foggier than he'd have hoped. A couple of hours of sleep just wasn't cutting it anymore.

A man in robes looking much older than he likely was appeared through a doorway concealed in the wooden wall beside the Bench carrying a laptop. He made his way up to his perch, sat down, set the laptop on the desk in front of him, and opened it up.

"You may be seated. Court is now in session," the clerk said.

Mike sat down at the Crown's table beside Bridget, and Mark Johnstone, wearing an orange jumpsuit, his hands still cuffed in front of him, sat down at the defense table beside his lawyer. By the way he sat, Mike assumed the leg irons hadn't been removed. The jurors also took their seats.

"Before we begin, Your Honor—" Bridget said, standing up, her robes making her appear taller than she was.

"Have you not already spent…what is it," the judge grumbled, looking at the tiny screen in front of him, "four days sorting this thing out?"

"We have, Your Honor," Bridget said.

"And so?" the judge asked, looking far too tired for this early in the day.

"I have Detective Michael O'Shea seated beside me."

"So I see," the judge said. "I assume he is there to assist you with your case?"

"Yes, Your Honor."

The judge sat up a bit taller, stiffening his back, his tired eyes shifting from Bridget to Mike before stating: "I have no issue with that."

"Your Honor," the lawyer representing Mark Johnstone said from the other side of the room as he jumped to his feet, the robes he wore clearly borrowed and ill fitting, making him appear short and dumpy. "I object."

"Already? And why is that?"

"Detective O'Shea is the alleged victim."

"Alleged victim, Counsel? I thought this was a murder trial. Unless I missed that day of law school, our victim must be deceased, and Detective O'Shea, judging by the look of him, is not."

The court clerk let a quick smile cross her face before regaining her composure. A few of the jurors snickered.

"No, he's not Your Honor," the defense counsel stammered. "But—"

"Again, feel free to tell me I'm incorrect, either of you when I say that there are no exclusions to or caveats in this particular definition."

"What I think my learned friend is trying to say," Bridget said slowly, using thinly veiled LawyerSpeak to denote that she believed her colleague to be an idiot, "is that Detective O'Shea is the victim of the attempted murder that Mr. Johnstone is also charged with."

"Is that so?" the judge said, looking at Bridget with a slight smile.

"Yes, Your Honor," she said.

"And that has that got to do with this? Mr. Johnstone is here before me today to answer to the charge of murder," he said, not waiting for an answer. "That Detective O'Shea is involved in another matter involving Mr. Johnstone is immaterial. Unless, as we've already discussed, Detective O'Shea is the victim of the murder, and I believe we're proven, beyond a shadow of a doubt, that he is not."

"Yes, but—" the defense counsel began.

"In the event that Mr. Johnstone is found not guilty on the charge of murder, it is reasonable to assume that the charges in relation to Detective

O'Shea will proceed. Hopefully, and most likely, with another judge presiding."

"Correct," Bridget said.

"Yes, I know that's correct, Ms. Calloway," the judge said. "I'm assuming none of us missed *that* day in law school. And so, I'm not seeing where having Detective O'Shea assist Ms. Calloway is an issue. Once he's given his testimony. As such, anyone having anything to do with this matter, please leave the court."

Mike stood up, gave a slight bow, and left the courtroom. He sat in the hallway of the old building, considering the marble floors and soaring ceilings, and wondered how such a stunning structure could be full of so much sadness and hate-filled people. He closed his eyes, glad that he'd taken a couple of aspirins this morning, but wishing he'd shaved. For some reason, he didn't think the stubble would be that noticeable. He smiled. *At least I showered. And didn't pop an oxy. Mostly because I don't have any left, but a win's a win.*

"Detective O'Shea?" a court security officer called out.

"That's me," Mike said, getting up, his body stiffer than he thought it should be as he went back into the courtroom.

The court clerk swore him in, and the judge invited him to sit down in the witness box.

"Good morning, Detective O'Shea," Bridget began.

"Good morning," Mike responded. He gave a nod to the jury.

"I'm sure you know why you're here this morning?"

"Yes. To give evidence in the murder trial of Sergei Kuzminov. The accused is seated over there," Mike pointed to Mark Johnstone, the handcuffs and, judging by the way he was sitting, leg irons both removed.

"Very good, Detective. And I believe you have some notes?"

"Yes," Mike said, reaching into his coat pocket for his memo book. It wasn't there. He checked again. Not there.

"You do have notes to refer to, don't you, Detective O'Shea?" Bridget said, forcing a smile as she turned to the jury, trying to distract them from Mike's bumbling.

"I do, but I seem to have forgotten my memo book, Your Honor," Mike said, addressing the judge to his right.

The judge looked down at him.

"Perhaps," Bridget said, pulling out a thick stack of papers from an envelope on her podium, "if my friend agrees, Detective O'Shea can use the photocopy of his notes that I have here in my file."

"No objections, Your Honor," the defense lawyer said, half standing up.

"Very well," the judge said. "You may approach the witness."

Bridget walked over to Mike with the papers, her legs stiff, her teeth clenched behind a tight smile. She handed him her copy of his notes.

"Thank you," he said.

"Now, will there be any other surprises this morning, or can we begin this trial?" the judge asked.

"No. We're good," Bridget assured him.

The usual gracious dance between Crown and Detective—Bridget and Mike—did not occur. Instead, they stumbled. Bridget had to ask Mike to pass her the copy of his notes numerous times so that she could highlight certain facts. Mike would have to ask for them back to avoid misremembering or completely forgetting key points Bridget needed to have introduced to prove her case.

As the day wore on and other witnesses were called, the judge made no secret of his dissatisfaction with Bridget's running of the trial. Adjournment for the day couldn't come soon enough. Finally, at just after 5 p.m., the judge dismissed the jury for the weekend.

"Want to grab a bite to eat?" Mike suggested as he struggled keep up with Bridget as she hurried down the hall to her office.

"No," she said, not slowing her steps or turning around. "Did you know that Mrs. Majewski barely speaks English and requires a translator?"

"Yeah," Mike said, recalling the difficulty he had had trying to interview her.

"But you didn't think to have a translator in court for her? Especially since she provided access to the crime scene? Without her statement, all the evidence from the scene gets tossed."

"It was actually Mr. Majewski who—"

She stopped short in the middle of the empty hallway and then turned abruptly to look at him.

"Really, Mike?"

"Yeah. And besides, ordering a translator isn't my responsibility," Mike said with a shrug. "Homicide—"

"And your memo book. Is that Homicide's responsibility, too?"

"No," he said, looking away. "That's on me."

"Yes, it is," Bridget snapped, pivoting on her heels to continue towards her office.

"It must be in my other suit jacket," he said, keeping in step with her.

"That's great, Mike. Just great. How many foibles do you think the judge will allow before he just kicks the whole case out?'

"You know it doesn't work like th—"

"You know what I mean."

"Yeah, okay. So you want to go grab something or not?"

"No, I don't. I'm busy," she said as they both arrived at the door to the Crown's Office.

"You still have to eat," he said with a boyish smile.

"But not with you. Good night, Mike. Have a good weekend, and I'll see you, and hopefully Detective Sergeant Black, on Monday morning."

Mike stood for a moment and then turned.

"Oh, and Mike?" she said.

Mike turned back with a smile that quickly faded.

"Find the memo book. I'll have another copy of your notes for myself regardless, but it looks really unprofessional on you."

"I'll, ah...I'll do my best," Mike said, turning away again.

Chapter Seventeen

5:17 p.m. Saturday, January 12, 2019

"Thanks for coming in, Mike," Amanda Black said, looking as sharp as ever, complete with her signature stiletto heels. "I know it's Saturday evening, and you don't get many weekends off, but, bluntly put, I'm screwed."

"I figured as much," Mike said, setting the tray containing two coffees down on his desk. One of the fluorescent lights flickered overhead. Another was burned out. All six sets lacked the industrial diffusers that would have cut the glare. "Is it darker in here than usual or…?"

"You are a godsend. My treat," Amanda said, striding over to the coat rack where her purse hung underneath her coat to give him some money for the coffees. She hesitated just before reaching for it, thinking she may have seen something scurry underneath the radiators.

"No, this one's on me," Mike said, draping his coat over the back of the chair at his desk. He looked around the empty office. "Where is everybody? Out buying candles?"

"At a scene. Stabbing," Amanda said, turning back and picking up one of the cups. She snapped the plastic lid open and took a sip. "Not life-threatening."

The flickering light began to make a buzzing sound. They both looked up at it.

"If that light burns out," Amanda said, "I'll be heading to Canadian Tire myself to buy a new one. Apparently, there are none downstairs."

"Landon's probably holding off until we get to the new station," Mike said, taking the other coffee. "So? What's going on?"

"I think there's an issue with my spin team, and I'm going to need you to be the eyes on our target."

"Surprise, surprise," Mike said, sitting down at his desk and typing his password on the keyboard in front of him.

"I'm just waiting for their call," she said, glancing down at her belt to check the screen on her cell phone. "On another note, I heard things didn't go so well with the Johnstone trial yesterday."

"Shit show, actually," Mike conceded, looking over at the flickering light. "You know, I think we should swap that light out for one in the hall."

"Callaway sounded a bit frantic, to be honest. You two have a lovers' spat?"

"She called you?" Mike said, sizing up whether or not he could get up on one of the desks to remove the fluorescent tube or if he'd have to get the ladder from the janitor's room in the basement.

"How else would I have heard about it? The Trial Pixies? Seriously, though, Mike. What the hell happened?"

"Well, the judge—" Mike said, pushing himself back from his desk.

"I know what happened, but what *happened*?"

"I have no idea," Mike said, standing up while looking around the office for a chair to use to climb onto the desk.

"I feel like I'm talking to one of my kids. Let me be more direct. Did you two have a falling out?"

"We were never *in*, so I'm not sure—" he said, wheeling the chair that Russ McLean used towards the desk he was going to climb on.

"Rumor has it that she's looking to join Munro and Associates."

"Really?" Mike said, puckering his face. He stepped onto the chair and then onto the desk, leaving a wet shoe print on the seat of Russ's chair.

"Yep. Word is that she's decided to go to the dark side. And, if that's the case," Amanda said, watching Mike quickly pull his hand back as he touched the exposed light.

"Shit, that's hot!" he said, shaking his hand.

"… she might as well go work with Joanie Munro. She's one of the best defense lawyers in the country. You couldn't buy Bridget some flowers or put out or something to keep her on our side, could you?" Amanda said with a wink.

"While I'm flattered," Mike said, climbing back down, "I don't think a romp in the hay with me would yield the same enjoyment as a half million or so bump in annual salary year after year would."

"True," Amanda said with a slow nod.

"Hey, tender ego, remember? You weren't supposed to agree with me," he said, pushing the soiled chair back to the desk where Russ McLean sat.

"Not going to swap it out?" she said.

Before Mike could answer, Amanda's cell phone began to buzz. She answered it and, after a few words, clicked the phone off and hooked it back on her belt.

"Confirmed," she said. "The spin team's been burned."

"Put me in, coach."

"Great," Amanda said and then, thinking out loud, continued. "So Hawthorne now knows that we're onto him. He probably had his suspicions earlier, which is why he was using public transit—"

"Some people actually like public transit," Mike said, pulling his coat on.

"Sure, but not guys that pick up hookers on street corners. Anyway, he's back at his residence now. Given that it's close to whoring hour," Amanda said, looking at her watch, "I think he'll be using his own car very shortly. Don't pull him over. Don't interact with him. Just shadow him until you can get a discard. We know he always buys a coffee when he's out, so be ready to grab that cup when he tosses it."

"Why couldn't your team have done that?"

"They tried last night. Saw him toss his cup into a bin on the street. One of the guys checked the bin and saw about a dozen other coffee cups inside. All from the same coffee shop. And that's how they got burned."

"Shit," Mike said, leaning over his desk to log himself off his computer. "So what makes you think tonight's going to be any different? With the trash bin, I mean?"

"Wishful thinking," Amanda said. "Don't worry about the discard. Just keep an eye on him tonight and I'll get another team to do the discard some other way tomorrow."

"I can gather evidence, you know," he said.

"Mike, just grab the least obvious unmarked car and get over to Hawthorne's address before he gets to the stroll and starts jerking off, OK?"

"You don't think he's going to be picking anyone up?"

"No. He's probably pretty paranoid right now and figures we've got decoys out there. The last thing he wants is to get stung in a John sweep."

"So I'm just supposed to follow him around the stroll while he—"

"Yep."

"Lovely," Mike said as he walked out of the office.

"Oh, and Mike?" she called after him.

"Yeah?" he said, popping his head back in.

"Don't get out of the car. And make sure the radio is off. If I need you, I'll call you on your cell."

* * *

Mike sighed as he sat in the dark Ford Taurus across from Jordan Hawthorne's house, engine off, feeling the dampness of the night more than the cold creep into his bones.

Couldn't look more obvious if I tried, he thought, looking at his watch.

Following the pattern of lights turning on and off inside, Mike imagined the activities of the occupants. A blue tinge in the dimly lit front room. Someone's watching TV. A light coming through a small window upstairs. Maybe a bath being run for one of the kids. The reflection of light coming through a main floor side-window. Someone grabbing a snack from the fridge?

Then the yellow front door opened, and out came Hawthorne, but not before he gave his wife a kiss on the cheek. She glanced over at the car Mike was in before stepping back inside and closing the door behind her. Hawthorne got into the minivan. His wife came to the front window and pulled back the drapes as she watched him reverse the van onto the street and drive away.

Mike waited until the drapes were closed again before turning on the car. He immediately blasted the fan on the heater, bringing the temperature inside the car from frigid to tropical within minutes. The minivan was nowhere to be seen.

Hoping that Amanda was right, Mike headed to the stroll. It was in the same run-down neighborhood where he first met Amanda standing on the corner as a decoy to catch johns to pump up the arrest numbers for Morality. It was also where he'd first met Ron Roberts back when Ron actually *was* a traffic man. And, as he got closer, Mike could almost believe that Sal was in the seat beside him, spitting sunflower seeds onto Mike's side of the car.

Fucking Sal.

Even though it wasn't true, the girls on the corner could have been the same ones he'd spent years trying to rescue back in the day. They had The Look: not what Hollywood said they looked like, but the real look: despair, fear, and addiction, all needing numbing. And an eager smile intended to attract men needing power, control, and a quick release.

By design, there was nowhere to park. Other signs prohibiting right turns, left turns, and proceeding through various intersections that were intended to keep johns from circling the block. Like every other guy in a car here did, Mike looped around the area using different streets that brought him back to where he began. Luckily, on his second loop, Mike noticed Hawthorne's van enter the informal roundabout and proceeded to follow him at a discrete distance.

Either waiting for someone specific or just out looking.

With each loop, Mike noticed one or two girls missing and another one or two returned. The cars they popped in and out of ranged from beaters to Beamers, some with *Baby On Board* stickers on the back, others clean and likely leased company cars.

Nothing changes.

He was stopped at a traffic light when there was a knock on the passenger window. Reluctantly, he rolled it down.

"Hey sugar," a girl that looked no more than fifteen said, her pouty lips glistening with newly applied red lipstick. "Lookin' for someone special or can I help you out?"

Sugar. Sugar-lips. That's what the girls used to call Robby Williams. Mike's mind went to Robby's apartment that afternoon. To Robby hanging over the balcony. To Robby just…letting go.

Shit.

"Suit yourself," the girl said when Mike didn't respond, her eyes looking over the roof of his car to another that was slowing down. She strolled over as it pulled up in front of Mike's car. As he watched, the young girl hopped into the car in front of Mike's and was gone.

Lisa had come by the station just after Robby fell, high as a fucking kite. Word had already passed on the street.

Everyone on these streets ends up dead.

Mike gave himself a shake and, the next time he saw Hawthorne's minivan, fell in right behind it. Too close. Hawthorne braked suddenly, and Mike rear-ended him.

Shit, Mike thought, backing up a few feet before putting the car in park and slowly opening the door.

Hawthorne was already out, standing between the cars, looking at the bumpers, cigarette in hand. The perfect discard.

"I'm sorry, man," Mike began, slowly walking towards Hawthorne, trying not to stare at the cigarette while calculating how long it would take to smoke it to its filter. "I just dumped off a girl and I guess I was still…you know…."

Hawthorne took a deep drag from his cigarette, still staring at the dent in his bumper. The jacket he had on wouldn't keep him warm for very long on a night like this.

"I'd offer you a few hundred to fix it, but I, uh, just gave—"

"Yeah, yeah," Hawthorne said with a shiver, blowing the smoke out of his mouth. "I get it."

Mike reached over to the bumper and gave it a wipe.

"Doesn't look too bad," he said.

"Yeah," Hawthorne said, taking another long drag from the cigarette. "It's just that, you know, kinda hard to explain to the wife—"

"Shit happens, man," Mike said, feeling the cold as he shoved his hands in the pockets of his coat, all while keeping an eye on the glow from the cigarette.

Hawthorne stepped away from the cars and took another long drag.

"Wife doesn't let me smoke in the van," he said.

Mike nodded.

Hawthorne took one last drag before flicking the cigarette towards the curb. He got back in his van.

"We good?" Mike asked.

"Sure," Hawthorne said without looking back as he pulled the door closed.

Mike stood where he was, watching the back lights of Hawthorne's van disappear as it turned the corner, heading away from the stroll. He checked the front bumper of his car again, gave it another rub, and then walked over to the cigarette butt. He pulled a clean tissue out of his pocket and carefully picked up the butt. Gently, he wrapped it up and got back in the car. He set the tissue and its contents on the seat beside him and then pulled out his cell phone.

"Detective Sergeant Amanda Black speaking."

"I got a DNA sample. I'm taking it over to Forensics now."

Chapter Eighteen

3:23 a.m. Sunday, January 13, 2019

"What the fuck!" Mike hollered.

Lights from down the hall and the third floor clicked on, and a small dog could be heard yelping.

"Michael, what have ye done to Wee Phil?" Mary-Margaret demanded as she pushed open his bedroom door.

"Phil?" Mike said, looking over his shoulder at his mother, her bathrobe wrapped tightly around her. "Shit!"

"Are you okay, Dad?" Max said, bounding down the stairs and into his father's room wearing only his boxer shorts.

"Come on out, luv," Mary-Margaret said, bending down as the dog came out from under Mike's bed.

"I am now," Mike said. "I thought there was a rat on my pillow."

"Now, now, Wee Phil," Mary-Margaret cooed, picking up the dog. "'Tis just our Michael, draggin' himself in at all hours, not realizin' that he's not the only one who lives here."

"This is my house."

"And thinkin' he's the lord and master of us all," Mary-Margaret continued. "In the meantime, Max, either go back to bed or get some clothes on. You'll catch your death. And now that I'm up, I'm goin' downstairs to make a cuppa. I'll make one for ye as well, Michael."

"I just want to go to bed," Mike said.

"I'll see ye downstairs," Mary-Margaret stated.

"Somebody's in trouble," Max said in a sing-song voice as he went back up to his bedroom.

"I'm not in trouble," Mike protested.

"Yes, ye are," Mary-Margaret said, making her way down the hall to the stairs, still carrying Phil.

* * *

"Sticheedoon, Michael," Mary-Margaret commanded, pointing to one of the wingback chairs in the living room.

Mike hesitated.

"Better yet, I'll sit meself down and ye can bring in the tea for us. And a biscuit would be nice, given the hour."

"Being in bed would be nicer, given the hour," Mike grumbled as he nonetheless got the tea ready.

"Right," Mary-Margaret said, taking a mug from him. "I'll not mince words: I think yer workin' too hard."

"Okay," Mike said, settling into the chair beside her.

"And it's takin' it's toll on everyone's health."

"How so?"

"Just look at us now, Michael. The lad and ye and me up at this hour because—"

"Well, if you went back to your own house and took the dog with you, I wouldn't have woken Max up because I thought there was a rat sleeping on my bed."

"Don't be ridiculous, Michael. Rats don't sleep on beds."

"Neither should other people's dogs," Mike said, shoving a biscuit in his mouth.

"Well, I'd have me bags packed and be gone by the morning, but there's somethin' else—-"

"What?" Mike asked.

"Michael, I'll thank ye not to use that tone of voice with me. I know ye

112

work in a very challengin' environment and all, but there's no need—"

"Sorry. I'm just tired."

"Exactly," Mary-Margaret said, taking a sip of tea. "And there's no point belly-achin' about me bein' here because—"

There was a knock on the front door. And then another. And then several more that quickly turned into a pounding.

"Are ye goin' to get that, Michael, or wait until whoever 'tis breaks the door down?"

"Who the fuck—" Mike began, getting up to answer the door.

"I'm so sorry, Michael," Carla said, barely able to stand.

"Jesus, Mary, and Joseph!" Mary-Margaret said, shooting up from her seat. "Michael, call an ambulance!"

"No," Carla said. "Just let me in. Please."

Mike grabbed her as she collapsed into his arms and gently guided her to the floor.

"You're bleeding," Mike said.

"I'm so sorry," Carla said, a catch in her voice, steadying herself as she got into a seated position.

"Michael, get her a whiskey," Mary-Margaret directed. "Better yet, get us all one. Can ye stand up, luv?"

"I-I think so," Carla said, gingerly getting to her feet.

"Grand, Let's get ye over to the dining room, there. Chairs are firm and the light is good. I can have a proper look at ye."

Mary-Margaret took hold of Carla's arm and walked her over to the chair Mike had been sitting in.

"I am *so* sorry, Michael," Carla said again, collapsing into the chair. "I just had nowhere else to go."

With that, she began to cry.

"Michael, put a rush on those whiskeys and get the box of Kleenex from the kitchen," Mary-Margaret said, and, once Mike had poured the drinks, handed Carla one of the glasses. "Here, luv. Take a sip. And then tell us all about it."

Carla pushed the whiskey away but took several Kleenexes from the box that Mike had set in front of her. Mary-Margaret leaned forward and gently rubbed Carla's knee while Mike remained standing, assessing Carla's injuries, unable to turn off the cop inside of him.

"I don't even know where to begin," Carla said, holding back another flood of tears. "I feel like such a—"

"Start where ye are," Mary-Margaret said, sitting back to allow the dog at her feet to hop up. "By the looks of things, ye had a bit of a run-in this evenin'."

"You can say that again," Carla said, allowing a slight self-deprecating chuckle to escape through her sniffles.

"I think you should go to the hospital," Mike said, leaning over her. "That gash on your head could use a few stitches."

"Did that begin to bleed again?" Carla said, wiping the wound first with her hand and then, seeing the blood, with a wad of Kleenexes. "I'm so sorry."

"Who did this to ye, luv?" Mary-Margaret asked.

"A guy I thought was my friend."

"Well, clearly he's not. That's one of the things ye'll have to learn as a woman, Carla. Men aren't always—"

"I don't think this is the time, Mom," Mike cut in, stepping back.

"She's right, Mike. I've known him for years. He was my neighbor. He called and said he'd heard what had happened between me and my wi...ex-wife and asked if I wanted to go out for dinner to talk about it."

Carla dabbed at her head.

"I asked if he knew the whole story, and he said he did, and I thought he did. I mean, he didn't seem at all surprised at how I look when I met him at the restaurant."

"What happened?" Mike asked.

"Michael," his mother scolded. "Let the girl speak."

"I don't know. Everything was fine. We had a lovely meal. We even shared a bottle of wine."

"Did he come on to you?" Mike asked.

"Yeah, he did. And I said no. I'm not ready for a relationship. And he's married."

"Dogs, the lot of them. Sorry, Wee Phil," Mary-Margaret said, patting the Jack Russell on her lap. "Didn't mean to insult ye."

"And...?" Mike said.

"And I said no, then we settled up at the restaurant—"

"I hope he paid," Mary-Margaret said.

"Mom!"

"He did," Carla said. "At least the restaurant part."

"Ach, luv," Mary-Margaret said, patting Carla's arm.

"I went to my car, he went to his, and I thought that was it. I drove around a bit because I still haven't found anywhere to stay—"

"Ye never told me that, Michael," Mary-Margaret said, glancing up at her son with a furrowed brow before looking back to Carla. "Well, there's no worries there now. Michael will make up the room downstairs and ye can stay as long as ye like, can't she, Michael?"

"I can't—" Carla began.

"Ye can and ye will. Michael, go get the blankets now and make up the spare room."

"So you were driving around and...." Mike said, ignoring his mother.

"He was following me."

"And ye know this how?" Mary-Margaret asked.

"She's a cop, Mom. She knows."

"I'm a cop, Mary-Margaret. I know," Carla echoed with a sad smile. "Meanwhile, I'm getting tired of driving around and decide to park at the station again for the night—couch surfing is more complicated than it looks—and I'm at a stop sign when he gets out of his car and taps on my window. I knew he was following me, but it still really scared me when I saw him right beside me."

"So what did ye do?"

"I rolled my window down just a bit and asked what he wanted. He smiled and said I could at least roll the window down the whole way, so, like a fool, I did. He reaches over me into the car, puts the gear in park, and then tries to pull me out the window by my neck. I ask him what the hell he's doing and tell him that he doesn't have to pull me out of the window and that I'll open the door instead."

"Ye weren't actually goin' to open the door to that madman, were ye?"

"No. I was going to knock the car into drive and get away, and I think he knew that, so he just kept trying to pull me out of the window, and when he couldn't do that, he just banged my head against the side of the door."

Carla shuddered and began to cry again. Mary-Margaret rubbed her arm even harder.

"H-h-he said that he was g-g-going to k-k-k-kill me," she sobbed.

"I'm calling the po—" Mike began.

"No!" Carla cried out. "I don't want to report this."

"What?" Mike said.

"I don't want any trouble. I just want—"

"That makes no sense," Mike said, his voice getting louder.

"Why don't ye go get the room set up, Michael," Mary-Margaret said. "I think she's had enough for one night. Am I right, or am I right?"

Carla nodded in agreement.

"Off with ye, Michael!"

* * *

"How could I have been so naïve?" Carla said as she sat on the edge of the bed. Without waiting for an answer, she began to cry.

Standing in the doorway of the bedroom he'd just made up for her, looking at her battered face, hearing the rawness of her sobs, Mike was at a loss. He went to the bathroom at the other end of the basement, grabbed the roll of toilet paper off the back of the toilet, and brought it to her. Carla took it without looking up and tore off sheets of it to wipe her nose.

"I should have known better," she said, looking up at him, her mascara streaked down her cheeks.

Mike cleared his throat and looked away.

"How could I believe that the rest of the world would just see me—the real me—now?" she said, releasing another volley of sobs, this time directly into the soggy wad of toilet paper.

Mike stood there, frozen for a moment before realizing that, as much as he tried, he also saw Carla as Karl dressed up like a woman. And then he realized that what he had really always seen was this woman, sobbing on his guest bed in front of him, caught inside of Karl. And he felt ashamed.

"I'm sorry, Michael. I've really burdened you. It's enough that you've— well, your mother has—let me stay for a while. You shouldn't have to deal with my emotional issues. Just like a woman to bring all her baggage with her when she comes for a few nights, eh?" Carla said with a smile, wiping away the tears from her cheeks.

Mike sat down at the end of the bed beside Carla and hugged her. Not the buddy-hug he would give one of the guys, or the awkward hugs he had given Amanda. This one was more like the hug he would give either of his sisters.

"Well," he said, clearing his throat again as he stood up, "if you change your mind about wanting to go to the hospital or report this, just—"

"I know, Michael," Carla said, sitting up straighter. "And thanks. For everything. I'll be out of here by—"

"No rush. As you can see, you're not putting anybody out," he said as he turned towards the stairs. "And I'm sure my mother would love to have another woman in the house for a while."

"Thanks, partner," Carla called after him.

She waited until a couple of minutes after the kitchen light at the top of the stairs was off, and then curled up on the bed and wept.

Chapter Nineteen

5:25 p.m. Sunday, January 13, 2019

"Just like ye to show up when all the work is done," Mary-Margaret said, the sleeve of the blouse under her apron rolled up. She lifted the lid off the big pot and stepped back, letting the steam escape before she leaned in to give the potatoes a poke with her fork. "But I'm glad ye had a good lie-in."

"Where's Carla?" Mike asked.

"She left hours ago," she said, replacing the lid.

"Is she coming back?"

"Surely. She lives here now, or at least until further notice."

"Oh."

"I told her dinner was at 5:30 and it's just goin' on that time now," she continued, wiping her brow with the back of her arm, mindful of the knife she held in that hand, and then began hacking away at the meat, "so I'm anticipatin' her walkin' through that door any minute. And while yer connectin' the dots on this straight line, can ye take Wee Phil out for a piddle? He's been waitin' on ye."

"I hardly think so," Mike grumbled, slipping his shoes on as he took the dog out the back door into the laneway.

In the few minutes Mike was outside with the dog, the house filled up for Sunday dinner. Barring the death of one's self, attendance at Mary-Margaret's table by the O'Shea children, their significant others–regardless of how temporary–and their offspring was mandatory. The penalty for failing to attend was unknown, since no one had ever considered such a contravention.

"Yer just in time, luv," Mary-Margaret said as Carla walked in the front door. "We were all just sittin' down for dinner. Fam, this is Michael's new partner, Carla. Carla, this is the fam. Now sit."

"Oh, I don't know," Carla said, trying to find a way to hide her swollen face. "I'm sure you're—'"

"No one sits there," Allan, Mike's brother-in-law, said, pointing to the two empty seats at the head of the table.

"That's not true," Paulie stated, intentionally bumping into his father as he made his way to the table. "What happened to your—"

Mary-Margaret always laid two extra place settings at her Sunday dinner table. The one at the head of the table was for her children's father. The other was set for Peter, the third of the O'Shea children, who now lived rough and whom Mary-Margaret never stopped believing would one day find his way back to her table, even if it wasn't in the house on Delaware Avenue now.

"Come on. Sitcheedoon," Mary-Margaret said. "We might seem a bit much at first, but ye'll get used to us."

"Unlikely," Allan said as he sat in his usual seat as far away from Mary-Margaret as was possible without being at the head of the table.

"Can we at least get seated before you two start in on each other?" Teaszy asked.

"No," Paulie said with a laugh as he sat down to the left of his grandmother.

"Where are the bags?" Mike called from the kitchen.

"Top drawer, left of the stove," Mary-Margaret called back. "Honestly, I do wonder how the lad survives. Men!"

"Not all men," Katie said, looking warmly at Ahmed.

"Most," Teaszy said, glancing at Allan before glaring over at Paulie.

"What?" Paulie said.

"Feel free to leave at any point," Katie whispered to Carla. "It doesn't get any better."

"For a little dog, he sure sh—" Mike stepped out of the kitchen and stopped, noticing everyone already seated at the table. "You guys don't waste much time, do you?"

"Don't just stand there, Michael. Sitcheedoon so that we can begin dinner. Poor Ahmed's wastin' away over there, aren't ye, luv?"

"Well, hardly wasting," Katie's partner said with a kind smile. "I'm getting pretty pudgy for an Indian guy."

"Yer an Indian-Irish lad now, luv, and yer too skinny," Mary-Margaret said. "Michael. Sit. Yer holdin' us up, lad."

As soon as he was in his chair beside Katie, the serving bowls began quickly making their way up and down the table, occasionally being removed to be refilled in the kitchen by one of the O'Shea women before being put back into circulation.

"Mom tells me you'll be staying here for a bit," Teaszy said to Carla.

"Hopefully not too long," Carla replied self-consciously. "No offence intended."

"None taken," Mary-Margaret said. "Yer welcome to stay as long as ye like, isn't she, Michael?"

"You should get a rooming house license, Mike," Allan said. "With Mary-Margaret and now Carla here, you could make yourself a little extra cash."

"Yeah. We should do that, Dad," Max said, eyes widening at the prospect of earning some additional income. "I could run the business end of things and you could—"

"I am the matriarch of this family, not some lost soul needin' a roof over her head, contrary to what yer da may have ye thinkin'," Mary-Margaret stated. "And our Carla is in temporary need of a place to stay until she can find suitable accommodation, not someone whose unfortunate situation is to be exploited by a money-grubbin' landlord whose own mother, if he had one, would be ashamed."

The table was silent but for the sound of cutlery on porcelain.

"So you work with Mike now, do you?" Allan asked. "I'm assuming you got into a little brawl. I see Mike hasn't got a scratch on him. Too scared to rescue your partner again, Mike?"

Except for Teaszy's fork bouncing off her plate before dropping to the floor, there was no cutlery on porcelain to be heard.

Mike saw a flash of white. Katie, who was sitting beside him, put her hand on his arm under the table and slid it down onto his clenched fist. She held his fist in her hand until he relaxed and opened his hand up. Katie gave his hand a gentle squeeze, the two holding hands just like when they were little, except this time, Katie was the protector. Mike took a deep breath, rotated his neck, and withdrew his hand to reach for a glass of water.

"I know I'm not at my best, Allan, is it?" Carla replied with a perky smile. "It's been a tough couple of days. And this has nothing to do with Michael."

When no one moved, Carla took a deep breath and continued.

"If you must know, I was attacked last night by a man I thought I knew well. Apparently, I don't. Which reminds me, Michael: do you think it makes more sense just to bring the top I was wearing yesterday with me as evidence when I go to the station to report this, or should I wear it?"

"I think just bringing it in would suffice," he answered with a slight smile.

"Swell. I think I'll do that tomorrow. Is there any more corned beef, Mary-Margaret?"

"Good on you for reporting," Katie said. "If we don't call these assholes out—"

"Language!" Mary-Margaret cautioned.

"Well, they are, Mom," Katie replied.

"Be that as it may, but there are young ears at the table."

"I'm sure Max has heard worse," Paulie said, smirking across the table at his younger cousin.

"I think she was referring to you," Max shot back.

"Anyway, I'm very proud of you for following through," Katie said.

"Does it make a difference that you're…." Allan said, not finishing his sentence, looking defiantly over at his wife.

"Christ, Dad. Do you live under a rock?" Paulie asked.

"No, but I just thought—"

"That'll be a first," Mary-Margaret said.

"I'm sorry, Mom," Teaszy began, glaring at her husband while sliding her chair away from him.

"How's Richard?" Katie asked. "He's still teaching English in Japan, right?"

"And dating a gender-fluid person," Paulie replied. "You knew that, right, Dad?"

"No. I didn't know that," Allan replied, trying not to choke on the piece of corned beef he'd just put in his mouth.

"I didn't know he was dating," Teaszy said. "How do you know?"

"Email. Twitter. Insta," Paulie said with a sigh. "I swear to god, I was adopted."

"He never said anything about...them...during our last Zoom call," Teaszy said.

"Duh," Paulie said. "You live with a troglodyte, Mom. Ritchie probably remembers how you lost your shit—"

"Language," Mary-Margaret said.

"Lost your *mind*," Paulie corrected, "when I came out to you guys."

"I didn't lose my mind," Allan objected.

"In fairness, ye didn't," Mary-Margaret commented. Everyone around the table looked at her, shocked. "Because that would presuppose ye had a mind to lose. Now, if we're done gossipin' about yer own flesh and blood, can we get on with the meal. Who wants more corned beef?"

"This has all been swell, everyone," Carla said, "but I think I'm going to excuse myself and go to my room, if you don't mind."

"Too much?" Katie asked.

"No, I'm just...tired."

"Well," Mary-Margaret began once Carla had gone downstairs, "I hope yer proud of yerself, Allen. Making our houseguest feel unwelcome."

Before he could respond, there was a knock at the door. Mike got up to answer it, almost tripping over the dog, who had appeared from under the table where he had previously been gorging himself on bits of corned beef that both Paulie and Max had, unbeknownst to each other, been shoveling at him.

"Oh, shit!" Amanda Black said, looking past Mike. "I forgot it was Sunday. Never mind, I'll come back—"

"Come in, yer out," Mary-Margaret called from the table. "There's plenty to eat."

"No, I can't—"

"Ye can and ye will," Mary-Margaret said, getting up and taking Amanda by the elbow to sit at the empty place at the head of the table.

"And ye all know Mandy, then?" Mary-Margaret said. Everyone at the table nodded. She looked down at the place setting. "Ach, Max, ye've not set a fork here."

"I'll get it, Mary-Margaret," Amanda said.

"Come on, luv. We'll fetch it together."

Amanda followed Mary-Margaret into the kitchen.

"Before we rejoin the unwashed masses," Mary-Margaret whispered, pulling Amanda close while glancing through the kitchen doorway into the rest of the main floor, "can I tell ye somethin'?"

"Of course."

"It's me Michael. He's not himself anymore."

"Well, I-I..." Amanda stammered.

"I know he's still strugglin' with Sal's death. I can't imagine, to be honest. Such a lovely young lad. And I know he's been enjoyin' more than his share of whiskey lately, but it's this bitterness that's got into him. It's not right, Mandy. It's not me Michael. Are the lads doin' anythin' to help him at your end?"

"I can't really talk about—"

"He's me son, Mandy. A piece of me. Like your girls are a piece of you. Mother to mother. Is he gettin' any help?"

"We're sending him to see a psychologist," Amanda blurted out.

"I thought he already was," Mary-Margaret said, looking down at her hands. "And that doesn't seem to be helping at all. The last one only made him—"

"This one's different. She specializes in PTSD."

"And the one he's seein' now doesn't?"

"Dr. Shimner-Lewis, that's her name, is an expert."

"I hope so, luv, because I'm really worried about him."

"We all are."

Chapter Twenty

10:00 a.m. Monday, January 14, 2019

"All rise," the court clerk said as the judge entered the courtroom and sat down behind the bench. "You may be seated."

Everyone but Bridget Calloway and Johnstone's lawyer sat down.

"Let us hope that today runs smoother than our last appearance together," the judge said as he sat down on his perch, rolling his neck before opening his laptop.

Bridget tried very hard not to purse her lips, extending her chin out as she took a deep breath instead. The defense lawyer smirked as he gave her the side-eye and sat down.

"Good morning, Your Honor," Bridget said. "I'd like to call to the stand Detective Griffiths."

A middle-aged, unshaved man with a mop of hair in a knock-off Armani suit stood up from the gallery and approached the witness stand.

"Are we not asking for an exclusion of witnesses today, Ms Calloway?" the judge asked.

"Uh, yes, Your Honor."

"Then let's do it, shall we?" he said before the words barely left her mouth.

"I'd like to ask for an exclusion of witnesses," she said, sounding more like a child that had been scolded than a top-notch crown prosecutor.

"Excellent idea, Ms Calloway. Madame Clerk, if you would be so kind?" the judge said, looking down at the court clerk seated in front of him.

"All persons having business pertaining to this trial are asked to leave the courtroom," the clerk stated without looking back at the judge.

A handful of people left the courtroom.

"And now I believe you have a witness to call, Ms Calloway?"

Detective Griffiths buttoned his suit coat jacket as he made his way to the witness stand. He smiled with a slight shrug at Bridget, nodded to the judge, and completely ignored the defense attorney.

"For the record," the court clerk said, turning to face the detective before passing the Bible to him. "Please state your name and rank."

The old clothes detective wearily stated his name and rank, swore on the Bible to tell the whole truth and nothing but the truth and began explaining his involvement with the Johnstone case.

And then, it was the defense attorney's turn.

"Just to clarify, Detective Griffiths," he said, swaggering around the table he had been patiently seated behind to approach his witness, "you were the one who held the warrant to authorize the search of the residence of the deceased. Is that correct?"

"Yes. That's correct."

"And you believe that the deceased was murdered in that room, correct?"

"Yes."

"What made you believe that, Detective?"

"Well, as I stated in my evidence in chief, there were signs of a struggle and a lot of blood."

"How much blood?" the defense attorney asked, narrowing his eyes and cocking his head to one side.

Bridget stood up.

"Objection, Your Honor. I don't believe my witness is qualified to quantify the amount of blood he saw."

"I don't believe our friend is asking for a measurement, Ms Calloway. Or am I mistaken, Mr.—-"

"The room was caked in blood," Griffiths cut in.

"*Caked*. Is that a police term or a medical term or…?" the defense lawyer asked.

"There was blood everywhere," Griffiths said.

"Everywhere?" the defense lawyer echoed.

"I believe my learned friend will get a better understanding of what Detective Griffiths means," Bridget began, flipping through her files until she found the scene photos taken by the forensics officer, "if he looks at these. I'd like to enter these photos—"

"Did you take these photos, Ms Calloway?" the judge said with a cringe-worthy smile.

"No, Your Honor."

"I didn't think so. Do you wish to call the individual who did?" the judge asked.

"I would, Your Honor, but the forensics officer is not available to—"

"Is the forensics officer a police officer, Ms Calloway?" the judge asked.

"Yes, Your Honor."

"Police witnesses are always available in my courtroom, Ms Calloway. I understand that civilian witnesses have lives outside of the judicial process, but police officers do not. At least not in my courtroom. I will take a thirty-minute recess now and I suggest you have the forensics officer in my courtroom when we resume if you intend to use that photo as evidence in this trial. Or you can consider all of them excluded."

With that, the judge got up and left the courtroom.

"A-all rise!" the court clerk spat out and then clicked her tongue at Bridget before clearing the courtroom.

Detective Griffiths stepped out of the witness box and approached Bridget.

"Hey, I'm sorry if I—" he began.

"No. It wasn't you. It was me. This judge…" She looked over at the defense attorney, who was sneering while adjusting his cufflink as the court security officers handcuffed his client to remove him to the holding cells in the basement until the trial resumed.

The lawyers followed the accused and his guards out of the courtroom.

"What happened?" Mike asked from the hallway as he watched Johnstone being led away.

"Where were you?" Bridget said.

"I was looking for parking. I didn't expect—"

"You never expect," Bridget said as she hurried down the hall to her office, leaving Mike and Griffiths behind.

"What happened?" Mike repeated, this time to Griffiths.

"Dunno," Griffiths said with a shrug. "Defense was taking a run at me, and she got flustered."

"Bridget? Flustered?"

"Maybe she heard about your tranny girlfriend."

"What?"

"That tranny partner of yours. Word is that you're living together. None of my business, bud, and I don't want to know. Nothing on this job would surprise me. Whatever. But not everyone thinks the way I do. And I'd be pissed if my girl dumped me for some trans…guy. Do they even have those?"

"What the fuck are you talking about?" Mike said, feeling his blood pressure rising.

"Listen, do yourself a favor. Own it. Fuckin' march in the parade with… her…next year. I don't give a fuck. Just…fuck, I don't know. If I was bangin' Calloway, I sure as hell wouldn't toss her over for a he-she, but that's your shit to figure out. I'm goin' for a smoke."

"Shit," he mumbled, making his way to the Crowns' office.

"I can't get hold of the forensics officer," Bridget said when Mike walked into her office.

"So?"

"So if I don't, we're going to lose all of the photos," she said, her voice breaking.

"No, we're not. Just withdraw your— Wait a minute. Why am I telling you how to run a trial? What's going on?"

"Nothing that concerns you," Bridget snapped.

"Listen, if it's about—"

"I don't know what you're about to say, and I don't care, because it's not anything about you. For once."

"Ouch," Mike said, wincing.

"I've got a murder trial to run. And then I'm—"

"What?"

"Never mind. Is Black around or are you standing in for her?"

"I guess I'm standing in."

"Great. So help me."

"But you—"

"Help. Me. Or get out."

Within minutes, the investigator and the prosecutor had a new game plan in place and returned to the courtroom.

"Your Honor, I'd like to call to the stand Constable Jergensen," Bridget said, glancing over at the defense counsel.

"That was not the plan," Mike whispered to Bridget.

"I'm assuming Detective O'Shea is not going to give further evidence?" the judge said, looking at Mike seated beside her.

"My apologies, Your Honor. Detective O'Shea was just leaving the courtroom."

"I don't know what you're doing, but I sure hope you do," Mike said to Bridget as he stood up to leave the courtroom.

"Of course I do," she said, frowning.

"Oh, and in case you missed her, Janelle Austin is outside," Mike said before he got too far away from Bridget to be able to whisper.

Bridget rolled her eyes before pulling out a copy of Jergensen's notes.

Chapter Twenty-One

11:47 a.m. Monday, January 14, 2019

"Hey Mike," a familiar voice belonging to someone whose name Mike could never recall said. "I heard you went to the dark side."

"Traffic? Not me," Mike said with a smile, stretching out his hand. "How the hell are you?"

"Curious as hell, Mike," the officer said, vigorously shaking Mike's hand. "I never pegged you as into that sort of thing."

"What are you talking about?" Mike said, still smiling.

"Tranny love, baby," he said with a laugh. "What's it like fucking a guy, or has he, you know...."

The officer circled the front of his pants with an open palm.

"Really?" Mike said, the smile disappearing from his face.

"Hey, brother, it's not a big deal. Love is love, right? I just never, you know, saw you as someone who would be open to that."

"Fuck you," Mike said and turned away.

"Come on, now," the officer called. "I'm not the one with the live-in tranny lover."

"Neither am I, you asshole," Mike shouted back.

Everyone in the hallway turned and looked at him.

"Fuck you all," Mike said, a little quieter.

"Bud, what the fuck?" Griffiths said, returning from his smoke break just as the two officers were yelling at each other.

"What do you think?" Mike said, looking Griffiths in the face.

"I don't know, bud. Don't tell me you didn't expect people would talk? It's not like it's anyone's business, but you don't find too many cops who are open about being into trannys. I mean, I'm sure lots of guys check it out online, but—"

"I'm not into trannys. Carla is a cop, just like you and me. And she needed a place to stay. It could have been any of us. So my mom—"

"Oh fuck. This just gets better and better, doesn't it," Griffiths said with a laugh. "No wonder Calloway's been banging one of the senior lawyers over at Munro & Associates. I wouldn't put up with that shit, either. Grown-ass man living with his mom. Never mind the kinky shit."

Mike recoiled, as if he'd been slapped in the face. Hard. He didn't hear anything else Griffiths may or may not have said.

The courtroom door flung open and Ricky Jergensen paused for a moment to bow to the judge and then stormed out.

"What happened?" Mike called after him, rushing to catch up with the young officer.

"Fucking defense. Got me all confused and then—"

Mike could hear the clicking of Bridget's heels as she stomped out of the courtroom.

"What—" Mike said as she rushed past him towards the Crowns' office.

"Don't even speak to me, O'Shea," she said without breaking stride. Mike hurriedly caught up with her. She stopped abruptly and turned on him.

"When were you going to tell me you knocked my arresting officer out cold, Detective?"

"What?"

"Did I stutter?"

"I told you."

"When? While you were helping me clear out my Dad's things?"

"What?"

"I don't know what the hell is going on with you, Mike, but you need to get your shit sorted out."

"We had a case conference about this, Bridget. I told you then."

"No, Mike, you didn't. You told me how Jergensen arrested Johnstone and then had to release him, and then you told me about how Jergensen saved your life. Shit, Mike. I had him set up to be the hero to offset what defense is now calling double jeopardy on the Johnstone arrest."

"What? There's nothing saying you can't arrest someone twice for the same crime. You just can't—"

"I know the law, Detective. I went to law school, remember? Didn't see you there."

Bridget turned and continued towards her office, stopping to punch the code in at the door.

"What the hell is that supposed to mean?" Mike said as Bridget fiddled with the door. "And here, let me do it."

Mike calmly pushed the buttons that unlocked the heavy door and opened it, gesturing for Bridget to enter first.

"I've been covering for you for a long time, and I'm done."

"What do you mean you've been covering?"

"Come on, Mike. Don't tell me you haven't noticed. Don't get me wrong. I love the brotherhood thing of policing, and I admire how loyal your colleagues are to you, but you've been slipping up in my court for a long time, and now it's just too much. This knocking Jergensen out thing has added a whole new level of shit to this show that I don't need."

Mike's jaw hung open.

"We're on our morning break and I'd like to have a few minutes to myself to enjoy a coffee. Alone," Bridget stated before Mike could offer to get her one. "I won't be calling you as a witness until at least tomorrow, so you're free to go."

Mike was speechless. He took a deep breath, pushed his chest out as he pulled his shoulders back and walked out of the reception area of the office with as much dignity as he could manage.

Once in the general hallway, Mike pulled out his cell phone and called the main police switchboard.

"Can you put me through to Dr. Shimner-Lewis's office, please?"

* * *

"Thank you for being so flexible, Mike. It is okay if I call you Mike, isn't it?" Dr. Shimner-Lewis said as she motioned to a leather chair for him to sit in. The interior office was a part of the Officer Wellness Unit at headquarters and was surprisingly calming. No broken-down furniture, stained carpets, or big box store prints on the wall here.

"Yes. Mike's fine. I didn't actually expect that you'd be able to see me so quickly," he said, sitting down in the soft chair.

"I had a last-minute cancellation, and we try to see members as soon as they reach out whenever possible, so I guess the stars just aligned for us today," she said with a genuinely warm smile. She sat in a firmer chair, steno pad in hand. "I hope you don't mind if I write down a few things while you talk. It helps me to—"

Mike flinched.

"If it makes you uncomfortable, I won't," she said, not taking her eyes off him. "It's just that it's easier for me to circle back if there's something you bring up, and it's not a good time to stop to discuss it. Don't worry. These are my notes, and they don't go anywhere. Unless you're suicidal or—"

"Yeah. I know the rules," Mike said. "I don't think there's any worry there."

"Good," she said with a slight nod. "So, Mike. What now?"

"I dunno," he said with a deep sigh. She waited for him to continue. He did not. Instead, he looked at the woman sitting across from him. She was slender and her long hair looked prematurely gray. It was her eyes that caught his attention. They were a very light blue and sparkled like sunlight on the lake.

He gave his head a shake.

She's a shrink. Not a blind date.

"Clearly, something has triggered you today," she said.

"Sure," he said with a slight laugh.

She waited for him to continue. He said nothing.

"You like crosswords, Mike?" she said, looking over her shoulder at a copy of *The New Yorker* that was sitting on her desk.

"Sure. I dunno. Why?"

"Since we have nothing to say and you're here for the hour, I've got a crossword I've been working on, and there are a few clues I'm just not getting. I thought I could read them out, and we could finish it together."

"I'm not that good at crosswords," he said with a smile.

"What are you good at, Mike?" she asked.

"Not much, apparently."

"Your partner was shot in your arms a few years back, wasn't he," she said.

"Yeah, he was," Mike said, his shoulders rising.

"Must have been horrible."

"Uh-huh." His breathing began to get shallow.

"Do you miss him?"

"Huh?" Mike said, taking a sharp breath.

"Your partner," she continued, unfazed. "Do you miss him?"

"I guess. I don't know," he replied before taking a very deep breath. "That was a long time ago."

"Our brains don't have a sense of time. Did you know that? It's in a kind of constant now. Or never, depending on whether you're an existentialist or not."

"What?"

"That was a joke. As you might imagine, I was that geeky girl who grew up to become this geeky doctor."

"I can see that," Mike said with a laugh.

"And so...?"

"Yeah. I do miss him, Doc."

"Rachel. Call me Rachel."

"Rachel," Mike said. "I miss him a lot. Every day."

With no warning, Mike began to weep. Tears flooded down his cheeks. Rachel waited a few minutes before passing him a box of Kleenex.

"I'm sorry," Mike said, wiping his face with some tissues while trying vainly to control his tears. He closed his eyes and saw his father's coffin being lowered into the ground. He saw his mother, looking so strong and stoic, holding Katie in her arms with Teaszy and Petie clinging to her legs.

He saw himself, not a boy but not yet a man, standing alone. There wasn't room for him. He felt so abandoned. And it was all happening right now.

"Take as long as you want, Mike," Rachel said. He glanced up at her and saw her smooth face and warm eyes.

"I'm sorry," he repeated, almost regaining his composure until he suddenly felt the blood on his coat as he cradled Sal's lifeless body, trying to will Sal back to life. He smelled Julia Vendrameni's perfume on the jacket she was wrapping around him. He felt the rain on his face, like tiny needles, exactly the way it was that day when he was strapped to the gurney, waiting to be loaded into the ambulance.

"Here," Rachel said, reaching over to open Mike's hands to take the wad of soaked Kleenexes from him. "I'll take those."

Mike was surprised by how warm and soft her hands were.

"I'm sorry," Mike said, wiping his nose one last time.

"Me, too," she said. "It sounds like you've had a shitty time of it."

"Are you allowed to say things like that?" Mike said with a slight smile.

"What? That things are shitty? Hell, yeah!" she said, smiling back at him. "Unless you'd prefer I not swear."

"Doesn't bother me at all," Mike said.

"That's one of the things I like about working with you guys. You're so down-to-earth." She set her steno pad aside. "Listen, Mike, I can't even imagine what you've been through as a cop, never mind the regular shit we all go through. If you'll let me, I'd like to help you work through it. All I ask is that you give me a starting point."

"I thought I just did."

"Okay. So where do you want to go with this?"

"No idea, but I have to go somewhere with it, I guess."

"Not necessarily. You can stay where you are or…not. Your call."

"I dunno," Mike said.

"Give it some thought. We can talk about whatever you want."

Mike's mind went blank.

"Anything at all, Mike."

Mike took a deep breath in and let it out quickly.

"I'm so fucking angry. And sad. And my whole body hurts."

"I can help you with that," Rachel said, nodding. "I'm good at that sort of thing. But only if you want me to."

"What choice do I have?"

"Depends."

"On what?"

"Do you want to stay on the job, or go off on long-term disability?"

Mike stared at her.

"If I leave, they'll never find Sal's killer," he said.

"Then I suggest we get our calendars out and line up a few appointments."

Just as he was pulling out his smartphone, it rang. It was an unknown number. He looked at Rachel.

"Go ahead," she said. "Pick it up. If you want to."

"Hello?"

"Crumply Pants. It's me. I need you to come in as soon as you can. We've got Hawthorne's DNA on Lisa's body, which puts him on the top of my hit list."

"Uhh," Mike hesitated.

"I know. Should be a slam dunk, but given Lisa's line of work, defense could argue consent for the DNA. I need you to spin him again, and I've got nobody. I've spoken to Langdon, and he hasn't got a car we can use, so I'm going to need you to pick one up from the carpool at headquarters. Let me know how soon you can be there so I can let them know at the duty desk to have one ready for you."

Mike looked at his watch.

"I can be there in ten minutes," he said, standing up and putting on his suit jacket.

"Shit, Mike. Why can't they clone you?" Amanda Black said before hanging up.

"Duty calls?" Rachel said with a knowing smile, looking up from her appointment book.

"Yeah. I've got—"

"I don't need to know, Mike. I'm not a cop, remember?"

CHAPTER TWENTY-ONE

"Right," Mike said.

"Next week too soon?"

"No. That's good. Around 4 pm is probably the best time. I should be out of court by then and can always adjust my start time at the station."

"Great," she said, flipping the page of her appointment book over. "Wednesday at four."

Mike entered the appointment in his phone with his thumbs as Rachel got up.

"Nice meeting you, Mike O'Shea," she said, extending her hand.

"Same," he said, shaking her hand. *So warm. So soft.*

Chapter Twenty-Two

6:00 p.m. Tuesday, January 15, 2019

T rying to recalibrate after his appointment with the psychologist, Mike almost ran into Amanda Black as he absently got out of one elevator while she, equally distracted by the dozen or so things she had to get done within the hour, was getting out of another.

"Where are you coming from, Crumply Pants?" she said with a start, looking at Mike as if she'd never seen him before.

"The shrink," Mike mumbled, the fear that he would be perceived as weak or unfit as a man or a cop because he had sought help rising in his throat.

"Oh good," Amanda said. "I'm glad you went. Rachel's lovely, isn't she?"

"I suppose," Mike answered, clearing his throat, unsure whether she was patronizing him or not.

"I send all my guys to her. You can't deal with what we do day in and day out and not be affected by it."

"Unless you're Ron," Mike said with a smirk.

"Yes, well. He's the exception that proves the rule. I'm going to miss that odd little man."

Mike nodded in agreement.

"Let's see what they've got for you," Amanda said, motioning for them to proceed to the security desk beside the plexiglass security doors.

"Hey Amanda," the salt-and-pepper-haired uniformed officer said as she stood up and walked around her desk, a broad smile on her face.

"Hi, Lynn," Amanda replied with equal familiarity. "How's your wife doing? She just had her hip replaced, didn't she?"

"Sure did, Boss," the officer said, shaking her head with a laugh. "And I'm pretty sure she's milking it for all it's worth. I come to work to get a break! I guess you're the one going on this secret mission for Amanda, eh, Mike?"

Mike nodded.

"Good luck," she chuckled, turning back to pull a set of keys and a journal from the desk drawer. She handed the keys to Mike. "Parked on the bottom level. Hopefully, it's been gassed up."

Mike took the keys and followed Amanda across the open-air lobby to another bank of elevators across from the duty desk.

"You want me to tail Hawthorne again, right?" Mike asked.

"No," Amanda said, stopping in front of the two sets of closed elevator doors. She looked up and saw that one of the cars was on P4, the other was on P2. "I need you to get out of the car and talk to the girls on the stroll. I need you to find out if there was anyone else that might have had it in for our victim."

"Isn't that your job?" Mike asked. "No offence, but you know...."

"That and a million other things. But hey, if you want to finish up my case prep for a prelim that starts on Monday, be my guest."

"No thanks. I'd rather hit the streets."

"Speaking of which, be careful, okay?"

"Always," Mike replied with a boyish shrug.

"I'm serious, Mike. If Lisa's death is tied into Sal's murder..."

"Whoa, whoa, whoa. Now who's sounding like a conspiracy theorist?" Mike said with a smile.

"I never doubted that there was something go on with Malcolm Oakes. He's too obvious. And too wanted. There's no way he should have been able to get past us for this long. He's either been dead for a very long time, or he's had help from people far above our pay grade. And if he was dead, we'd have found out about it by now, so...."

Mike's eyes narrowed as he looked at her.

"There are snakes in the grass everywhere, Mike," she continued, looking up at the elevator car indicator. The one that had been at P2 was now at P1. "Slowest goddamned elevators in the world. Anyway, you and I both know about those insidious little fuckers and that's what makes this job so hard. Especially when the snake is wearing a white shirt."

"What are you saying?" Mike said, absently looking up at the number above the elevator, needing Amanda to confirm what he hoped she was saying.

"Keep all of this under your hat, Mike, but know that I'm working on it."

"Just you?"

"Bridget Calloway..."

Mike didn't hear the rest of what Amanda said.

It's not the money. She's leaving the Crown's Office because she can't stay. They're onto her, and she knows it. If she stays, they'll smear her reputation. Or worse. Shit. I have to find Malc—"

"Ground Control to Major Tom," Mike heard Amanda say.

"Huh?" he replied, looking vacantly at her.

"Are you there, Bueller?" Amanda raised her hand to his forehead, preparing to flick him with her middle finger. "Oh. Right. Almost forgot. They frown on us, flicking subordinates in the head."

"Sorry, I was just thinking—"

"Don't think. Just do. Get out there and talk to some of the girls."

There was a ping, and then the elevator door opened. Three ruddy-faced young officers in uniform got out, clearly having just come from the gym two floors below. Mike followed them with his eyes, remembering when he was just like those young officers. And when he went to the gym.

"Call me if you find anything out," Amanda said as Mike got into the elevator, adding, "and be careful! And I can't believe you let me call you a subordinate without—"

The elevator door closed.

Mike pushed P4 and looked at the license number on the key fob. He leaned back on the mirrored wall and stretched his neck before realizing that he didn't have his gun with him. He didn't have his handcuffs or memo book, either. He didn't even have a steno pad to make some notes.

CHAPTER TWENTY-TWO

Hopefully, there'll be some napkins or something in the car to write on.

The door slid open, and he walked down the narrow hallway with all of its blind corners until he got to the parking garage door. A couple of the overheads were blown out, giving the passage a cave-like feel with shadows appearing and disappearing on the walls as Mike walked by them, wondering why it was so difficult to make just a straight-run hallway. His leather-soled shoes clicked as he walked, almost echoing.

He stopped for a moment, looking at the panic bar on the metal door in front of him. He thought he had heard the door click shut just before he made that last blind corner, but he wasn't sure. Beads of sweat began to drip down his back, absorbed by the white cotton t-shirt he wore under his dress shirt. He loosened his tie.

He pushed the panic bar with too much force, causing the door to hit the wall on the other side and bounce back quickly, hitting him. He pushed it again, his heart racing as he looked into the dark parking lot. He heard tires screeching before seeing headlights coming around the blind corner from the floor below. He reached for his gun and then remembered that he didn't have it.

Last time, he didn't reach for it.

But this wasn't the underground where Sal was shot. This wasn't that afternoon. The car that screeched by him didn't carry the murderer. This wasn't then. This is now, in the underground parking lot of police headquarters, and Mike was looking for an unmarked police car to use.

He took a deep breath and noticed his hands were shaking. He wondered if seeing the psychologist triggered something in him or if he'd been this fucked up for a while, like Bridget said.

Dunno.

He continued to where the unassigned cars were parked and looked around until he found his. He opened the door and noticed sunflower seed shells on the floor.

Fucking Sal.

Chapter Twenty-Three

7:03 p.m. Tuesday, January 15, 2019

I t got dark early in January. Usually by about 4:30 or so, especially on days like this, when it seemed as if the sun never really came out at all. At least it wasn't snowing. Or raining. The temperature hovered just around freezing, which would have made for a messy night. Not that it would make any difference for Mike's purposes.

He turned the familiar corner to see those same half a dozen or so girls in various stages of disarray, looking hopefully at every car that drove by. If the car sped up, they yelled obscenities at it. If it slowed down, they sauntered over to it, ready to sell.

Tonight, he noticed another group of women standing across the street a dozen or so yards away from these girls. At first glance, they looked more like what most people would think a sex trade worker would look like: big hair, tight short dresses, unbelievably high heels. Mike knew that they were the transgender sex trade workers.

Mike took a deep breath and slowed down. Seeing one of the young women approach his car, he stopped and rolled down the passenger's side window.

"Hey, baby. How ya doin'?" she said, slurring slightly. The night was almost as young as she looked. Plenty of time to get completely stoned. And wholly destroyed.

"Good. You?" Mike replied, leaning across the passenger's seat.

"Better for seein' you. Whatcha lookin' for, darlin'?"

Her eyes began to brighten as much as they could under the veil of whatever drug she was on.

"I'm looking for a girl named Lisa," Mike said.

The girl stepped back from the car and then inspected one of the scabs on her arm.

"You know her?" Mike continued.

"You a cop?"

"I'm her friend."

"I dunno where she is, honey, but I'm sure I can do whatever she did for you better."

"Do you know her?"

"You look like a cop."

"I've been told that before."

The woman sized Mike up and then looked at the car.

"You even drive a cop car. One of those undercover ones."

"It's not mine," Mike said.

"Don't matter. Even if you are a cop, you wouldn't be the first I've sucked off. You want me to suck you off?" she said, opening the passenger door.

"Do you know Lisa?"

She stopped and looked at his crotch.

"What if I do?"

"Listen," Mike said. "I'll pay you whatever it'd cost for a blow job if you just hop in and tell me about Lisa. We can drive around the block while you talk. No one needs to know."

"You got it bad for her or what?" the woman said, getting in, holding her hand out for the cash. Mike gave her a few bills and then drove off with her in the car.

"She's a friend of mine," Mike repeated.

"At least she's got one friend," the woman said, looking out the side window.

"What do you mean?"

"She was a bitch."

"Was?"

143

"Oh. Yeah. She's dead. Sorry, not sorry. You got any smokes, darlin'?"

"How?"

"Fucked if I know. I'm not a cop," she said with a self-deprecating laugh. "Any ideas?"

"As if. That old piece of shit's lucky she lasted as long as she did."

"What do you mean?"

"You knew? Fuck me. She was like, what, twice as old as us? Thought she knew how to turn a trick better 'en any of us and always ended up standin' on the corner waitin' for her regular."

"Regular?"

"What the fuck, bud," she said, reaching for the door handle.

"No, wait," Mike said, pressing the automatic door lock.

A look of terror washed over her face.

"I won't hurt you. I'll take you back to the corner. I just want to know…"

"Listen, you fuckin' creep. Lisa was bad news, okay? She fuckin' scared more johns away with her fuckin' rantin' and such. The only thing that kept her alive on these streets was that jerk-off regular of hers."

"Do you know what kind of car he drove?"

"No. Fuckin' let me out, you perv. Fuck."

Mike rounded the corner and let the woman out, but not before she took the opportunity to throw a hard right at his jaw, breaking the skin. As she pulled her fist back, it got caught in the breast pocket of his shirt and ripped the fabric.

"It was a minivan, you fuckin' weirdo. Now fuck off!"

Mike massaged his jaw and made sure he hadn't lost any teeth in the transaction. A bit of blood from his lip spilled down onto his shirt. His attempt to wipe off the droplets only caused them to smear, turning the blood spots on his shirt into something that looked like it would have come from a much harder punch to the head.

Shit. I've gone too far.

Mike drove away from the group of women on the corner, seeing the one he had just dropped off pointing to his car out of the rearview mirror.

Burned.

Mike pulled around the corner, parking the car outside a convenience store. He got out and went into the store to buy a bag of gummy bears for himself.

"Rough neighborhood ," he said as he set the bag of candy on the counter.

"Not so much," the small but very pregnant Korean woman said, sliding the bag over the scanner. "You get to know them."

Mike pulled a five-dollar bill out of his wallet.

"Ever seen an older-looking woman—"

"They all look old," the woman said, giving Mike his change.

"How about this one?" Mike said, pulling up a mugshot of Lisa on his smartphone.

"That one!" the woman exclaimed. "She not allowed in here."

"Why not?"

"She owe me money."

"How much?" Mike asked.

"I don't know. A hundred? She come in here all the time, wants smokes, say she have no money. I go to call the cops, but she say she'll trash the place before they come. First time I try, she right. Place trashed. And they never come. So I give her a pack. And then she start coming in all the time. She take whatever she want from the store. I call the cops again. She just laugh at me. I call cops after she leave. They tell me I have to give her trespass paper or something. I tell them I want her arrested. They tell me they're too busy. I tell them what I pay taxes for? Useless."

"So what happened?"

"I have enough. I tell her she banned. Nothing. My husband working a few day ago and she come in. Same thing. She tell him she have no money and to give her cigarettes. He tell her get the hell out."

"Did it work?"

"Must have because I no see her around for last day or so."

"Thanks for the candy," Mike said. "Oh, and you can't sell that stuff."

"What stuff?" the woman said, following Mike's eyes to the shelf behind her. "Bear spray? It's our best seller. Best price in town."

"It's illegal."

"No. Pepper spray is illegal. Bear spray is not. I know the law."

"Those little bottles in plastic baggies don't look too legit to me," Mike said.

"I get them from eBay. One hundred percent legit," the woman countered.

"I doubt that, but I'm not the patent police," Mike said as he picked up the candy from the counter and left.

He turned the car on and cranked the heat, opening the package of gummy bears, picking out one at a time as he considered his next move. He finished them, crumpled up the package, leaned over to stuff it in the glove box, and then put the car in gear.

Maybe another loop.

Before he got back to the stroll, he saw a group of people huddled in front of a storefront.

This is new.

He slowed down. A large man was standing at the doorway, smiling as he welcomed the people inside. Mike pulled the car over and turned off the engine.

"Welcome to the Church of the Liberator," the large man said as Mike approached the storefront.

"Uh, thanks," Mike said. "How long have you been here?"

"God has always been here, my brother," the man said with a large grin.

"No, I mean the...this..."

"If you have to ask, you must be new to the neighborhood. Come in. Enjoy some fellowship," the man said, ushering Mike in. "Pastor Chloe will be preaching shortly, and there'll be coffee and sandwiches afterwards. Coffee isn't great, but it's hot."

Mike looked around at the handful of people all seated on the folding chairs facing the back of the storefront. A couple of them looked certifiable, while another looked like he had passed out. Mike could smell the alcohol from where he stood. A toothless woman with scraggly bleached hair came in behind him with two small, miserable-looking children in tow. One of them smiled, or maybe scowled at Mike, his baby teeth blackened with rot.

"Welcome to the House of God, brothers and sisters," the big man who had greeted Mike at the door said, making his way to the back of the building. "Pastor Chloe will be here in a moment to—"

"Where's the fuckin' food?" the previously passed-out man hollered, looking around him as if he'd just been dropped into a parallel universe.

"Watch yer fuckin' mouth, motherfucker!" the woman with the two small children hissed at him. "I got kids here."

"Let us welcome Pastor Chloe!" the big man said, clapping wildly as a middle-aged bohemian-looking woman leapt out from behind the back wall to the stage. Mike looked around him as the drunk man seemed to pass out again and the other men nodded. The woman with the children smiled her toothless grin as her two children clapped madly.

For fuck sake.

The woman began, and Mike had to admit, her fire-and-brimstone sermon was something to behold. Certainly not like anything he'd ever heard back in the day when he was hauled to Church every Sunday. She quoted scripture, she lowered her voice to a whisper, and then got so loud that Mike thought the front windows would rattle. She sang. She danced. She wept. And then she told everyone that God loved them while the big man put two large trays of sandwiches on a table along with an urn full of coffee.

Everyone in the place except for Mike, the big man, and the pastor pounced on the sandwiches. It was like a cage match watching this small group scramble for a few dozen squares of bread with processed cheese between the slices. The woman with the small children shoved sandwiches into her pockets amidst the protests of the drunk man. While with not quite the same level of despair, the urn of coffee was emptied into cup after cup with everyone, including the small children, practically dumping the scalding beverage down their throats.

And then they all cleared out. Except for Mike, the big man, and the pastor.

"Is it always like this?" Mike asked.

"Pretty much," the big man said.

"We feed their souls and their bodies," the pastor said with a wide smile.

"Why?" Mike asked.

"Because God put the word in me," the woman said.

147

"And God told me to support my wife," the big man said.

"So you do this yourselves?"

"No. God's with me," the woman said as the big man cleaned up around the table.

"Who pays for this?" Mike asked.

"God's other children," the woman said. "The church I pastor at truly understands Christ's teachings, and they know that I've been called to spread the Word."

Mike tried not to grimace.

"Do you ever get any of the girls on the corner coming in?" Mike asked.

"The prostitutes?" the woman asked. "Once in a while, but we're here during their working hours."

"Does that bother you at all?" Mike said, his eyes narrowing.

Both the big man and woman looked at him.

"I mean that there are sex trade workers...young sex trade workers...just over there while you're trying to preach—"

"God chooses those with the worst past for His brightest future," the woman said.

"Who are you?" the big man asked.

"I'm a guy looking for a woman named Lisa. She worked on the corner."

"We know Lisa," the pastor said. "The Devil keeps trying to steal her soul, but she's always fighting back."

"What do you mean?"

"Drugs," the big man said. "The Devil's trying to keep her down with drugs, but God keeps pulling her out."

"So you know her?"

"She was coming to my other church for a while," the pastor said. "But then the enemy put shame into her, and she fell back into the Devil's pit."

"Is this the Devil's pit?" Mike asked, looking out the front window.

"One of the many pits the Devil put in her way," the pastor said.

"There were others?"

"Every man who picked her up was sent by the Devil," the big man said.

"Are you a Christian?" the pastor asked.

CHAPTER TWENTY-THREE

"I'm Catholic, if that's what you mean."

The husband and wife looked at each other.

"When was the last time you went to Church?" the pastor asked.

"I don't know. A few years a—"

"God has brought you into this storefront today to deliver you from whatever the enemy has put in your way that has kept you out of His house," the pastor began.

"Thanks, but no thanks," Mike said. "I appreciate you telling me about my friend, but I've gotta go."

"We're here every Tuesday night, my brother," the big man said as Mike exited the storefront. "God is telling me that you're running from something, and He is the answer."

Mike got back in the unmarked police car, sweat beginning to drip down his back.

Fucking Sal.

Chapter Twenty-Four

10:01 a.m. Wednesday, January 16, 2019

"Ms Calloway," the judge said, his words dripping with exasperation, "I am curious about the manner in which you're conducting this trial."

The court transcriber paused and looked up at the judge as she mumbled his words into her steno mask.

"Your Honor?" Bridget replied from the podium.

"Yes. Detective O'Shea has been in the court, excluded from court, on the stand, and now he's assisting you with your trial. It makes no sense to me."

"Me either," the defense attorney said, motioning to stand up without actually rising from his chair as he spoke.

"If you'd like to call for a recess, I'd be happy to explain it to you in your chambers," she offered, looking back at Mike, who was sitting at the prosecution's table, steno pad at the ready.

"And now you're telling me how to run my courtroom. I'm not amused, Ms Calloway."

"Hrumph!" the defense attorney muttered.

"I will, however, grant you a *voir dire* to explain yourself," the judge said.

"Thank you, Your Honor," Bridget said, walking as purposefully as she could back to her table.

"I guess I'll wait outside, huh?" Mike said, gathering his coat and briefcase.

And so the morning went, most of which Mike spent sitting in the hallway outside of courtroom 205. A few of the accused being brought into other courtrooms nodded to him, as did some of his peers, although most of the latter avoided him. Or so he thought.

Fine. Fuck 'em. Brotherhood, my ass. As long as you toe the line.

Mike rubbed his face, gently touching his swollen lip, noticing that, in an effort not to re-open the cut, he may have missed too large a patch while shaving that morning.

Carla's fucked. They're going to eat her alive once she gets out from under Landon's wing.

He looked at his watch. Just after eleven. Not a good sign.

Or is Landon part of it, too? And he's throwing both of us to the wolves once he moves on. They always move on. Nothing sticks to them that way. Teflon. All of them.

The thick wooden door to courtroom 205 burst open. Two uniformed officers escorted Mark Johnstone out of the courtroom and down the hall, his lawyer following. Bridget, checking her watch, wasn't too far behind, purse under one arm, a bundle of papers shoved in a folder under the other.

Mike decided not to try to catch up with her. Instead, he stayed seated on the bench and watched her hustle to the Crown's Office. He waited another few minutes, leaned his head back to stretch his neck, and then went to grab a coffee and a sandwich from the shop across the street before going in to see her.

* * *

"So?" he said, poking his head in Bridget's office.

"Where have you been?" she asked, looking up from her.

"Across the street for a bite to eat."

"Did you bring me back anything?"

"No. I figured—"

"Never mind. And what happened to your lip? Again, never mind. Okay. Clearly, we're close to going off the rails with this trial. Time to regroup. If I can't have you on the stand to bring the pipe into evidence for the murder, we need another angle."

"It's obvious," Mike said as he sat down in the chair across from her desk. "The pipe was seized in relation to another offence and was found to have the deceased's blood on it. That's a no-brainer, Bridget. You know that."

Bridget didn't answer, looking back at the file on her desk instead.

"Is there something going on that I need to know?" Mike asked.

"Like what?" she said, staring blankly up at him.

"Like that you're quitting the Crowns office and going to the dark side?" Mike asked.

"What if I was?"

"And that you're involved in the same load of shit that I'm involved in?" he continued, careful to tread lightly, just in case she was on the other side.

"I have no idea what you're talking about," she snapped, looking back down at her papers.

"Come on, Bridget. We've known each other for how long now? And through how much shit?"

"Exactly. And right now, I've got a burrito full of shit that I've got to turn into a successful prosecution in front of a judge that's disappointed that I'm not just more T&A wanting to sleep with him."

"So you're leaving the Crown's Office to—"

"Yes. I am. Okay? I haven't submitted my resignation papers yet, so I'd appreciate it if you'd keep it under your hat, but yes. I'm joining Munro & Associates at the end of the month."

"Wow. That's quick."

"Two weeks' notice. That's all they require."

"But what about all of your cases? What about—"

"I'm sure they'll find someone else to take them over."

"Like that dipshit that was in here a few weeks ago?"

"Likely. He's good. Getting better."

"But he's no you."

"Your powers of observation are staggering some days, Mike," Bridget sneered.

"Well, at least I'll still see you," Mike said, trying not to sigh.

"Not unless you're planning on moving out west."

"Huh?"

"They're opening up a new office on the west coast. I'm going to be overseeing it."

"Oh."

"There's nothing holding me here, Mike. Now that my father's gone, I can start doing the things that I want to do."

"Like move out west?"

Bridget looked at Mike. He noticed the darkness under her eyes.

"Yeah. Like move out west. Like oversee a law firm. Like be surrounded by beautiful scenery instead of these ugly building. Like get on with my life."

"I thought you were getting on with your life," Mike said. He felt a tightness in his chest.

"No, Mike. I was just biding my time until my father passed. And now he's gone, and I'm done. It's me time."

"But what about—"

"Well, look at that, will you?" Bridget said far too brightly. "Court will be in session in about ten minutes. Just enough time for me to go to grab a coffee from the machine, freshen up, and get back in there. If you'll excuse me?" she said, getting up.

"Yeah. Sure. Of course. See you back in court."

* * *

The afternoon went marginally better than the morning had gone. While she couldn't prove it, Bridget was fairly certain that the judge, having engaged in the decades-past habit of having a martini or two at lunch was likely the cause. And that would likely mean this case would end up going to appeals if the defense lost. For now, all Bridget could do was carry on, getting the pipe in as evidence, while Mike's testimony was excluded. At least they were moving forward.

And then the judge dropped a bomb.

"Just a reminder that we will not be sitting tomorrow," he said. "In fact, we will not be reconvening on this matter until a week Tuesday."

"Your Honor!" the defense lawyer said, shooting up to his feet, patting his agitated client on the shoulder as he did so.

"The court coordinator knew my schedule before she scheduled me for this trial," the judge said, his voice rising. "She knew that I had another commitment beginning tomorrow that is expected to last a week."

"But my client?" the defense lawyer whined.

"Indeed. I am sure Mr. Johnstone's pre-trial custody will be taken into account in the event he is found guilty. In the meantime, you have my sincere apologies, Mr. Johnstone. But there's nothing that can be done about it."

"Your Honor," Bridget said, standing up.

"Nothing, Ms. Calloway, can be done about it," he repeated and then looked over at the court clerk.

"All rise!"

Chapter Twenty-Five

5:07 p.m. Wednesday, January 16, 2019

Mike was not in a good mood when he came through the front doors of 6 District. The chipped asbestos-tile floor that was probably giving them all cancer was even filthier than usual, and the corpse-gray walls were just a reminder of how they'd all end up. He'd had to park a couple of blocks away from the station because it was shift-change, and no one, in their infinite wisdom, had thought that every person assigned to the station would have a car that needed to be parked. And, once again, the sun had failed to break through the clouds, so it was already very dark outside—not that it mattered because the windows inside were filthy.

He pushed his way past the crowd of uniform officers who were either forcing the fob the scout car keys were affixed to in or out of the board that some brain surgeon had decided to mount right by the back hallway. He noticed that most of the guys looked like they hadn't shaved in a week, while the women, flagrantly disregarding the hair regulations with their ponytails popping out from behind their issued baseball caps, looked more like minimum-wage rent-a-cops than real police officers. As he continued down the hallway towards the detective office, he wondered when he got so old.

"What happened to your lip, Crumply Pants?"

"What? This? Got clocked by a hooker," Mike said, taking his trench coat off. "How are you always so—cheery?"

"I surround myself with cranky old men like you, so, in comparison...." Amanda said with a shrug.

"Thanks," he said as he hung his coat up. "But on the upside, I may have gotten saved last night."

"She hit you so hard that it was a come-to-Jesus moment?" she asked, looking down at the cell phone that she'd placed on the desk.

"Not exactly, although I did end up at some revivalist bible-thumping thing."

"I'm not even going to ask. So,what have you got for me?"

"Nothing that we didn't already know, really," he said, sitting down at his desk and typing in his password, his upper back already tight. "Lisa was still on the strip, not very well-liked, owed the convenience store a pile of money for smokes."

"While we can't rule them out, I wasn't thinking the convenience store owners were the killers," Amanda said with a smile, scrolling through a series of images on her computer screen.

"No, but I think this establishes that Lisa wasn't well-liked by anyone, which opens up a can of potential suspects."

"Except that Ron—god, I'm going to miss him—was able to light a fire under someone's ass to get me some CCTV footage from the city showing the vehicle Lisa's body was found in going into the parking lot. Here. See? Look. I want you to see the original first. Here's the car going into the parking lot. You can see a driver and a passenger. We see the car proceed towards the far corner of the parking lot. The camera swings back to scan the entrance and then, when it goes back to the lot, we see the car that was carrying our victim–"

"Lisa," Mike said, leaning over to look at the screen.

"Lisa and the driver going off the pavement onto the sand towards the lake. Another pause while the camera scans the parking lot, and then we see the car engulfed in flames, and one person getting out of the driver's side of the car."

"Well, that beats my update. Where's Carla?"

"In the ladies."

"TMI," he said.

"You asked."

"So are we still ruling out suspects or…?"

"Hang on. Take a look at this," Amanda said, opening another file. "Tech Support was able to enhance the video. You can see that it's Jordan Hawthorne getting out of the car."

"Slam dunk."

"Pretty much."

"Sorry. Got talking to one of my guys in the hallway. Oh, hi, housemate!" Carla said. "What happ—"

"Girl trouble," Amanda quipped.

"I didn't take Bridget to be the physical kind," Carla said with a wink as she sat at her desk across from Mike's.

"Why does everybody think—"

"Kids? Do you mind? We've got a homicide to investigate here," Amanda said.

"Right. About that. I've never typed up a warrant before," Carla began.

"No better time to learn than now. And you've got the best teacher right there," Amanda said, looking at Mike.

"Sure. Pull up a chair," Mike said.

"TV chick's at the front desk," the uniformed station duty officer called from the hallway. "Says she wants to talk to someone about the hooker that got fried."

"That wouldn't be Janelle Austin by any chance, would it?" Amanda said.

"You got it, boss," he said.

"Shit. Tell her—"

"Says she's not leaving until she speaks to someone involved in the case."

"Get Staff to kick her out."

"Are you kidding? He's too busy getting his balls licked by her."

Carla screwed up her face and gave Mike the side-eye.

"Likely told him he's god's gift to women," the uniformed officer continued, hoisting his pants up over his ample midriff.

"Mike?" Amanda began hopefully.

"No," Mike said, doubling down on his efforts to assist Carla in writing the warrant for Hawthorne's arrest.

"Fine. Tell her I'll be out in a minute," Amanda said. "But I'm only giving her two minutes."

The uniformed station duty officer waddled back up the hallway towards the front desk.

"And tell her she can get in line like everyone else going forward," Amanda called after him.

"Sure thing, boss," the officer hollered back.

* * *

"You must be very brave," Janelle Austin practically cooed to the uniformed staff sergeant behind the front desk.

"Well," he began with false modesty, the civilian station duty officer sitting at the desk a few paces behind him, trying not to roll her eyes too conspicuously.

"Inspector Black!" Janelle called, dropping the ego of the man in front of her like a hot potato when she saw Amanda walk towards her.

"Detective Sergeant, and let's get this over with."

"My apologies. Tara?" Janelle said to the cameraperson beside her.

"You'll have to take that outside," the uniformed station duty officer called out, seeing that his boss was still under Janelle's spell and temporarily incapable of taking control of the situation.

"Of course," Janelle said, motioning for the cameraperson to get the shot set up outside the police station.

"I've got two minutes," Amanda said.

"We're both articulate women, Detective Sergeant," Janelle said. "I'm sure that's all we'll need."

Amanda rolled her eyes.

"Janelle Austin here with Detective Sergeant Black, the lead investigator in the Lisa Clayton murder. Tell me, Detective Sergeant, do you think this is the beginning of a series of murders involving sex trade workers?"

"No."

"I understand you've got your department's only transwoman working on this case with you. Is that correct?"

"I've got the best investigators in the city working on this homicide, yes."

"And one of them is a transwoman. The only transwoman detective in the city, if not the country, correct?"

"I wouldn't know."

"And did you specifically request a transwoman investigator because you felt that this murder is linked to the numerous unsolved murders of transwomen in this city that date back—"

"I'm investigating the murder of Lisa Clayton. If anyone has any information about her murder, they can contact me at Homicide or call Crime Stoppers. Thank you, Janelle," Amanda said and walked back into the station.

"As we've just heard, the investigation into the murder of Lisa Clayton has opened up the reality that this city continues to be plagued by the unsolved murders of sex trade workers, some of whom are transwomen. If you, or anyone you know, have any information about this or the unsolved murders of other sex trade workers, please notify Homicide or Crime Stoppers."

Janelle gave her most serious look at the camera for a few seconds before her cameraperson hoisted the camera off her shoulder.

"Send that in ASAP, Tara. I'm sure they'll want it for the 6 o'clock news."

* * *

"How'd it go?" Mike asked, looking up from his computer screen.

"Are you going to be on the news this evening?" Carla asked.

"I hope to hell not," Amanda said. "Somehow, word got out about you, Carla."

"I know and I'm sorry, Amanda."

"Why are you sorry?" Mike asked.

"Don't worry," Amanda said. "I'll get Corp Comm on it. They'll manage the message."

"What message?" Mike asked.

"I just want to be me," Carla said, beginning to cry. "And not bloody-well cry at work every day! Excuse me."

Carla got up and strode out of the office.

"What was that all about?" Mike asked.

Amanda just looked at him.

"I live under a rock, don't I?"

"You live under male privilege," Amanda said. "How's that warrant coming along?"

"Done."

Mike pressed the Print button.

"Good. Let's get it sworn to and arrest that fucker."

Mike got up and walked up the hall. He noticed the washroom door was closed.

"You in there, Carla?" he called.

"Yes."

"Can you unlock it? I'm coming in."

Mike waited to hear the click and then gently pushed the door open.

Carla was standing in front of the mirror, wiping away the mascara that had drizzled down her cheeks.

"It's going to be okay," Mike said. "Just give it a few weeks, and you'll be old news."

"Oh, Michael. What was I thinking? I should have known this was going to happen. I should have—"

"Shoulda, coulda, woulda, didn't," Mike said. "We're here now, so let's just deal with it."

"We?"

"Yeah. We're partners, remember?"

"You're going to make me cry again, Michael."

"Yeah. About that...."

* * *

It was just after 3 a.m. when Mike got home. Carla had booked off several hours earlier and was asleep downstairs. He reached up and pulled the half-empty bottle of Jameson down and poured three fingers' worth into the waiting glass.

"Ye can't beat out the darkness with darkness, me son," Mary-Margaret said, covering her pink flannel pajamas as she wrapped her bathrobe around her.

"I'm just pouring myself a nightcap, Mom," Mike replied, turning around to see her come into the dining room. "Sláinte."

"Ach, I've only been yer mam for how many years? I know when me lad's heart is hurtin' and no amount of Jameson will heal it."

"It's just a nightcap," Mike repeated.

"Tell that to all yer mates and all, luv, but a mother knows. What's troublin' ye? Carla told me her troubles, but I'm sensin' there's something else goin' on with ye," she said, now standing beside him, eying the whiskey.

"Do you want one?"

"A proper shot, yes. I'm not lookin' to make a meal out of it, as ye clearly are. And 'twas I who replaced the empty bottle ye'd left on the shelf, so don't think I don't know what's goin' on with ye."

Mike nodded as he poured her a shot, and they both sat down at the dining room table. Neither of them spoke again for several minutes.

"Bridget's moving out west," Mike finally said.

"Do ye blame her, son?"

"Whose side are you on?" Mike said, taking a sip of his whiskey.

"Neither, but the night is short, and so is me time remainin' on this earth, so let's not mince our words. Ye've had years to win her over, but ye chose not to. She practically threw herself at ye, but ye didn't see it. And now, she's realizin' that her ship with ye will never come in, so she's moved along."

"Not helpful, Mom," Mike said, taking another sip of his whiskey.

"Ach, I know it hurts, Michael," she said, putting her hand on his arm, "but ye can't honestly be gutted. A bit o' pride bruised, maybe. Loss of familiarity, sure. But did ye really think she was the girl for ye?"

"I don't know."

"Well then, that says it all, doesn't it," Mary-Margaret concluded. She took a sip of the whiskey in her glass and pushed it aside. "Now, don't be sittin' here over an empty bottle when Max gets up for school."

She stood up and kissed him gently on the forehead before heading up to bed. "And let me know how it's goin' with yer Dr. Shimner-Lewis."

"How do you know?"

"Girl talk. Mind yerself on the stairs comin' up, me son. No one needs to be a stumblin' drunkard."

Chapter Twenty-Six

2:01 p.m. Thursday, January 17, 2019

"Whathat happened in Court today?" Amanda asked.

"The judge argued with Bridget, who argued with me," Mike said, dumping his coat over the back of his chair before sitting down.

"You two need to come out as a couple and get rid of all of this pent-up sexual tension," Amanda said.

"Kinda hard to do when she's moving across the country," Mike said, pounding the keyboard in front of him to unlock his computer.

"What? I thought she was just going to the dark side."

"Yeah. The dark side on the West Coast," Mike said. "They're opening up another office and she's going to be the lead."

"Oh."

"So," Mike continued flatly, "what's on tap for today, Boss?"

"You know I hate it when people call me Boss, right?"

"Sorry."

"You and Carla are going to go arrest Hawthorne," Amanda said, squinting as she leaned closer to the screen, scribbling out an address. "I really should pick up another pair of those damned readers."

"Isn't that why they pay you the big bucks?"

"Really?" Amanda said, turning to look at Mike. "Unless you'd rather—"

"I know. Prep a case for court next week."

"No. Go to the Hope Care Facility to register my sister."

"That's for disabled elderly people, isn't it?" Mike asked, scrolling through the rows of unopened emails, most with little red exclamation marks beside them.

"Yep. My parents can't take care of her anymore."

"What about caregivers?"

"Caregivers cost. A lot."

"Yeah, but you must have got a good settlement…?"

"From who, Mike? Randy Valencourt? That piece of shit who shot her in the neck and left her for dead? Not likely."

"What about —"

"That thousand or so bucks a month doesn't go very far. God forbid we give victims of crime a livable income."

Mike remembered the huge manhunt years ago for the guy who walked into a convenience store one hot summer night and shot the part-time clerk in a botched robbery attempt and how they caught him a week or two later up north. The media was all over it right up until the trial ended, plastering both of their pictures everywhere. He was found guilty. She was left a quadriplegic. Both were soon forgotten.

"Is he still in jail?"

"No," Amanda said. "He's been out for five years. Served his time. Never apologized. Never showed any remorse. Just bided his time for thirteen years."

"Well, at least they caught him."

Amanda turned sharply and looked Mike squarely in the face.

"We'll catch Malcolm Oakes, Mike," Amanda said, and then, her voice softening, added, "but don't give up your day job to become a grief counselor."

"Sorry."

"In the meantime, you and Carla are going to make the door knock. I don't need to tell you, but I will. Try to keep it simple."

"You're talking to the right guy," Mike said. "Mister Easy-Does-It."

"I've known you a long time, Mike. You're anything but."

"Speaking of which," he said, looking over at Carla's empty chair, "where is she?"

"In the washroom."

"Don't tell me she's crying."

"No. She's fixing her makeup to try to cover up those bruises on her face. Tell me she's going to report whoever did that to her."

"I think she should tell you."

"Tell you what?" Carla said, bursting into the room with a big smile.

"Amanda wanted to know—"

"If we have time, Amanda, let's pop out for a coffee and I'll tell you whatever you want to know, unless Michael's already annoyed you enough to assign us both a horrible detail?"

Carla sat down at her desk and began to log herself in.

"I was just telling Mike that I want the two of you to pick up Jordan Hawthorne."

"Is that all?" she said, looking up at them both. "Swell. Maybe we can grab a coffee on the way back. See you in ten?"

"Amanda wants to know if you're going to report…." Mike said, making circular motions with his hand around his face.

"Already done," Carla said, looking back at her computer screen. "And yes, photos were taken. Anything else?"

Amanda looked over at Mike.

"I'm going to leave you to sort this out, Crumply Pants," she said. "The arrest warrant is in here. Call me when you've got him."

"Well, Michael, let's grab a car and arrest our man," Carla said.

"Please don't cry," Mike said, seeing Carla's shoulders begin to shake.

"It's hormones, Michael. It's not my fault."

"Well, maybe you should take less."

"Really, Michael? That's your answer?" she snapped. "Well, maybe you should just address the root cause of your problems."

"What?"

"You heard me. Deal with it! And I'm driving. I hate your driving. You drive like an old man!"

"Because I *am* an old man."

* * *

"Oh no," Carla said as they parked across the street from Jordan Hawthorne's house.

"What?"

"Look," she said, pointing to a small bicycle left near the front porch. "Kids. He's got kids. I hate arresting people in front of their kids."

"I know. Hopefully, he'll come without any trouble."

"Let's hope."

"Let's get a game plan," Mike said.

"Simple. I'll knock on the door. Dressed as we are, they'll probably think we're Jehovah's Witnesses and not answer, so then we'll knock again, announcing ourselves, warrant in hand. Sound like a plan?"

"Hardly, but let's go."

"You know, you're sounding more like Ron Roberts every day."

"Not remotely accurate. Or helpful," Mike said as he fumbled, getting out of the passenger's side.

"And don't break your ankle on the curb, Michael. If I'd known I would throw you off this much by driving, I'd never—"

"Shit. He's seen us," Mike said, focusing on the upstairs bedroom window. "I think we've been burned."

"I'll still do the door knock at the front. You go around the back."

Carla went up to the front door as Mike walked to the back of the house, getting there just as Hawthorne was coming out the back door.

"Stop. Police!" Mike yelled.

Carla ran around the side of the house to see Hawthorne at the back of the yard, looking up at the 6-foot-high wooden fence.

"Jordan Hawthorne," Mike called out. "You're under arrest."

Hawthorne grabbed the top of the fence and struggled to pull himself over. Mike ran to the back of the fence, looking for something to stand on to help him get over it.

Carla, meanwhile, headed into the next-door neighbor's yard, where a chain link fence separated this yard from the one behind it, and saw

Hawthorne scramble up from where he had landed and start to run away.

"This way, Michael!" she yelled as she ran to the back of that yard and hopped the fence. Despite her Cuban heels and skirt, she still managed to lessen the gap between her and Hawthorne.

Mike saw that Hawthorne had cut between two houses, running along the street that paralleled the one he was on. He saw Carla disappear between the houses after him. Knowing that it was unlikely that he'd be able to catch up, Mike ran back to the car with the intention of driving around the block to cut Hawthorne off. When he got to the car, however, he realized that he didn't have the keys.

Shit!

Suddenly, Mike saw Hawthorne round the corner, running towards the minivan parked in the driveway. Mike ran at him. Hawthorne didn't notice him until he was almost at the van, at which point he deked to the right, past Mike and the van, Carla not too far behind.

"Here," she panted, tossing the car keys at Mike. "I'll keep following him. You get the car."

Mike ran to the car and started it up. The tires screeched, and he was gaining on them. Within seconds, he had passed Carla and the hood of his car was about five yards away from Hawthorne. With a quick spin of the steering wheel, Mike bumped the man with his right bumper, causing him to fall to the ground. Mike threw the engine in park and ran around to arrest him.

Hawthorne got back on his feet and was running back past the unmarked car towards his own house with Mike in full pursuit.

Seeing Hawthorne heading towards her, Carla positioned herself so that he ran right into her. She tackled him to the ground with ease and, as he began to flail his arms, he hit her several times in the head.

"I am Detective Carla Hageneur," she yelled, "and you're under arrest for murder, Jordan Hawthorne. Stop resisting."

She grabbed one of his arms and wrenched it around his body with such force that, to stop it from snapping, he let it go limp, rolling onto his stomach as she pulled his arm into the air.

"Handcuffs, Michael. Quickly," she said as Mike caught up with her. "And then let's get him off his belly so he can breathe easier."

"Here," Mike said. "I've got it."

Mike clicked the handcuffs on Hawthorne's wrists and then sat him up.

Hawthorne leaned back, gasping for air.

"Positional asphyxia. It'll get you every time," Carla said, wiping the sweat from her brow.

"Good job," Mike said.

"You, too," she replied, sitting beside Hawthorne, her legs outreached in front of her, noticing a hole in her pants. "Not very ladylike, am I?"

"You're a fucking woman?" Hawthorne gasped. "With a tackle like that, I thought you were a football player."

"I was," she said.

Chapter Twenty-Seven

5:00 p.m. Thursday, January 17, 2019

"Well done, Dream Team," Amanda said as Mike and Carla came into the detective office. "Did he give you any trouble?"

"Nothing my partner couldn't handle," Mike said.

"You're too kind, Michael," Carla said. "Now, if you'll excuse me, I have to clean myself up a bit."

The booking officer appeared through a door that came from the cells. "Says he wants to talk to you."

"You read him his rights, didn't you?" Amanda asked Mike.

"Of course I did."

"Just checking," Amanda said. "Has he lawyered up?"

"Yep. Just got off the phone with her," the booker said.

"Do you know who she is?"

"Yeah. Got it written down," the booker said, looking at the name he had written on the palm of his hand. "Carr. Rejeanne Carr."

"I'll wait until she gets here," Amanda said.

"He says he wants to talk to you now," the booker said.

"No. There's no way in hell that I'm going to take a statement from a guy up on a murder charge without his lawyer present."

"I'll let him know," the booker said, disappearing back into the cell area.

"What did I miss, kids?" Carla asked.

"Hawthorne wants to spill," Mike said.

"Is that normal?" Carla asked.

"No. Unless *he's* having a come-to-Jesus moment," Amanda said.

"Or he wants to make a deal," Mike said.

"On what? He has no idea what we've got yet," Amanda said.

"Maybe Lisa's not the only one," Mike said softly.

"Michael..." Carla said, shaking her head.

"Wouldn't that just be the fucking dog's biscuit," Amanda groaned. "I was hoping to be able to swing by my house at some point this week."

"As long as we get him before the courts for one count, we can take our time on the others," Mike said. "Maybe he's related to—"

"*If* there are others. Let's just wait until Carr gets here and see what our boy has to say."

"Do you want us in on this or not?" Mike asked.

"I'd like *you* in with me, Mike. Nothing personal, Carla."

"Nothing personal taken," Carla said. "Do what you have to do."

"I'll ask any questions, Mike. You scribe. At the end, if you think there's something I've missed, let me know."

"Sounds familiar," Mike said.

"Just making sure we're on the same page. I'm going out to grab a coffee while we wait for his lawyer to get here. You two want anything?"

"Do we know his lawyer's coming? He may not have said anything to her," Carla said.

"Good point. Mike, go ask—"

"I'm on it, Boss."

"I hate when you call me Boss."

* * *

"I'd like to speak with my client," the tall, thin woman at the front desk said, authority exuding from her Vera Wang skirt suit.

"And your client would be...?" the uniformed station operator asked with indifference as he casually got up from behind his desk.

"Jordan Hawthorne. I believe—"

"Oh, yeah. Hawthorne. The guy who's in for murder," the station operator said louder than necessary, sauntering towards the front desk.

"*Charged* with murder, yes," she clarified in a flat tone, her dark eyes almost as intense as the dark makeup around them. "I'd like to speak to him. Now."

"Gimme a second," the station operator said, turning around and waddling down the back hallway towards the detective office.

"Hey. Dickhead's lawyer is here," he announced to no one in particular.

"I'll be right there," Amanda said. "Just let me have a sip of my coffee. Always the way, isn't it? I can't remember the last time I had a coffee from start to finish."

* * *

Rejeanne Carr and Detective Sergeant Amanda Black were not strangers to one another. They had had many homicide trials together and were equally matched in both intellect and intensity. Mike also remembered Rejeanne Carr clearly, having been cross-examined by her a few times. Rejeanne Carr did not remember Mike.

"I'll just go over the cautions again while Detective O'Shea gets the video equipment going," Amanda said, sitting across the table from the defense lawyer and her client.

"Rolling," Mike said, clicking the timeworn video recorder on.

"My client has nothing to say," Carr said.

"Your client said he does," Amanda countered.

"My client misspoke," the lawyer volleyed back. "Please call the booking officer to return my client to his cell pending his court appearance, which, I'm assuming, will be in a few hours?"

"Wait," Hawthorne said. "I want to—"

"No, you don't," his lawyer advised.

"Yes, I do," he protested.

"As your lawyer, I'm advising—"

"As your client, I'm saying—"

"At the direction of my client, Detective Sergeant Black, I will allow you to speak to him. If, however, I feel that you, or my client, are saying anything incriminating or prejudicial in terms of him receiving a fair and impartial hearing before a judge, I will shut you both down. Do you understand?"

"Absolutely," Amanda said. "Now, Mr. Hawthorne, for the video, do you agree that you have chosen to speak with me without inducement or threats of any sort?"

"Yes, I do. I want to talk to you."

"And, again, for the video, are you aware that anything you say will be used against you in a court of law?"

"Yes, I am."

"And finally, for the video, do you acknowledge that you are aware that I am the officer in charge of the investigation into the murder of Lisa Clayton and that you have been arrested in relation to said murder?"

"Yes, I do. Now, can I tell you—"

"A moment alone with my client, please, Detective Sergeant?" his lawyer interrupted.

"Certainly. Mike, let's step outside."

"No. My client and I will step outside or go to whatever secure, private space you have available."

"This is a secure—"

"But not always private, is it, Detective Sergeant? We all know that, sometimes, that tape recorder," she gestured to the plastic device Amanda had set down in the middle of the table, "doesn't always get turned off when the cops leave the room."

"I know my rights, Rejeanne. I think I can manage this without your input," Hawthorne said.

She looked thoughtfully at her client for a few minutes before acquiescing. Amanda tried to control her breathing as she exhaled with relief. Mike took a pen from his suit coat pocket and readied it on the steno pad in front of him.

"I know you think I killed Lisa," Hawthorne began and then hesitated.

"You don't have to say anything," his lawyer reminded him.

"I didn't kill her," he continued.

CHAPTER TWENTY-SEVEN

Mike and Amanda both looked at him.

"Yeah, she got in my car. But not like that. She said she was going straight, and I just wanted to talk to her."

Mike looked down at the blank page in front of him, trying not to groan.

"I get how you'd think otherwise, but I just wanted to talk to her."

"Had you ever had sex with her before?" Amanda asked.

"You don't have to answer that question," Carr stated.

"Yeah. Lots of times," Hawthorne replied.

"Did you pay her for her services?"

"You don't have to answer that."

"Like as a hooker? Sure. Yeah. That's how we met."

Carr took a deep breath and let it out slowly.

"What? She's a hooker. I'm a guy. How do you think we met?" Hawthorne said to his lawyer. "And, truth to be told, I was kinda sorry when I heard that she was giving it up, you know?"

"So, on the morning in question," Amanda began.

"Yeah, so, that morning, I was driving into work and saw her on the stroll and I thought 'hey, there's Lisa. Maybe one last…you know…?' So I pull up and she gets in my car. I head towards the beach, likely out of habit."

"Jordan are you sure—" his lawyer began.

"When I park, I kinda get that old feeling, you know?"

"I don't think my client—"

"I'll admit, I may have gotten a bit carried away—"

"Okay. I think we're done."

"But before I could actually, you know, *do* anything, this guy comes up beside the car and starts banging the window."

Mike looked up from the steno pad.

"Go on," Amanda said.

"Yeah. This guy…he looked like he knew Lisa. He bangs on the window and then douses the car with what I figure out is gasoline."

Amanda looked at Mike, who shrugged back.

"The car just went up. I know it sounds kinda cowardly, but it was just instinct, I guess. I shoved my door open and got out and, before I could even think about Lisa, the car was totally on fire. Like, I just figured that there was no getting out of that, you know, so I, uh....”

There was a pause.

“Can you describe the man?” Amanda asked.

“I dunno. White? I didn’t get much of a look at him.”

“So what I’m hearing is that my client was also a victim of what may have been a targeted attack on the deceased,” Carr stated. “Not the cause of her death.”

“What I’m hearing is that your client has created a convenient alternate suspect,” Amanda retorted.

“Prove him wrong, Detective Sergeant,” the lawyer taunted.

“Mike?”

“I don’t recall seeing anyone on the CCTV cameras,” Mike said.

“But you’re not sure, are you? Until you can completely rule out this other individual, I believe that you’ve got no other option than to release my client.”

“Really?” Amanda mused.

“Insufficient grounds for detention, at the very least. Wrongful arrest if we want to go that route.”

“I believe that there are reasonable grounds to suggest that your client is responsible for the death of Lisa Clayton.”

“Well, we’ll see how that goes in court tomorrow,” Carr said with a tight smile. “In the meantime, can you call your booker so that we can get my client back into his cell. And I suspect he’s a bit hungry. What’s on the menu tonight?”

* * *

“We need to find Gasoline Guy,” Amanda snapped at Mike as the two of them hurried into the detective office.

“There *is* no Gasoline Guy,” Mike said.

“Prove it,” Amanda said.

“How’d it go?” Carla asked, and then, seeing how flushed Amanda’s face was and how pale Mike’s was, added: “That badly, eh?”

"We need all of the CCTV footage for that parking lot near the beach," Amanda said, pacing back and forth in the dingy office.

"We have that already, don't we, Mike?" Carla asked.

"Yeah."

"Well, we need it in a disclosable file ASAP," Amanda said. "Tomorrow's bail hearing is a done deal, but I'd bet my last dollar that Carr is going to put in an application to get the charge tossed just as soon as she gets her client out of custody."

"That shouldn't be a problem, Amanda. I can do that," Carla said. "In fact, I can get that sorted now and send it to you if you'd like."

"Great," Amanda said, taking a couple of strides before sitting down at the desk beside Mike's.

"But before you get too settled in, I think I have something you might be interested in," Carla said as she logged into her computer. "Take a look at this."

Both Mike and Amanda came around to look at Carla's computer screen as she pulled up a video file.

"Where did you get this?" Amanda asked.

"From my–the Foot Patrol guys. Lawrence gave it to them when they were doing their canvassing of the area."

"Who the hell is Lawrence?" Amanda asked.

"The guy who owns that restaurant just on the corner there when you turn into the parking lot. Wonderful deli that used to get broken into on a regular basis, until Lawrnece installed a few video cameras, including one that looks directly out at the street. Here. Have a look."

"What's that?" Amanda asked, leaning over Carla's shoulder to look at the footage.

"It looks like someone walking into the parking lot, " Mike said, leaning over Carla's other shoulder.

"Is the date stamp correct?" Amanda asked.

"According to what I was told, yes," Carla answered.

"Ok," Amanda said, now practically breathing down Carla's neck as she leaned in closer. "I'm seeing someone walking from the right side to the left side of the screen."

"Right," Carla said. "That's the way to the parking lot."

"Okay," Amanda said. "What else should I see?"

"Give it a minute," Carla said.

The three investigators stared at the video, observing an empty street dimly lit by a streetlight several yards away. Suddenly, they noticed a flash that turned into a glow emerging from the left side of the screen.

"Wait," Amanda said. "I take it that's coming from the parking lot?"

"Correct," Carla said.

Within a few seconds, they saw what appeared to be the same man moving quickly across the screen in the opposite direction.

"Could this guy be the guy Hawthorne was talking about? Mike asked, noting the time at the bottom of the video.

Amanda stepped back from the screen and straightened up and then took a deep breath.

"When did you get this?" she asked Carla.

"While you were in with–"

"Shit," Amanda said. ""Okay. I need you to get this to Video Services right now and have them pull a still of this guy. We'll get it out to all of our people ASAP. I want him identified now. Sooner than now. Like, yesterday."

"I'll find out who's working now and send them the file," Carla said.

"Great," Amanda said, sitting back down at the desk beside Mike's.

"What do we do with Hawthorne?" Mike asked, following her to his own desk.

"Nothing. Until we know better, let's keep everything as it is. In the meantime, good work, Carla."

"Thanks. You know, I wasn't always just a pretty face," she replied.

"In the meantime, I want this guy found and spoken to. Shit. Shit. Shit."

Chapter Twenty-Eight

3:12 a.m. Friday, January 18, 2019

After exhausting all their leads as well as themselves by about 3 a.m., Amanda told Mike and Carla to knock off for a few hours, reminding them that they were required at the team briefing in six hours. Given that they lived together, Mike and Carla drove in together, which didn't do anything to quell the rumors about them as a romantic couple.

"I've never been talked about so much in all of my life," Carla said. "We're practically the Brad and Angelina of the station."

"Hardly," Mike said. "But this, too, shall pass. Soon, it'll be somebody else's turn."

"Yes, I know. Although I have to admit that I am a bit surprised at how long we've been at the top of the hit list."

"What can I say? A hot-looking chick like you hanging out with a stud like me? Bound to turn heads and get them gossiping."

"Thanks for being such a good sport, Michael."

"That's me. The good sport."

* * *

The Major Crime office usually stunk more like a by-the-hour motel than an office within a police facility. The stench of stale booze and unfettered body odor permanently hung in the air. This morning was no exception.

"Okay, gentlemen," Amanda Black said, trying not to cough by reminding herself that she'd smelled worse things, "and once again, I have to ask myself why there are only gentlemen in this room, but that's a battle for another day."

"I don't see any gentlemen, do you?" Billy-Bob said to the other men seated around the room. "Well, maybe Nerdster here, but—"

"As I was saying," Amanda continued just as Mike opened the door.

"Jesus!" he said, turning his head as he moved back into the hallway. "Did someone die in here?"

"Oh my," Carla said, stepping around Mike. "Is there not another room we can use?"

"Central Audit's in the parade room, so...no. And, if anyone has to use the washroom, you'll have to use the ones in the changerooms upstairs. The one downstairs is plugged," Amanda said. "Find a seat. You get used to the smell. And I stand corrected, boys. We've now got representation."

"I don't see any representation, unless you mean *that*," someone muttered loud enough for the words to be heard but not loud enough for the speaker to be identified.

"You two already shacked up?" Billy-Bob asked.

"Insubordination is a thing," Amanda said around the room. "Find a seat, detectives."

Mike and Carla came into the crowded office and found a couple of chairs in the far corner. Carla sat down in the one that looked least likely to collapse before looking over at Mike, who remained standing, stared stoically ahead, not focusing on any of the half dozen or so major crime officers.

"Now, if everyone's ready to get to work, I'm going to turn it over to you, Mike," Amanda said.

Mike cleared his throat.

"Thought your new partner would be doing that," the anonymous voice said.

"Okay. If I have to redirect my briefing one more time, you'll all be back in uniform before the day's over," Amanda advised. "And I'll make it my personal mission to make sure that each of you gets every single goddamned awful detail going for the foreseeable future."

The room was silent.

"So, as everyone knows," Mike began, "Jordan Hawthorne was arrested for the murder of Lisa Clayton yesterday—"

"Thanks to the excellent police work of Detectives O'Shea and Hageneur," Amanda said, looking as proudly at the two as if they were her own children.

"And is likely before the judge as we speak, trying to get bail," Mike continued. "Which he likely will."

"System's fucked," Billy-Bob said.

"And his lawyer, Rejeanne Carr, is likely going to put in an application to have the charge tossed because of some theory she has about a different guy who brought his own gasoline to the—"

"Did someone say Vaseline?"

"Shut. Up," everyone in the room cried, looking towards the detective sergeant.

"Anyway, Carla—Detective Hageneur—was able to identify a man whom we believe did bring something into the crime scene at about the time the car was torched."

"Well, actually," Carla said, "it was a foot patrol officer who got the video from–"

"Regardless," Mike continued, "we have footage of a man in the area, but we don't know who he is. Video Services made some stills from the footage, but they're pretty grainy. They've been handed out to the uniforms on both the midnight and dayshift parades, and I've got a stack here that I'm going to pass around. If anyone has any ideas—"

"By which he means: I need this guy ID'd now," Amanda said.

Mike handed out the stack of photos. Each officer took one before passing the rest along.

"No. Don't tell me," Billy-Bob said with a grin. "Nerdster, is this Anson the Arsonist?"

"Ummm, yeah. I think so," the young officer replied, taking a closer look at his copy of the photo.

"Got a full name on him?" Amanda asked, cocking her head to one side. "And what's his deal?"

"Anson Meyersen. Lives near the beach. Loves to burn shit up."

"Tell me more," Amanda said. "And then tell me why it's the highest maintenance guys who yield the best intel."

"You know more about him than I do, Nerdster. You tell her," Billy-Bob said, elbowing the young officer. "And we're not high maintenance, Boss. We're just…distinct."

A knowing chuckle rippled through the room.

"Ummm. Like Billy-Bob said," the young officer began, "he lives near the beach. Mostly with his mother, although he sometimes just crashes down by the water, weather permitting. We're looking at him for a string of arsons in the division. We don't have enough to arrest him yet, but he's our prime suspect."

"When do you think you will have enough?" Amanda asked. "I don't suppose he'd come in for questioning."

"Well, here's the thing, Boss," Billy-Bob said. "We been working on Project Ash for a few months now, and if we bring him in—"

"I've been working on a homicide for a couple of days now. If you don't bring him in, and the guy whose lawyer is trying to spring him walks, then somebody's going to be doing a lot of shitty details for a very long time," Amanda said. "And it might not just be you."

"Gotcha. Me and Nerdster'll drop by his mom's after this. If he's not there, he'll be hanging out on the beach," Billy-Bob said.

"Great. I want this Meyersen character brought in—not under arrest, by consent—and be sure to seize any property he may have with him, particularly if he's living on the beach."

"Do you think he'd still have the gas can?" Carla asked.

"We don't catch the smart ones," Amanda said. "Okay. You guys go fetch. I want my detectives to hang back and put together the best briefing notes they can so that I can try to break this guy down."

"Grabbing the gas can will be a no-brainer if he's on the beach, Boss," Billy-Bob said. "Gotta be some law against having a gas can on a public beach."

"I doubt it," Nerdster said.

"Anson the Arsonist doesn't have to know there isn't one, does he?" Billy-Bob replied.

"This bullshit-baffles-brains thing only goes so far," Nerdster objected.

"Maybe, but I haven't gotten that far yet," Billy-Bob said.

"What about his having a lawyer?" Carla asked.

"He's coming in for a talk, not under arrest, *right*, Billy-Bob?" Amanda said.

"He still has rights," Carla said.

"Not if he knows what's good for him," Billy-Bob said.

* * *

"What's it like to bang one?" Billy-Bob said, relieving himself at the urinal.

"I don't know what you're talking about," Mike said, pulling the last piece of paper towel out of the dispenser.

"Come on, Mike. It's just you and me in here. What's it like?"

"I'm not banging anyone," Mike said, tossing the paper towel in the waste bin, his hands still wet.

"Sure. But does it kinda freak you out knowing—"

"You know, if Ron wasn't gone and I wasn't sure that Carla had the wherewithal to cover it up, I'd crack your fucking head open on this sink right now," Mike said, pulling the changeroom door open. "But if you continue, I might just take my chances with IA while you spend the rest of your life relearning how to eat with a spoon."

"All good?" Carla said, almost running into Mike in the hallway.

"Just tickety-boo," Mike said. "Want to grab a coffee before Nerdster and his knuckle-dragging partner convince Anson the Asshole or whatever his name is that he wants to come in to talk to us? I've got the car keys in my pocket."

"You read my mind, Michael," Carla said. "It seems like it might end up being one of those days."

"Mike?" Amanda called, just as they were passing by on their way towards the back doors.

"Huh?" Mike said.

"Listen," she said, stepping out of the detective office. "I've got a bad feeling about Billy-Bob and his partner going out to pick up our guy for questioning. Would you and Carla mind heading out instead to see if you can convince him to come in?"

"What about—"

"Even though I don't like being called it, I'm still the boss, remember?"

"Right...Boss," Mike said with a slight smile.

"Crumply-Pants," Amanda said softly, smiling back at Mike before pulling the vibrating phone from her belt. "Detective Sergeant Black speaking."

Chapter Twenty-Nine

10:49 a.m. Friday, January 18, 2019

"Nothing like a drive on a sunny day, wouldn't you say, Michael?" Carla said, pulling a pair of sunglasses that would have put Jackie O to shame out of her purse. She leaned over and checked herself in the side-view mirror. "Oh, good. You can't see the bruising as much. You know, I really should pick up some of that coverup that I saw on—"

"Are you always this toxically positive, or is it the hormones," Mike grumbled as he cranked up the heater, scouring the street ahead of him for someone who matched the photo he'd placed on the console between them.

"It's nice to know that Ron's spirit lives on," she said. "There. In the bus shelter."

"What?" Mike said.

"It's him."

"How did you—"

"Toxic positivity. Or maybe it's the hormones. Do you want me to initiate, or are you going to?"

Mike glanced around for a place to pull over. Finding nothing convenient, he drove the car up over the curb and stopped right by the bus shelter.

"Let's see how it goes," Mike said, hopping out of the car.

Both Mike and Carla approached the bus shelter. The lone occupant was a man sitting on the bench. His clothes were disheveled but not filthy. His

183

hair was greasy but not ratty. From his appearance alone, it looked as if he had a place to be but chose not to be there. He was likely younger than he looked, and clearly suffered from some mental health issues. He was also holding a plastic grocery bag tightly on his lap.

"Hey!" Mike called.

The man looked warily at Mike.

"We just want to talk to you," Mike said, reaching into his coat pocket and pulling out his badge. Carla stayed a few feet behind.

The man's eyes widened. He clutched the grocery bag tighter.

"Is your name Anson Meyersen?" Mike asked, putting his badge back into his pocket before.

"Yes, it is."

"I'm Detective O'Shea, and this is my partner," Mike nodded behind him, "Detective Hageneur."

Meyersen looked at them both by way of acknowledgement.

"What have you got in the bag?" Mike asked.

"None of your business."

"Mind if I have a look?" Mike said, moving closer.

"I said it's none of your business!" Meyersen said, his nostrils starting to flare, steam coming out with every forced exhale.

"Why don't you stand up for me."

"I haven't done anything wrong. Go away."

Meyersen began to rock slightly, his breath returning to normal.

"I just want to talk to you."

"Talk to me here. Before my bus comes."

"What bus are you waiting for, Anson?" Mike asked.

"None of your business. Am I in trouble?"

"You might be."

"You know that makes no sense, right? I mean, you're either in trouble or you're not. Which one is it? If I'm not in trouble, then leave me alone. I have a bus to catch," Meyersen said.

"I have a picture of you in a parking lot the other day," Mike said slowly. "I want to talk to you about that picture."

"Is it a crime to be in a parking lot? I don't think so, but it is a crime to take someone's picture without their consent, isn't it? Otherwise, we'd be a police state. Like in *1984*. But that was a long time ago. I wasn't even born then. But here we are, back in *1984*. When I wasn't born. So you're not even talking to me. Because I don't exist. I'm not even here. So leave me alone."

Mike held his ground.

"Go, Detective Police Man."

"I'm going to give you a choice," Mike began, looking over his shoulder again at Carla, who began to shorten the gap between them.

"Choices are arbitrary, dependent upon who is giving them and who is supposed to pick them. I reject that. I reject your arbitrary existence. I reject your invading my space. I reject—"

"Either you come with me voluntarily or I arrest you and—"

"Arrest. Arrêt. Stop. You've already stopped me. I was already stopped when you got here. I've already been arrested. A-rest. But there's no rest. I'm not rested. I'm stopped. I'm delayed. I'm in transit. I'm en route. I'm—"

"Okay, Anson," Mike said, glancing at Carla to see how close she was to him before stepping closer to Anson.

"Don't touch me!" he shrieked, pulling a mason jar out of the grocery bag. He held it close to his face before lifting it over his head, preparing to throw it in the direction of Mike and Carla.

"What—"

"It's gasoline, Mike!" Carla said, stepping back.

Meyersen reached into his pocket, dropping the shopping bag, causing the glass containers within to smash, gasoline spilling out around him. He then opened the lid on the jar in his hand.

"You touch me, and I'll throw this gas all over you and burn you to a crisp," Meyersen said, clearly oblivious to the gasoline around his feet. "I got a lighter. See?"

Mike stepped back when he saw it, as careful not to let the approaching liquid on the pavement reach his shoes as to give Meyersen space. He looked over at Carla, who, by this time, had stepped several paces back and was on her cell phone.

"This is Detective Hageneur. I've got a guy who just doused the area with gasoline and is threatening to light it up. I need a Critical Incident Team here along with a hazmat team," Mike heard her say. "No sirens if possible. Yes. That's correct."

"You need to come out of the bus shelter now," Mike said calmly.

"You need to leave me alone," Meyersen replied, flicking the lighter.

"You're going to blow yourself up if you stay there," Mike said.

"Blow up. Glow up. Flow up. Grow up."

"Anson," Carla called out gently, moving closer to the bus shelter, her cell phone still in her hand. "Your mother wants to talk to you."

"What?".

Mike looked over at his partner.

"Your mother. She loves you, doesn't she?" Carla continued, now standing beside Mike. "And you love her, don't you."

"Yes, I do," Meyersen replied quickly.

"And she wouldn't want anything to happen to you, would she?"

"No."

"And you wouldn't want her to be sad, would you?"

"No."

Carla held the cell phone to her ear and nodded slowly.

"She's telling me that you need to get out of the bus shelter."

"But I need to get the bus."

Carla nodded again, the phone still at her ear.

"She's telling me," Carla said, pulling the phone away from her face, "that it's more important for you to get out of the bus shelter than stay there waiting for the bus."

"How does she know?"

"Doesn't your mother usually give you good advice, Anson?" Carla asked.

"Yes, she does."

"And doesn't your mother usually do what's best for you, Anson?"

"Yes."

Carla pulled the phone back up to her ear and nodded a few more times before putting the phone against her chest.

"She's telling you to put what's in your hand on the bench beside you and walk towards the nice man in the suit."

"How does she know?'

"She says it's the right thing to do, Anson. You want to do the right thing, don't you?"

He considered this for a moment.

"You're lying to me!" he shouted. "You're not talking to my mother. You don't even know who she is. You're lying. You're crying. You're frying. You're—"

Mike was about to jump onto Meyersen when he saw the Critical Incident Team SUV pull up.

"Anson, you know you're not supposed to have incendiary devices. What the heck are you doing?" a familiar voice called out.

Anson's attention went directly to the uniformed officer who was just stepping out of the SUV.

"I'm sorry, Officer Preston. It's just—"

"Put that lighter down and come on over here. I want you to meet my new partner, Nurse Jess."

To the amazement of both Mike and Carla, Meyersen put the lighter down and walked over to the vehicle. The passenger in the SUV got out and stood at the back corner of it.

"Hi. How're ya doin' today?" the short, heavy-set woman wearing a Kevlar vest asked, hand outstretched. "I'm Nurse Jess, and I hear we'll be seeing a lot of each other. Let's get a wet wipe and give your hands a clean."

Both Mike and Carla gave a sigh of relief as they saw Meyersen engaging with the nurse.

"Hey, Detective. Detectives," Preston McAfee said, smiling broadly as he approached his colleagues.

"I'm so glad you finally got the CIT spot, Preston," Carla said to her former foot patrol constable, giving him a hug.

"Thanks. I just started a couple of months ago. I guess you were away...."

"I always knew you'd be a great officer," Carla said.

"Thanks. I owe it all to both of you," he said with a slight blush.

"You might have saved that guy's life," Mike said.

"Come on, Michael. You're not *that* ferocious," Carla said with a smile.

"I thought he was going to turn this bus shelter into a space launch gone bad," Mike said. "You obviously know him?"

"Oh yeah. He's a frequent flyer," Preston said. "How did you guys get involved with him?"

"He might be a homicide suspect. Certainly a person of interest," Mike said.

"Okay. So I guess you're going to want to talk to him. Is he under arrest yet?" Preston asked.

"No. We were hoping to bring him in as a friendly."

"Hmm. I'm thinking he might be beyond that. Based on what's in the call and what we're seeing now, we're likely going to have to apprehend him and take him to the hospital. Sorry, Boss. Bosses."

"Shit," Mike said. "In that case, all bets are off with us."

"Yeah. Sorry about that."

"Hey. Anson," Mike called. "Why did you torch the car?"

"I know you're anxious, detective, but this boy isn't really in a posi—" Nurse Jess began.

"A guy told me to keep an eye on his girl and it got outta hand," Meyersen blurted out.

"What guy?"

"Her guy. Monty. Monkey. Marky. Maxwell. Mitchell. Morty. Montel. Malcolm."

Mike's heart was pumping so hard that he couldn't respond. He took a couple of breaths and was just about to say something when, out of the corner of his eye, he saw the METRO TV SUV pulling up. Janelle Austin wasted no time getting out as a hazmat truck pulled up behind them.

"Get your camera up," she called to her driver-cum-cameraperson.

The young woman leapt out of the SUV, grabbed the camera from the back, and ran after the seasoned reporter.

"Sergeant McAfee," Janelle said, her whitened teeth sparkling almost as much as her eyes as she approached the young officer.

CHAPTER TWENTY-NINE

"That's constable," Preston said, his cheeks reddening again.

"My camerawoman and I were just driving by when we saw your SUV speeding by us, and now you've got one in custody. What do my viewers need to know?"

Out of instinct, Preston looked over at Mike.

"Detective O'Shea," Janelle said, redirecting her attention, motioning to her cameraperson to follow her.

"We're that familiar with each other now, are we?" Mike said.

"I'm sorry?"

"You're not going to even try to give me a field promotion?"

"I don't—" she began, feigning confusion.

"Never mind," Mike said.

"I know there's something good happening whenever I see you, Detective. What can you tell me?" she continued, motioning to her cameraperson to turn the camera on.

"Nothing."

"This is Janelle Austin reporting from what looks like a volatile police interaction," Janelle said, trying to bait Mike into responding.

"Come on, my friend," Nurse Jess said. "Let's get you out of here."

"From the Hazardous Materials truck to my left," Janelle continued, the camera following her gesticulation, "and the detectives involved in the Clayton homicide investigation in front of me and the Critical Incident Team behind me, I'm curious to know how the pieces fit together. Detective Hageneur?"

Carla looked over at Mike.

"We don't have to say anything," Mike said.

"Of course, you're right to wonder," Carla said, ignoring Mike as she swept towards Janelle. "My partner, Detective O'Shea, whom you are correct to say has been instrumental in so many major arrests in this city over the years, and I were—dare I reinforce the stereotype—just out for a coffee when we saw an individual known to police—"

"Pardon me for interrupting, Detective, but you did say *known to police*, did you not?"

"Absolutely."

"In relation to your current homicide investigation?"

"As you know, Janelle," Carla said, lowering her voice, "we are not in a position to rule anyone out at this time—"

"So the person now in the back seat—"

"Is on his way to receive the help he needs, thanks to Constable Preston McAfee and Nurse Jess, both of whom we're just so darned proud of."

Carla gave a nod and smiled brightly at Janelle, who lowered her microphone and turned to her camerawoman.

"Let's get back in the truck," she said.

"Well played," Mike said, watching the reporter slink away.

"Thank you, Michael. And I'm sorry if you thought that I was disregarding your suggestion to keep quiet. It's just that, well, I want to stay on her good side. I may need her later."

"I think that's what keeps her going," Mike said, turning back to the car.

Chapter Thirty

5:00 p.m. Friday, January 18, 2019

"Jesus, Crumply Pants, you sure have a way with people, don't you?"

"Apparently," Mike said, he and Carla barely having stepped through the back doors of the station.

"I understand that Anson Meyersen is currently on his way to the hospital," she continued.

"News travels."

"Preston put it over the air," Carla said brightly, removing her coat and hanging it up on the rack before noticing something crusty along the side of it. "Has anyone ever washed this thing?"

"Have you seen the place?" Mike said with a grimace, hooking his jacket on one of the available pegs.

"You know, one thing I've never understood is how coats get left here. I mean, you wore your coat in, so you wear it home," Carla continued.

"Excuse me, people," Amanda said. "We have a homicide investigation going on over here. I'm sure there'll be many long, boring nights in the future when you two gifts to the investigative arts can figure that one out."

"Sorry, Amanda," Carla said, going over to her desk, eyes downcast like a child who had just been scolded by a teacher.

"Seriously, though, how did you go from finding Meyersen to...this?" Amanda asked.

"He just kind of went off," Mike said with a shrug.

"As you've noted, Amanda, Mike has a way with people," Carla added.

"Did he say anything?" Amanda asked.

"Yeah. He torched the car," Mike said.

Amanda froze.

"And you're just telling me this now?" she said. "It didn't occur to you to maybe call that information in?"

"Yes, we probably should have done that, Michael," Carla conceded, typing her password on the keyboard. "I really should get my eyes checked. I think it's the hormones. You just started needing readers recently, didn't you, Amanda? You're probably menopausal, right?"

"When did I lose control of my investigation?" Amanda asked, throwing her hands up.

"Well, at least we know where he is," Mike said. "Do you smell gasoline, or is it just me?"

"It's likely on your shoes, Michael," Carla said. "By the end there, you were standing in a puddle of it."

"Great."

"Good thing neither of us smoke," Carla said.

"People? Over here? The show is over here," Amanda said, pointing towards herself. "Talk to me."

"Oh, right," Carla said. "Michael, maybe you should tell her since you were the lead."

Mike gave Amanda an annotated version of what had just happened, omitting the part about Janelle Austin pulling up on the scene.

"Shit. Shit. Shit," Amanda said.

"But this also pulls Malcolm Oakes back into the picture," Mike said.

"Hardly," Amanda said. "I want solid evidence before I go off on some wild goose chase."

Carla glanced over at Mike, who stared at Amanda.

"Afraid you won't get the next bump if you pursue this?" Mike said sourly.

"Pardon?"

"I think what Michael meant—" Carla began.

"I meant what I said," Mike said, looking at Amanda.

"I'm a homicide investigator, Mike. Not a politician."

"But you're a career officer. Emphasis on the career," Mike shot back.

"Carla, would you mind—" Amanda began, turning away from Mike.

"I think I've got to check something at the front desk," Carla said, quickly getting up and leaving the office.

Amanda watched her go before speaking.

"What *the hell* are you up to, Mike?"

"You want to know? I'll tell you. Malcolm Oakes has been on the loose for almost twenty years. He killed a cop. He also killed other people. And he's got one hell of an obvious marking on his face—"

"What does that have to do with this murder investigation, Mike?"

"You said it before. You agreed with me," Mike said through clenched teeth. "He's been on the loose and, from what we're seeing, still active as a pimp, because people bigger than us want him to be. Either he has something they want, or he's got something on them that they can't get back, even if he's in jail. Or dead."

"Okay," Amanda said, her voice steady. "And what does that have to do with my—"

"Now you're involved," Mike yelled.

"Excuse. Me?" she said very quietly.

"He may not have lit the fire that killed Lisa Clayton," Mike said, his voice lowered, "but we now know that he was seeing her and that he had some kind of hold over her."

Amanda held Mike's glare.

"Do we?" she said.

"Yeah. We do."

"I'm not buying it. At least," she said, stepping away, "not lock, stock, and barrel."

"I know. Why her? What interest could Malcolm Oakes have in a burned-out drug-addicted hooker well past her prime?" Mike asked, anger beginning to give way to reason.

"Your guess is as good as mine, Mike, but right now—"

"I knew Lisa long before Sal was shot. Before Chelsea Hendricks. Before any of this bullshit started. Robby Williams and I used to arrest her almost nightly. The night Robby jumped off his balcony, she stood right out there," Mike said, gesturing towards the front of the station, "offering her condolences."

"I heard he fell."

"Fell. Jumped. Same thing when you're intentionally dangling off your balcony," Mike said, sitting down again. "I say he jumped, and his kid brought me a box full of papers. I haven't gone through it yet, but I'm thinking it'll tell us why he jumped."

"It's been how long, and you haven't looked at it?"

"I know. It's in Ron Roberts' basement."

"What the—" Amanda said.

"I-I got busy. And probably drank a bit too much too often."

"Mike," Amanda said gently, "that stuff might all be evidence."

"I have no idea, but even if it is, why would I submit it?" Mike asked, his voice breaking. "If they can lose a cop killer given all the resources on the planet, why would I trust them to safely store something that might break open whatever's going on?"

"You never looked inside the box?" Amanda said, shaking her head slowly.

"No," Mike whispered.

"Fuck, Mike."

"I know."

They looked at each other, both lost in their own thoughts.

"Let's get the Clayton murder sorted out and then do a deep dive on this Oakes thing," Amanda said.

"What about your career?"

"I've got a career, Mike. No one can take that away from me."

"Don't be so sure. Look what happened to Sal. And Robby."

"Sal was shot, point blank. Robby slipped from his balcony."

"Still…."

"You know what I tell my girls, Mike? If they think they're being followed, then they should walk in the middle of the street."

"And that has what to do with this?"

"That way," she continued, "if they really are being followed, they've created lots of witnesses. And, if whoever is following them is stupid enough to do anything, lots of people will have seen it happen."

"Lots of people saw Sal get killed."

"No, Mike. You saw him get killed. Lots of people saw his funeral."

Mike was silent.

"Times have changed. Policing has changed," Amanda said.

"Do you think it's changed that much?"

"The political climate has changed. Leave it with me for a bit. Then we'll do some digging. When we know we've got something—"

"Oh, we've got something," Mike said, the hair on the back of his neck starting to tingle.

"Once we know we've got something," Amanda repeated, "then I propose that we go public with everything and be as available as possible to answer questions."

"Trial by public opinion?" Mike asked.

"It'll be a bit of a circus, but we'll make sure that we are so visible that no one will touch us."

"Yeah, but—"

"You've been carrying this monkey on your back for so long that you don't want to let it go, even if you have the chance to. And that chance is coming. I promise. And when it gets here, you have to take it and let the monkey go."

Mike looked at the filthy windows.

"What about Carla? Do you trust her?" Amanda asked.

"Yeah, I do.".

"Great. Go on up to the front desk and get her before she—"

"Is everybody decent in there?" Carla called from the hallway. "Some of us have work to do, you know."

"Come on in," Amanda said. "We were just talking about you,"

"Apparently, so is everyone else. Great to be so popular, but honestly, you all need a hobby. Any word on how Anson's doing? And Preston. Wasn't he just remarkable? You know, not every copper is right for the road, and I'm not sure it was Preston's forté, but I think he's just perfect for this job, don't you, Michael?"

Mike looked over his monitor and smiled across at her.

"I'm going to get you to do up a warrant for Anson's arrest," Amanda said. "Once he's cleared at the hospital, I want the two of you to arrest him."

"You don't fool around, do you?" Carla said. "What's this? My second minute here, and already I'm doing warrants and—"

"And then I—" Mike began and then corrected himself. "Sorry, we need your help."

"Swell. What do you need? I'm very good at matching colors. Honestly, it's like the estrogen took me from black-and-white to technicolor!"

"We're going to catch the guy who killed my partner," Mike said.

"Oh, that," Carla said with a nervous laugh. "Sure. And what's on the agenda for after lunch?"

"There's likely a lot more to this than just Malcolm Oakes," Amanda said. "Mike may have some new information that will substantiate his claims of high-level corruption, and we need to go through it before deciding whether or not to proceed."

"Sounds like police work to me," Carla said. "I believe that's what I signed up for."

"You're not obliged to—" Amanda began.

"Are you arresting me?"

"What we're saying," Mike said, "is that this is going to get messy. I'm okay if you want to be left out of it. You've got enough—"

"Mess?" Carla asked.

"On your plate is what I was going to say," Mike concluded.

"Michael, I'm a lot of things, but first and foremost, I'm a cop. If you're giving me the opportunity to catch a cop killer and bring down dirty cops, I'm all in."

Chapter Thirty-One

10:37 p.m. Friday, January 18, 2019

"So what do we do about Hawthorne now?" Mike asked.

"He didn't get bail. Let's continue as planned," Amanda said.

"But what about Meyersen's—"

"Hardly the most credible witness," Amanda said. "And I know his statement was given before he was read his rights—"

"*Res gestae*," Mike stated. "He just blurted it out. Didn't get a chance to caution him."

"Regardless, given his mental state at the time and the fact that he wasn't cautioned about the implications of giving a statement, I'm thinking no court would accept it."

"But when we add it to what Hawthorne said about the car being doused, Meyersen starts to look pretty good," Mike said.

"Let's just leave things as they are for now," Amanda said. "I don't want to release him now and then have to rearrest him later."

A cell phone rang. Mike reached over into his suit coat pocket. Carla opened her purse. Amanda clipped hers off the belt on her dress.

"Detective Serge—oh, sorry. I didn't realize it was that late. Everything okay? Have both girls gone…." she said, walking out into the hallway.

"If we're not a hundred percent sure, I think we ought to release him," Mike muttered. "Sounds a bit sloppy to me."

"If you're becoming Ron Roberts," Carla said, opening the bottom drawer of the desk to set her purse in, "then does that mean I'll turn into you? I'm not sure I'm good with that, no offence intended."

"Just type, okay?" Mike replied.

* * *

"Michael, wake up!" Mary-Margaret said, clutching the top of her dressing gown with one hand while shaking him vigorously with the other.

"Wha—?" Mike said as he opened his eyes. He grabbed his cell phone. 4:27. He looked at the curtains covering the window and saw only the muted glow of the streetlight outside.

"Our Mandy is downstairs. I've got the kettle on," she said as she left his bedroom. "And put somethin' on. No one wants to see ye in yer skivvies!"

Mike got up and pulled on the pair of pants that were lying on the floor by the bed. When he got to the bottom of the stairs, he stopped. He had known Amanda Black for a very long time and in all kinds of situations, including at some horrific homicide scenes, and after being awake for more than forty-eight hours. He'd never seen her look the way she did now, sitting at his dining room table, a mug of tea and a plate of McVitie's in front of her.

"Sticheedoon, Michael," his mother said.

Mike had seen that look in his mother's eyes before, and it always scared him. He sat down in the chair beside Amanda.

"Have a cuppa, me son," she said, passing him a mug. "I'll just be in the kitchen. Come on, Wee Phil."

Mike took the mug and put it down. Mary-Margaret turned to leave, the Jack Russell following her. Amanda looked down at her mug, took a deep breath, and then turned to Mike, her eyes puffy.

"There is no easy way to tell you this, Mike, and I wanted you to hear it from me. Bridget Calloway is dead. She was shot at close range in the underground parking lot at the courts sometime between 11:30 p.m. last night and 1:00 a.m. this morning. She was pronounced dead at the scene. The shooter or shooters are still outstanding."

Mike stared at her.

"As you know, we're in the infancy of the investigation and…"

Stairwell. Underground parking lot. Shot. Point blank. Dead at the scene.

"Malcolm Oakes," he said flatly.

"As I said, Mike, we're—"

"It's exactly like Sal."

"Mike," Amanda said, placing her hand on his arm, "lots of people get shot in undergrounds."

"Why now? Why Bridget?"

"We don't know, Mike. But we will."

A wail could be heard from the kitchen over the whistling of the kettle.

"Mom," Mike said, getting up, Amanda following him into the kitchen.

"I'm sorry, lads," she said, weeping into a dishcloth. "I didn't think ye'd hear me, what with the kettle and all. I boiled more water than a midwife would ever need for months after yer da, God rest his soul, died. And now…."

"It's okay, Mom," Mike said, wrapping his arms around her. He held her for a moment and then he and Amanda, one on either side of her, walked her to one of the chairs in the living room.

"Such a lovely girl, our Bridget," Mary-Margaret said, wringing the dishcloth.

"I know," Mike said, kneeling before her.

"The two of ye were made for each other, Michael," Mary-Margaret continued.

"I don't know about that."

"Ach, I hate yer world, me son. I hate yer business. I hate…ach, 'tis no use. She's gone. Before she even had a chance. She would have made a wonderful mother, our Bridget. She had that light in her eyes. She was a keeper, Michael."

Amandas eyes welled up.

"So who's next? 'Tis not like I don't already worry every time ye leave the house, Michael. And for what? It's over. I canna take it anymore. By the grace of God, ye've survived all yer bashin's and run-ins with this lot. Ye should have left after Sal—"

"Stop, Mom," Mike said firmly, getting to his feet.

"Mike, she's upset," Amanda said.

"We're all upset. Death is upsetting," he said.

He walked over to the wall unit that held the whiskey.

"Death is a part of God's plan," Mary-Margaret said sharply. "Murder is not."

"It's all the same," Mike said, pouring himself a drink. "Anyone else?"

"No, I'm still working," Amanda said.

"That won't help, Michael," his mother said.

"Said no Irishman ever," Mike said, throwing back the shot and then pouring another.

"They're pulling the video surveil—" Amanda began.

"Don't bother," Mike said, cutting her off. "I know what that looks like. And the shooter will have a Glasgow smile. But we'll never catch him. Imagine that."

Mike threw back this shot as well.

"I think ye've had enough, Michael," Mary-Margaret said.

"Do you now?" he said, looking over at her. "Since when—"

"Mike, I need you to come in sober in a couple of hours," Amanda said.

"Who said I won't be?" he said, pouring himself a third shot of whiskey.

"Lower yer voice, lad. No need to wake the whole house up," Mary-Margaret said.

"We're not thirty anymore," Amanda said. "Why don't we call it a night, and I'll see you in a—"

"I told you this was going to happen," Mike said, looking at the bottle. "I told you that Malcolm was here and that something was happening and that—"

"We'll catch him, Mike. I promise," Amanda said.

"And will you bring Bridget back?"

Amanda looked down.

"And, while you're at it, how about Sal? Are you going to bring him back, too? Janice would be happy to hear that. I still talk to her, you know. She calls me on the anniversary of his murder. And I call her on Mother's Day."

"That's lovely, Michael," Mary-Margaret said.

"Yeah. But not nearly as lovely as it would be if her own son was calling her, is it?"

"Well," Mary-Margaret said after she'd caught her breath, "you're goin' to have to excuse me. I canna take much more this evenin', and I'm sure there'll be plenty to do in the mornin' to get things sorted for our Bridget's funeral."

"I'm sure she has family, Mom," Mike stated flatly.

"Well, I don't know, but we'll discuss that in the mornin'. Good night, everyone."

Amanda helped Mary-Margaret to her feet, and she and Mike watched her climb the stairs to her bedroom.

"Do you think you were a bit harsh, Mike?" Amanda asked, sitting down at the dining room table.

"Maybe."

"They'll find out who did it, Mike."

"And what do we do in the meantime? Drink tea and eat biscuits?"

"No. We're going to keep an eye on your Mom. I think she loved Bridget more than you did," Amanda said and then looked at her watch. "I'm going to head out now. I've got a few things to do before I have my hour and a shower. Try to get some rest, and I'll see you when you get in tomorrow afternoon. Want me to put the bottle away for you, Mike?"

Chapter Thirty-Two

5:30 a.m. Saturday, January 19, 2019

Mike lay on his bed until he couldn't any longer. His mouth was dry and his mind was numb. He heard his mother pacing in her bedroom down the hall. He also heard her occasional muffled cry, but he knew better than to go knock on her door. She would want her privacy. Her dignity. Her right to mourn in private. At least right now.

Eventually, he heard her bedroom door open, her heavy footsteps as she went into the bathroom, the sound of the tap going on and off while she wiped her face and brushed her teeth, and the flush of the toilet. And then he heard her go downstairs into the kitchen, talking merrily to that little dog as she went. He closed his eyes and fell asleep.

* * *

The sound of his mother's normal routine and cheery voice let Mike believe, for a moment, that it might still be a dream. A wistful smile crept across his face as he realized it was not. But it was a new day, and there were things to be done.

"Ach, yer up," Mary-Margaret said as Mike walked into the kitchen, her hand resting on the knob of the open back door, waiting for Wee Phil to return. She looked him up and down. "And dressed. Off to work, then, are ye?"

"Yeah," Mike mumbled, grabbing a mug from the cupboard.

"Well," she said with a heavy sigh as Wee Phil came bounding in. "That's somethin'."

"Good morning, my wonderful friends!" Carla said, emerging from the downstairs suite. "What was all that commotion last night? I thought I heard something and was going to come up but then thought—"

She stopped, seeing the looks on their faces.

"Oh my," she said. "This isn't good, is it?"

"Bridget's dead. Shot in the head last night. Point blank," Mike said without turning around to face her, scooping the coffee into the coffee maker.

The blood ran out of Carla's face as Mary-Margaret shored up against her to prevent her from collapsing.

"Not much of a bedside, have ye?" she muttered sourly, ushering Carla towards a chair in the dining room.

"Sorry, but it's the truth," Mike said, still standing where he was.

"Sitcheedoon, luv," Mary-Margaret said as she set Carla into the chair. "I'll go get ye a cuppa, and we'll have a moment, shall we?"

"Jesus, Mary, and Joseph, Michael. Where's yer brain at?" Mary-Margaret hissed. "'Tis enough that we've lost that lovely girl just a few hours ago without ye—"

"What, Mom? Making it worse?" Mike cut in, splashing coffee on his hand as he poured it into the cup. "Shit!"

"Well, the least ye could do—"

"Is what?" he said, jamming the pot back into the coffee maker.

Mike locked eyes with his mother.

Mary-Margaret reached up and pulled her son into her. All of the tenderness she was too far stretched to give to him when his father died flowed through her now. Mike leaned down, buried his face in her neck, and cried.

"'Tis goin' to be all right, me son," she said after a few seconds, stiffening her body as she pushed Mike away and then looked at the mug of coffee on the counter behind him. "Give that a dump in the sink. I'm gettin' the kettle on, and we'll all have a proper cuppa."

"Right. I'll get the mugs out," Mike said, wiping his eyes.

"And a plate of McVities."

Mike glanced over at his mother.

"'Tis a difficult mornin', Michael. Don't be thinkin' we'll be havin' biscuits for breakfast every day now. And it'll be just a moment now before Max is up. Don't ye be sayin' a word. I'll tell him."

"It's Saturday. He won't be up before noon."

"Just as well. Meanwhile, ye might be wantin' to pop upstairs and give yer face a wee wipe. But run a razor across it first. 'Tis the least ye can do to honor our Bridget, God rest her soul."

Mike turned to go.

"Oh, and Michael," his mother called out after him, her voice firm. "This house is in mourning. We won't be having a Sunday Dinner."

* * *

"Did you hear—" Russ began even before Mike and Carla were in the office.

"Yeah," Mike grunted.

"No moss on you, eh?" he said with a laugh.

"Huh?"

Carla held out her hand, took Mike's coat, and hung both his and hers up.

"You never stop with the surprises, O'Shea," Russ said, shutting down his computer.

"I'm just going to powder my nose," Carla said, not wanting to put up with Russ right now.

"Anything happen last night that I need to know about?" Mike said.

"You tell me," Russ said.

"What do you mean?"

"You're the one with the new girlfriend. Must be kinda hard to have a romantic evening when you're living with your mother, but I've never been with a tranny, so maybe…" His words trailed off.

"No bodies in the cells that need their paperwork done before the wagons get here?" Mike said.

"What's it like with a tranny?" Russ continued, shuffling over to the coat rack, plucking his wrinkled trench coat from it.

"A crown prosecutor got shot point blank in the head last night, and all you have to talk about is your fantasy of having sex with a trans—"

"That's another thing," Russ said with a grin. "How do you go from bangin' Calloway to bangin' that thing?"

"Oh good," Amanda Black said. "You're in, too. I saw Carla out front, but I wasn't sure if you'd be in. And you're just leaving, aren't you, Russ?"

"You bet," he said, his trench coat over his arm. "Unless you're willing to pay me overtime?"

"Have a good day, Detective," Amanda said.

Russ almost bumped into her as he shuffled out the door.

"Given that we have a clothing allowance, you'd think he'd buy shoes that fit, wouldn't you?" Amanda said. "Anyway, how are you doing?"

"Peachy keen," Mike said.

"Liar."

Mike didn't respond.

"They're doing the autopsy on Bridget in an hour or so," Amanda said.

He looked up at her.

"No, I won't be going. Not my investigation."

"Whose is it?"

"William Gill. He's an excellent investigator, and he'll do a fine job."

"Sure."

"Mike, I know—"

"It was Malcolm Oakes."

"You have no—"

"It was Malcolm Oakes," he repeated.

"Listen, Mike. Lots—well, not lots, but some people get shot in stairwells. It happens. It's not exactly a signature, especially since the last time it happened was—"

"You said that Bridget was involved."

"I said—"

"You know that Malcolm is active. Very active."

"I said—"

"Bridget knew something, and they didn't want her to talk."

"Bridget's car was in a parking lot and she was in the stairwell of that parking lot for reasons yet unknown. A person, or persons, unknown, approached her, and she was shot in the head. That's what we know right now."

"Why would she be in the underground parking lot at 11:30 on a Friday night?"

"I don't know. Working late? Having dinner with someone after work? I don't know, Mike," Amanda said with a shrug.

"If she was working, she could have done it from her kitchen table. Everything she may have wanted is available electronically. And meeting someone?" Mike said with a harsh laugh. "Who?"

"Right now, we—and it's not even my case—have to consider everything. No tunnel vision, remember?"

"I'd be looking at where Malcolm Oakes was last night."

"Mike—"

"But we won't, will we? Because, for reasons unknown, the entire law enforcement world hasn't been able to find Malcolm Oakes since 2005. Even though we now know that he was Lisa Clayton's boyfriend. The Lisa Clayton who *is* your case. The Lisa Clayton who lived less than twenty minutes from here."

"I'll make sure Gill knows," Amanda said, turning to walk out of the detective office.

"You be sure and do that."

"In the meantime," Amanda said, "Hawthorne's on ice, and I'm debating whether or not to bother reinterviewing him while we have his undivided attention. I doubt he'll say anything with his lawyer perched beside him, but it might be worth a try."

"Sure."

"They've got coffee and fresh pastries at the front," Carla said as she came into the office, a cup of coffee in one hand and a danish in the other. "Oh! I've come in at a bad time, haven't I?"

"No. Not at all. I was just telling your partner that they're doing Bridget's autopsy this afternoon," Amanda said.

"I'm so sorry, Michael."

"Can we stop talking about this, please?" Mike said. "I've been told that this investigation has nothing to do with us."

"I disagree, Michael," Carla said. "I think—"

"Nobody cares what you think!" Mike snapped.

Carla recoiled as if she'd been slapped in the face.

"I think you should get a coffee and a pastry from the front," Amanda said. "I'll go see what they have."

"Sorry," Mike mumbled as soon as Amanda left the office. "I'm...sorry."

"Maybe a nice car ride would help," Carla said.

"I'm not a fucking puppy," he spat.

"Then stop shitting on everyone, Michael."

Chapter Thirty-Three

2:16 p.m. Saturday, January 19, 2019

"I gotta go," Mike announced.

"Are you sure that's a good idea, Michael?" Carla asked, looking at him over her half-moon glasses.

"Since when did you get glasses?" he asked, brow furrowed.

"Since I realized I couldn't see the letters on the screen in front of me. So where are you going?"

"I've got something to pick up."

"If it's flowers, I quite like a bird of paradise."

"No. It's a box of files."

"Not giving me much to work with."

Mike thought for a minute before answering.

"It's a pile of papers my old boss left behind after he jumped off his balcony."

"I would think it highly unlikely that he'd take them with him, Michael. Do I need to pack a lunch to hear this story or...?"

"Robby Williams was my boss when I worked at Juvenile Prostitution. He ended up doing a header off of his balcony a couple of years back."

"I seem to remember that."

"Yeah. So, his kid brought in a box from the storage locker and said I might want to have a look at it," Mike said as he walked over to the coat rack.

"And...?"

"I never did."

"Because…?"

"Because I got busy," he said.

"And now…? Honestly, Michael, you're aging me!"

"And now I think it might have something in it that might have something to do with Sal's murder."

Carla removed her glasses, placing the end of one arm in her mouth.

"And we're going to check that out this afternoon while we're involved in a homicide investigation, and Bridget's been dead less than," Carla looked down at her watch, "twelve hours."

"I think they're all tied in together."

"I'll get my purse."

Carla turned her head slightly.

"Hold on to your hats, kids," she said. "Here she comes."

"I just got off the phone with the pathologist," Amanda said as she strode into the detective office.

Mike looked quizzically at Carla.

"I'd like to say it's my superpower, but I heard her heels," Carla said.

"I have no idea what you two are talking about, but the pathologist says Lisa Clayton didn't die from the fire. Her throat wasn't singed at all. He thinks her lungs were likely clear but won't know until the specimen is examined at the lab."

"So what killed her?" Carla asked.

"Hawthorne," Mike said.

"Her larynx was crushed, which is consistent with being strangled," Amanda said.

"So it's a slam dunk?" Carla asked.

"There's no such thing as a slam dunk in homicide," Amanda replied. "You look even worse than you did ten minutes ago, Mike. Glad to see you're on your way home to get some rest. You *are* on your way home, right?"

"No, I've—" he began.

"Nobody's in the cells, are they?" Amanda asked. "And, if something comes in, I'm sure you can manage it, can't you, Carla?"

"My pay grade does say detective," she replied.

"So go home, Crumply Pants."

"But–"

"Go. Get some sleep. You look like hell," Amanda said. "And stay away from the whiskey."

"Whatever,'" Mike said with a sigh as he stepped past her.

* * *

It took Mike a few minutes longer than he'd have liked to get his car out of the crowded back lot. He knew he should have parked it out front, but there were no spaces available when he came in, and he couldn't be bothered to park down the street. Rather than turning right once he got to the roadway, he turned left and made his way to Ron Robert's house.

Mike put the car in park in front of Ron's house and got out. Not surprisingly, the place was immaculately maintained. No chipped paint on the eavestrough or downspouts. The mortar joints between the bricks were flawless, and the metal handrail leading up to the front door was solid. Mike gave three sharp raps on the front door.

Within seconds, Ron answered, along with a skinny cat that was weaving its body between Ron's legs.

"What's with the cat?"

"Not mine," Ron said, his hand still on the door.

"It's in your house. Possession is nine-tenths of the law, so they say."

"It's a long story," Ron replied, looking down at it.

"Can't be that long."

"It would take about a cup of coffee to explain. Want to come in?"

Without waiting for an answer, Ron turned around and headed towards the kitchen. Mike and the cat followed.

"I'm kind of surprised to find you here," Mike said.

"Then why did you come?" Ron said, turning stiffly.

"I guess I was hoping—"

"That I wouldn't be home, and you could jimmy the basement window to get in? Doubtful."

210

Ron opened the fridge door and pulled out a small container of milk. He brought it up to his nose.

"Milk's gone. You're going to have to do without."

Mike wanted to make a snide remark but stopped himself.

"How's Marie?" he said instead.

"Dying," Ron said.

He poured two mugs of coffee, setting one on the table for Mike. He paused for a minute as if he'd forgotten what he was doing before setting the other on the table for himself. He then sat down across from Mike.

"Right," Mike said, looking into the mug.

The two men sat looking at their coffees.

"So about the cat...?" Mike began.

"Yes. It's not mine."

"So you said."

"It's my neighbor's."

"You know, I never saw you as the hospitable type of guy," Mike said.

"I'm not, but it started coming over here last winter when it was so cold. I left a note on their door telling them that their cat was here, but they didn't respond."

"So you're going to keep the cat?"

"No. As soon as it warms up, I'll drop the cat at their doorstep. It's too cold to put it out now."

"Fair enough," Mike said, taking a sip of his coffee. "Shit, this is bad coffee! How long has it been sitting in the coffeemaker?"

"I just put it on, and it's good coffee," Ron said. "You're just used to drinking bad coffee hidden inside lots of milk."

"Maybe. Listen, I didn't come here—"

"I know about Bridget," Ron said.

"How?"

"Word travels. I'm sorry, Mike. She was a really good prosecutor."

"I think she knew something," Mike said.

"I'm sure she did," Ron said, reaching down to scratch the cat's ear.

"No, I mean about Malcolm and that whole shitshow."

"Oh. That."

"Yes, that. But, as much as I'm enjoying your company—"

"The feeling is mutual," Ron said. "Are you finally going to take that box that's been in my basement or not? Although if you think there's something to your conspiracy theory…"

"Can I just have the box, please?"

"It would make more sense for you to leave it here," Ron said without moving.

"Why?"

"Well, off the top of my head, I'll have the time to go through it. You haven't so far, and I highly doubt you will in the near future," he said, taking a slow sip of his coffee.

"Yes, but Robby's son gave the box to me to look into."

"Yes, and you gave the box to me. Nine-tenths of the law, remember?"

"Right," Mike conceded. "But are you sure you want to get involved? I mean, you'll be a man of leisure—"

"A man with nothing to do but wallow in grief," Ron said. "I don't pretend for a moment that the next few months are going to be easy, and I'd like to have something familiar to keep my mind busy."

A phone rang. Mike looked around and was surprised to see an old-school rotary-dial telephone attached to the kitchen wall.

"Phone company wanted to take it out, but I paid for it, so I kept it," Ron said as he lifted the receiver out of the cradle on the second ring. "Hello? Yes. This is he."

Mike shook his head and was about to laugh until he saw the look on Ron's face.

"I see. Okay. I'll be there as soon as I can."

Ron's shoulders slumped as he dropped his arm down, the receiver still in his hand.

"It was the hospice. Marie…I have to go."

"I'll drive you."

Ron didn't argue.

* * *

The two old partners sat beside each other in Marie's room for the entire night, getting mugs of coffee for each other from the kitchenette down the hall that neither of them drank. They spoke very little. Each man's mind raced with his own thoughts of loss: one for the woman whom he had loved above all others for decades, the other for the woman whom he should have loved but had been too afraid to.

As the birds began to chirp outside, the night shift nurses began to leave, and the sun started to shine through the curtains of Marie's room. Eventually, her uneven breathing came to a stop with a final inhale. Neither Ron nor Mike made any attempt to contact the attending physician. It was over. She was dead.

After a few minutes, both men stood up.

"You're a good man, Michael," Ron said, extending his hand.

"I'll be outside," Mike said after shaking Ron's hand. "Take your time."

Chapter Thirty-Four

3:30 p.m. Sunday, January 20, 2019

Amanda Black poked her head into the detective office.

"Since you're here, you might as well come with me to interview Hawthorne at the detention center," she said. "Where's Carla?"

"In the booking hall," Mike said, looking up from the papers on his desk. "Releasing a prisoner."

"Jesus, Mike," she said. "What the hell happened to you?"

"I was up all night."

"I know Bridget's—" she began.

"With Ron."

"Oh."

"Yeah. She died this morning," Mike said.

"Shit."

"Yeah."

"You should go home."

"And do what? Walk the fucking dog?"

"He's not your dog, is he?" Amanda asked.

Mike began to laugh.

"What a fucking pair we are. I've got my mother's neighbor's dog, and Ron's got his neighbor's cat—"

"I don't even want to know," Amanda said. "Anyway, if you're not going home, I'd like you to come with me to talk to Hawthorne."

"I'll let Carla know that she's in charge back here," Mike said.

* * *

The drill was always the same. Had always been the same. Was likely always going to be the same. Guns locked up prior to entry into the secure area, pockets checked, bodies wanded, any metal removed.

Once they'd cleared security at the detention center, Mike and Amanda were directed to a small windowless room where they were met by Hawthorne's lawyer.

"Didn't think you'd get a run at my client without me being here, did you?" Rejeanne Carr said, looking up from the files she had spread out on the metal table that was bolted to the cement floor.

"He must be paying you one helluva big retainer to get you here on a Sunday afternoon," Amanda said.

"Not that it's any of your business, but he is," Carr shot back. "Ah, here he is. How are you doing, Jordan?"

"Thanks for being here," Hawthorne said to his lawyer, slipping onto the bolted metal chair beside her.

"Twenty minutes enough time?" the guard asked.

"More than enough," Carr replied.

"Since we're the ones who called the interview, I think we should be the ones to determine how long we anticipate it going, don't you?" Amanda said.

"Don't matter to me," the guard said. "I'm here until 1900 hrs. How 'bout one of you poke your head out when you're done."

"Are we going to be adversarial right away, Detective Sergeant, or can we at least begin the proceedings in a civil manner?" Carr asked.

Amanda put the tape recorder she had in her purse in the middle of the table.

"I'll make sure you have a transcript of this as soon as practicable," Amanda said.

"No rush," Carr replied, pulling out her Smartphone and placing it in front of her. She opened an app and pressed PLAY. "I'm sure we'll end up with the same material."

"Fine. Let's begin, shall we?" Amanda said. She stated the date, time, location, and identified everyone in the room before asking her questions.

"As I'm sure you're aware, Jordan, we now have someone whom we believe set your car on fire."

"That weirdo? No. He didn't do it."

"I'm not sure I know who you're referring to," Amanda said.

"That little arsonist guy. Anson? No. He didn't torch the car. Didn't have a chance."

"Why is that?"

Hawthorne looked over at his lawyer. She shook her head.

"Dunno."

"But you seem to think—" Amanda began.

Hawthorne looked at his lawyer again. She looked back at him.

"If you have anything to say, this would be a good time to say it," Amanda said.

"I, uh, I dunno. I don't even know who the guy is. Just some random…." Hawthorne stammered, his voice trailing off.

"A moment ago, you seemed quite sure—"

"I was mistaken," Hawthorne said, looking down as he crossed his arms.

Amanda waited.

"I believe my client is done," Carr said after several minutes of silence.

"May I?" Mike asked.

"Be my guest, but I don't think my client has anything further to say."

"Listen, Jordan," Mike said, leaning across the table. "A woman is found dead in a burned-out car registered to you. We've got you in that car with her prior to the time she was dead. We've got video of you getting out of the car when it was on fire. We've got some guy willing to say he set the car on fire. You might have an opportunity to save yourself here."

Hawthorne looked over at his lawyer, who shook her head.

"Your lawyer?" Mike continued. "One of the best, no doubt about it, but as soon as we're finished here, she gets back in her fancy car, drives to her fancy house, and spends the night sipping fancy cocktails. What's your evening looking like, Jordan?"

Hawthorne looked at his lawyer again. She rolled her eyes.

"I want to talk."

"As your lawyer, I'm advising against it," Carr said. "And, for the record, Detective, I won't be getting in my fancy car. I took an Uber."

"I still want to talk," Hawthorne said.

"Then let's talk," Mike said.

"Yes, Lisa was—"

"That's Lisa Clayton?" Mike said, looking at the two recording devices sitting between them. "Just to be clear."

"Yes. Lisa Clayton. I started…coming to her…a few years back. Things weren't going so well at home—"

"I don't think you need to get into that," Carr said.

"Okay. So I've known her for a few years. I guess you could say that I was one of her regulars. She was mostly clean on the nights when I'd pick her up. I don't know. And then she started to try to get really clean, which was good for her. We still hooked up, if you know what I mean, so that was that."

Mike nodded while Amanda jotted down some notes.

"So that last time, which shouldn't have even happened–"

"Meaning?" Mike interrupted. Amanda looked over at him.

"That I was just on my way to work and saw her there."

"Really?" Mike said. Amanda shot Mike a sterner look.

"You don't have to answer that," Carr said.

"Really," Hawthrone replied. "I drive that way every morning. Not to, you know, but because it's the most direct route. Not many girls, or my type of girl, out there at that time anyway. But on that day–"

"The day Lisa Clayton was murdered," Mike said, and then, looking at Amanda, added, "just to clarify."

"You don't have–"

"Yeah. That morning, I see her and I'm wondering why she's there. I pull over, she comes over to the car, I tell her I just want to talk, catch up, you know. We drive to the beach, park…and then this guy pops up out of nowhere."

"Anson Meyersen?" Amanda cut in.

"You don't have to answer that," Carr said.

"I don't know his last name."

"But you know who he is," Amanda said.

"No. But he seemed to know Lisa."

"From where?" Amanda asked.

"I dunno."

"Doesn't matter. We'll find out. Sorry. Carry on," Amanda said.

"Yeah, so, this guy shows up reeking of gasoline. Like, I mean, *stinking* of it. So I tell him to fuck right off. I don't want my car smelling like that. He ignores me and looks right at Lisa. She tells him to fuck off too, and then he tells her that he's been sent by some dude to keep an eye on her."

Mike looked over at Amanda.

"Did he say who it was?" Mike asked.

"No, but Lisa starts freaking out. Like, *really* freaking out. I've seen her when she's had a bad trip or whatever, but this was much worse."

"Did she say anything?"

"Well, kinda."

Hawthorne looked at his lawyer, who was doodling on the notepad in front of her.

"A name?" Mike asked.

"I'm not sure. Something with an M. Mark...? Marty...?"

Mike looked over at Amanda again. She held her hand out.

"Go on," Mike said.

"Anyway, she starts freaking. And I've got this weirdo all over my car, so I kinda start freaking."

"You don't have to—" Carr began.

"I tell her to shut up, but she's totally lost it," Hawthorne continues. "Like some crazy dog locked in a crate. I flick the door lock button open, hoping she'll just get out of my car, but she starts banging her head on the side window and slamming her hands on the dashboard. I'm thinking she's going to break something, so I grab her."

CHAPTER THIRTY-FOUR

"I think my client is—" Carr said.

"You have to remember, it's all kinda crazy about now. This guy pulls out this jar from this plastic bag and empties it on my car. At first, I was kinda hoping, I dunno, but then I smell it. The crazy bastard doused my car with gasoline. And then I've got Lisa freaking, so I grab her by the—"

"We're done," Carr said. "My client doesn't have anything—"

"—throat, and she's like a wild animal," Hawthorne said, speaking over his lawyer. "Next thing I know, she's gone kinda limp, so I look to see what that weirdo's doing, and I'm thinking he's going to torch the car or something, so I start to get out."

"We're *DONE*," the lawyer said.

Hawthorne stopped speaking. The tape in the recorder continued to wind. Carr did not pause the app on her Smartphone.

"Did the person you saw approach your car light it on fire?" Mike asked.

"No."

"Do you know how the fire started?" Mike asked.

"No."

"Did you kill Lisa Clayton?" Mike asked.

"Don't answer—" Carr began.

"I don't think so," Hawthorne said.

No one spoke for several minutes.

"A surveillance video we have clearly shows one person outside of the vehicle at the time it caught on fire," Mike said. "We believe that person is you. We now have additional video showing a person entering the crime scene and leaving it shortly thereafter. That additional video suggests that, while that person was in the crime scene, your car began to burn. We believe that person is Anson Meyersen. You and Anson Meyersen are the only two people we have both entering and exiting the crime scene. The body of Lisa Clayton was found in the burned vehicle. She was alive when you picked her up and drove her to the beach, and now she's dead, her body found in your burned-out car on that beach."

Mike stopped and waited.

"Help me out, Jordan," Mike said. "Did you kill Lisa Clayton?"

"The interview is over. My client has nothing further to say," Carr said, grabbing her phone before getting up to summon the guard.

Chapter Thirty-Five

10:00 a.m. Monday, January 20, 2019

Bail Court was always chaotic. It wasn't anyone's fault. It just was. Too many people held in custody, only one prosecutor to get through the never-ending list, a harried court-appointed defense popping up to speak to matters he'd just been advised of by the defendant in the cells only moments before, a courtroom full of tired detectives intent on keeping the accused in custody, and a smattering of surprised or drained family members as equally intent on getting their loved one out. The judge appointed to sit on the bench was a rotating position. Today's recipient of that dubious honor was an old man who looked like he'd be more content lying in an open coffin than deciding on who would stay and who would go.

Given the appearance of Anson Meyersen in her investigation, Amanda assumed that Jordan Hawthorne would be released from custody pending trial and had Mike sit in for her. Not surprisingly, Hawthorne's wife was also there, ready to leverage the house for her husband's liberty. When Hawthorne was brought into the courtroom, wearing an orange jumpsuit, hands shackled in front of him, Mike looked over at her. She sat statue-still, only looking at the back of her husband's head when he was brought into the accused's box.

Unlike many who preceded him, Hawthorne had his own lawyer present to argue that he had no priors, had a wife and kids, was the sole breadwinner for the household and that the evidence against him was circumstantial at best.

After confirming that Hawthorne could fulfill his employment requirement remotely, the judge released him on house arrest.

"You understand, Mrs. Hawthorne, that this means that your husband is not to leave your home except for medical or legal appointments, and then only in the company of you," the judge said, looking down at her.

"I do," she said for the second time in her life.

"Except for medical emergencies," Rejeanne Carr chimed in.

"Yes," the judge said wearily. "Except for medical emergencies but, given that your client will not be away from his wife, I think it's fair to say that he would be attending to any medical emergency in her company, wouldn't you?"

"It's just standard—" Carr began.

"I am quite aware of what the standard is, Madame Defense. I was likely where you are now when that standard was set," the judge said with a slight smile. "Who's next on the docket, please?"

Hawthorne was led back into the cells, where he would be released wearing his orange jumpsuit. His wife hurriedly left the courtroom to fill out the paperwork and then retrieve her husband. Mike waited a moment before standing up, walking to the heavy wooden doors, and then bowing to the judge before leaving the room, weaving his way between the drug dealers, hustlers, and petty criminals that populated the hall.

* * *

"Don't you have an office somewhere else?"

"Well, good afternoon to you, too, Crumply Pants," Amanda said, setting her cell phone down. "How'd it go in court? I'm assuming he's out?"

"Yep. Wife was there to bail him out. I wouldn't want to be a fly on the wall in the Hawthorne household this evening."

"Me either," Amanda said. "How are you doing?"

"Peachy keen. Why do you ask?" Mike said, hanging up his coat.

"Have you got a follow-up appointment with Dr Shimner-Lewis?"

"I'm not that tender a snowflake, am I?"

"We all have a breaking point, Mike," Amanda said. She looked over at the clock on the wall. "What time does Carla get in? Two?"

"As far as I know. Any word back on the autopsy?"

"Which one?"

"Both. Either," Mike said.

"Bridget's was as expected. Single bullet in the skull. Close range. No other cause of death, although we're waiting on tox."

"What, like she ODed on crack moments before her brains got blown out?"

"And nothing back on the Clayton murder from the pathologist," Amanda continued, "but I just got off the phone with the Fire Marshall."

"And?" Mike asked.

"He says the fire likely started on or near the center console of the car, likely on the passenger's side."

"That makes no sense."

"Sorry I'm late," Carla said, bursting through the doorway while peeling off her coat. "The traffic. You'd think it couldn't take more than half an hour to get from your place to here, Michael, but honestly. And what is it that makes no sense?"

"Wow," Amanda said. "Where did you get that outfit? I have *got* to pick up my game."

"Thanks, Amanda. But you've got me beat in spades when it comes to shoes," Carla said, hurrying over to her chair and turning on her computer.

"Excuse me," Mike cut in. "Police Station. Detective office. Supposedly male-dominated environment. Talking about the Fire Marshall?"

"Right. Says the fire likely started on the passenger's side of the center console."

"So our little firebug didn't torch the car?" Carla asked.

"Not according to the Fire Marshall."

"And he knows this how?" Mike asked. "Aside from being the Fire Marshall."

"The level of heat was greatest on that console," Amanda said.

"And so?" Mike asked.

"And so what Hawthorne said about Meyersen not torching the car could be true."

"But we have video of Hawthorne scrambling out of a burning car, don't we?" Carla asked.

"We do," Amanda said. "I'm going to pull up the pathologist's report and see if there's anything about Clayton's pelvis."

"Why her pelvis?" Carla asked.

"Her hip would have been the closest thing to the console. Could there have been something in it that started the fire?" Amanda wondered.

"She was pretty much burned to a crisp," Mike said. "I'm not thinking he'd have much to work with."

"You never know. Polermo is a virtuoso when it comes to this sort of thing. Let's just see if the report has been uploaded."

After a few seconds, Amanda found it.

"Jesus, I know he's a genius, but I wish he would either print or learn to write legibly."

Both Mike and Carla came around to Amanda's computer to look.

"There. On the diagram," Carla said, adjusting her glasses while pointing to a diagram of a female body lying face up. "What's that squiggly line mean?"

"I'm hoping it means he's found some irregularity on the left pelvis," Amanda said. "But hoping and knowing are two different things. Let me give him a call."

Amanda pressed a button on her phone. She had the chief coroner's phone number on speed dial.

"Hi, Doc. Amanda Black calling. Listen, I know you're…thanks. Yes, we're all still trying to come to terms with…yes. I don't know who to release the body to. Hang on."

Amanda looked over at Mike.

"Any idea who Bridget's next of kin might be?"

"No," Mike said.

"No. Sorry, but leave it with me. What I'm really calling about is something on the diagram of the Clayton autopsy report…no, just this squiggly line you've got on…oh? An irregularity? Like a birth defect or…? Oh. I see. Yes, this was the woman who was found burned in the car…. Sure, I can wait,"

Amanda looked over at Mike and Carla. "He's just pulling up the file now. Yes, I'm still here…. I've got two of my detectives here with me. Do you mind if I put you on speaker?"

Amanda set the receiver down as Mike and Carla pulled a couple of chairs up.

"Go ahead, Dr. Polermo. I've got Detectives Mike O'Shea and Carla Hageneur here with me."

"I'm sorry for your loss, Detectives," the pathologist said.

"Yeah," Mike grunted.

"Thank you, Doctor," Carla said.

"Now, about the irregularity on Lisa Clayton's left pelvis," Amanda said.

"Yes, as I'm looking at the diagram, which I'm sure you've also looking at—" Dr. Polermo said.

"Yes, we've got it here," Amanda confirmed.

"And as I'm reading in my notes, I'm seeing that the deceased's pelvis was particularly brittle on the left side."

Amanda looked at both the detectives.

"Would you say that this brittleness, as you've noted, was a pre-existing condition or…?" Amanda asked.

"Depends. Was the deceased ambulatory in life?"

"Huh?" Mike asked.

"Could she walk unassisted," the pathologist clarified.

"Absolutely," Mike said.

"Then I'm going to say that the brittleness was likely caused by the intensity of the fire being much greater on the deceased's left side than her right."

"What, exactly, does that mean?" Carla asked.

"That the fire that burned the deceased's entire body was much more intense in the pelvic region," the chief coroner clarified.

"Thank you, Dr. Polermo," Amanda said, picking up the phone while taking it off speaker.

Mike and Carla returned to their own desks.

"So what I'm hearing," Mike said once Amanda had finished her phone call, "is that the fire may actually have started inside the car, maybe in the console?"

"Or maybe on Lisa," Carla said.

"I don't think she torched herself," Mike said.

"What if she had some sort of incendiary device on her person?" Amanda asked.

"Like what?" Mike asked, frowning.

"Like bear spray," Carla said. "In her left pocket."

"Why the hell—" Mike began.

"Because men are assholes," Carla said.

"Oh shit," Mike said. "You're right. About the bear spray. Not the asshole bit."

"I think she might be right on both, but go ahead, Mike," Amanda said with a smile.

"The convenience store near the stroll sells it. There was a whole shelf of what's probably knock-off spray behind the counter. Girl there said it was their best seller."

"Knock-off?" Amanda asked. "How do you know?"

"The little aluminum spray bottles were in plastic baggies."

"I'd say that's a clue," Carla said. "Road trip, partner?"

"Hold tight," Amanda said. "If Lisa had the bear spray in her pocket, and it was the bear spray that set the car on fire, then that would mean that Lisa was left-handed and that she would have had to light the spray on fire herself. That makes no sense."

"I can pull up an old arrest file now to see if she was left-handed," Mike said, already opening the arrest app.

"Did the woman at the store say where they got that bear spray from?" Carla asked.

"eBay," Mike said, opening report after report, looking for some notation that Lisa Clayton was, in fact, left-handed.

"There's lots of off-market crap that's chockablock full of butane," Carla said. "That stuff'll blow up if you just look at it sideways."

"Here," Mike said. "Left-handed."

"Print that out for me," Amanda said, already on the phone. "I'm getting one of my guys at the office to get a tele warrant so we can seize all of that bear spray for analysis."

Chapter Thirty-Six

11:59 p.m. Monday, January 20, 2019

"There's plates in the oven for ye both," Mary-Margaret said, stopping on her way up the stairs as Mike and Carla came in the front door. "And don't forget to take Wee Phil out before ye turn in for the night, Michael."

"Thanks, Mom," Mike said, taking his coat and shoes off before going towards the kitchen, the tiny dog leading the way.

"Aren't you going to join us?" Carla asked after taking off her coat and shoes as well.

"Ach, no, luv. Look at the time. I've not got it in me," Mary-Margaret said with a sigh.

"What about a cuppa?" Carla offered. "And maybe a biscuit?"

"Ye drive a hard bargain, Missy," Mary-Margaret said with a smile as she turned and came back down the stairs.

"I know," Carla said, giving Mary-Margaret a much-needed hug. "How are you holding up?"

"I canna believe it, to be honest," Mary-Margaret said.

"None of us can, Mary-Margaret. Michael, put the kettle on."

"I see yer face is healin' up nicely," Mary-Margaret. "And I hope yer goin'—"

"Done. I gave a full statement, and charges have been laid. Not that I wanted—"

"None of us do, luv, but if we don't, aren't we just condonin' the violence?"

Mary-Margaret said, walking back into the kitchen, Carla following her.

"Well, that was my thought. Not like I wanted to announce my new self like this."

"What he did to ye has nothin' to do with ye," Mary-Margaret said sternly. "Ach, Michael. Could ye not have put the kettle on while ye were standin' by the back door? And didn't I tell ye to go out with Wee Phil, not just let him prance about on his own? He could get lost in the darkness."

"We should be so lucky," Mike muttered.

"Here," Mary-Margaret said, turning on the burner underneath the kettle before shoving the dog's leash at her son, "get out there and find Sally-next-door's dog."

"Why doesn't Sally-next-door just take her—"

"Away with ye, before someone takes him in as their own," Mary-Margaret said. "And where are yer shoes? Ye canna go out in your stockin' feet. Ach! Just when I was beginnin' to think I could go to me own house—"

"I'm sure Wee Phil—" Carla began.

"Phil! Wee Phil!" Mary-Margaret hollered out the door.

The little dog came bouncing through the kitchen and into the living room.

"Thanks be to St. Roch! Now, pull that dinner out of the oven before it's dried up on itself. And there's me kettle. Ach, Michael, go just sitcheedoon so as I can get ye lot fed and a cuppa into me before it's too far after midnight!"

Mike took a seat at the dining room table. Wee Phil jumped up on his lap and, before Mike could push him off, had snuggled in.

"A man and his dog," Carla said with a smile, bringing the plates from the oven in for them using a tea towel to prevent her fingers from getting burned. She paused after setting them down. "My god, I've turned into a 1950s housewife."

"Is that a good thing or a bad thing?" Mike said.

"It's a false construct made by lads with no real power," Mary-Margaret said as she came in carrying three mugs of tea and a plate of McVities.

"Rise up, Sister!" Carla said.

"Here we go," Mike said.

"Rise up me arse. 'Tis that sort of thinkin' that continues to permit a society to normalize any sort of violence at the hands of a man. Did ye know that our Carla had charges laid against the maggot that did this to her, Michael? I'm proud of ye, luv. Now yer lot just need to find out who killed our Bridget, God rest her soul."

"The same fucker who killed Sal," he muttered, pushing a forkful of food into his mouth.

"Michael," Carla said softly, "we don't know that."

"I'd put money on it," Mike said.

"Let's not—" Carla began.

"Let the man speak, Carla," Mary-Margaret said. "Ye seem quite sure of yerself, lad. And ye know this how?"

"Same M.O.," Mike said, shoveling another forkful into his mouth.

"Lots of people get shot in stairwells," Carla said.

"Do they now?" Mary-Margaret said, "I've only known two over the past twenty-odd years. So tell me— why do ye think it's the same lad, Michael?"

Mike paused and swallowed hard while Carla bit her lip.

"Or are the details of it all far too complex for ye to get into at the moment?" Mary-Margaret said.

"Yeah. It's complicated," Mike said, wiping his face with the back of his hand.

"Ach, Michael," his mother said softly. "Ye weren't raised in a barn. If ye need a napkin, just ask, luv."

"Sorry. I'm just…really tired. If you'll excuse me?"

Mike got up from the table with his plate.

"Just leave it, luv. I'll take them all in and put them in the dishwasher when I go to bed. Off with ye, then."

Mary-Margaret and Carla watched Mike go up the stairs.

"I think it's all been a bit too much for him," Mary-Margaret said once he was gone. "What, with his pal Ronny retirin', Marie's passin', and this horrible business with Bridget, God rest her soul. I'm worried about him, luv."

"He'll be okay, Mary-Margaret," Carla said.

"He is seein' that psychologist lady now, isn't he?"

CHAPTER THIRTY-SIX

"Yes. I think he had an appointment."

"And he's got another?"

"I don't know."

"Ach, I wish Father Brian was still around. I'd send Michael to talk to him."

Carla didn't respond.

"Do ye believe that our Bridget's death, God rest her soul, is related to that horrible thing that happened all those years ago?"

"I…" Carla faltered. "I don't know enough about the case, Mary-Margaret."

"Or do ye think me Michael's just losin' the plot?"

"No," Carla said with a smile. "I don't think he's losing anything."

"When he first started out, full of piss and vinegar back in the day, I worried that he'd get shot or something like that. And then, when it was his partner instead, I have to admit, I did thank God that it wasn't mine. And then I prayed for forgiveness for puttin' that on another mother."

"I'm sorry."

"And then I worried that he'd get himself hurt," Mary-Margaret continued. "And he did. So many times. I think God was gettin' back at me for wishin' another woman's son dead."

"You didn't wish anyone dead."

"The real reason I came to live with Michael wasn't to keep my eyes on him—although he clearly needs some mortal guidance—but to have God keep watch over him. With all his talk about not believin' and havin' no faith and all, I'm sure God's fed up with him, and I thought that if I stayed close to me son and kept my faith strong, God couldn't help but see me Michael and keep him safe while he was watchin' over me. God must know what a pure heart and good soul he has."

"I'm sure your god does," Carla said.

"But he's losin' his mind, isn't he? The stress. The losses. The drinkin'. Me lad's belfry is fillin' up with bats. I can see it," Mary-Margaret said and began to cry.

"I think we all just need a good night's sleep," Carla said. "Why don't you go on up to bed, and I'll clean up here. What is it they say? Tomorrow's another day?"

"Ach, I'm sorry," Mary-Margaret said with a sniffle. "Yer right, luv. Must just be the fatigue talkin'. Tomorrow is another day. Are ye both up early or...well, regardless, I'll have a pot of rollies on for ye both."

Mary-Margaret got up from the table and looked at the mugs and plates.

"I'll get them," Carla said. "You go on off to bed, and I'll see you in the morning."

"Ye are a godsend," Mary-Margaret said, giving Carla a hug.

Chapter Thirty-Seven

9:30 a.m. Tuesday, January 21, 2019

"Well, that didn't last long," Amanda Black said, rounding the corner into the detective office, her attaché case in one hand, cell phone still in her other.

"Our unrequited love affair?" Mike asked, winking over at Carla.

"No. That's still ongoing. And you still don't have a hope in hell," Amanda said.

"Damned," Mike said. "Now that Bridget—"

He stopped.

"Sorry," he said. "Too soon,"

"There's nothing wrong with gallows humor, Michael," Carla said, looking over her screen. "As long as you're dealing with the issues underneath."

"Thank you, Doctor Carla," Mike said. "What's going wrong now, Amanda?'

"I just got off the phone with Hawthorne's lawyer," she said.

"What's she doing calling you?" Carla asked. "Shouldn't she be calling the Crown's Office?"

"It's even more of a shitshow than ever there since...."

"So what did she have to say?" Mike said.

"The Fire Marshall's report—that even I haven't seen yet—got leaked, and now Rejeanne Carr is saying that Clayton brought her means of death with her."

"Sounds like victim blaming to me," Carla said.

"Whether it is or not, Carr is arguing that the fire was caused by the cheap shit bear spray," Amanda continued, hoisting a file out of her attaché case onto the desk.

"For fuck sake," Mike groaned.

"And that, even though her client admits that he "may have"," Amanda continued, making air quotes in front of her, "strangled Clayton a bit, the actual cause of death was the fire that was started in the car. By the bear spray that Lisa Clayton had on her person."

"But didn't the pathologist say that there wasn't any smoke in her lungs?" Carla asked.

"That was his opinion, yes," Amanda said, rifling through some documents. "But we need the tox report to confirm. And, with the backlog—"

"I'm sure you can pull some strings," Carla said.

"It's homicide that's creating the backlog. And we all have the same string to pull on," Amanda said.

"So we wait. Hawthorne's on house arrest and nothing's going to happen until all the evidence is in anyway," Mike said.

"The clock is ticking. We have exactly," Amanda said, looking at her watch before returning to her files, "ten months, twenty-seven days, and three hours to get this case to trial."

"We know Hawthorne killed her," Mike said. "We know she was dead before the car went up in flames. Don't worry about it. Carr's just trying to get under your skin.".

"Well, she's doing a good job. Maybe I should call Dr. Shimner-Lewis and make an appointment for myself," Amanda said.

"I've got one in a couple of days. You can have my time slot if you want," Mike offered.

"Thanks, but no thanks," Amanda said, yanking the receiver away from the phone on the desk as she punched in some numbers. "I've got too much on the go right now."

"Isn't that the kind of attitude that puts people on her couch to begin with?" Carla asked.

Mike and Amanda stopped what they were doing and looked at each other.

"She's new," they said in unison.

The phone on Mike's desk rang.

"Detective O'Shea, how may I make your life better?" he answered.

"Make sure he gets to that appointment," Amanda mouthed to Carla and then turned her attention to the phone call she was making. "Hey. It's Amanda Black. Can you email me a copy of..."

"Sure. Let me check my calendar, and I'll get back to you, okay, Ron?" Mike said.

"Tell him we're all thinking of him," Carla said.

"Yep. After work? Wherever you want. Okay. Talk to you then."

Mike hung up the phone and returned to his typing.

"So? How's he doing?" Carla asked.

"Dunno. Good, I guess. Marie's been cremated already, and he was just asking what day worked for me for her memorial service."

"Jesus, Mike," Amanda said, hanging up the phone. "That's huge."

"I guess. Doesn't really know anyone outside of...me...us...so it kinda makes sense that he wants to make sure I'll...we'll be there."

"We're a family," Amanda said. "And since when does it matter what works for you? He should just pick a date, and we'll be there."

"I guess," Mike said.

"What the hell is wrong with you, Mike?" Amanda asked as the cell phone on her skirt waistband began to buzz. "Detective Sergeant Black.Yes. Thanks. Great. Okay. Thank you."

Amanda shoved the phone back onto the belt on her skirt.

"Meyersen's been admitted. There's no way he can be a witness at the trial."

"We don't know that for sure, do we?" Carla said. "What if the trial isn't for another six months? He might be better by then."

"He's going to Willow Ridge Psychiatric," Amanda replied. "We're not going to be seeing him any time soon."

"Oh," Carla said.

"What if we went to speak to him now?" Mike suggested.

"Are you crazy?" Amanda said. "Sorry. Poor choice of words. But still."

"If we want to ask him anything about Malcolm Oakes, it's now or never."

"Can you give it a rest, Mike?" Amanda said. "We've already got this homicide on the go, and then Marie's memorial service, and when is Bridget's funeral going to be?"

"Really?" Mike said, his voice flat. "You're going to let info on a cop killer get buried in some insane asylum because your schedule is too busy? What the fuck is that?"

Amanda's nostrils flared as her face reddened.

"I think we need to go grab a coffee," Carla said.

"What about the guy in the cells?" Mike said.

"He won't make it to court today anyway. Let him sit. In the meantime, grab your coat. I'm buying."

* * *

"I'm driving. Get in the passenger seat and shut up," Carla ordered.

"When did everyone we work with lose their minds?" Mike said.

"They didn't. They…we…are all just stressed to the max. Have you got a steno pad with you?" she asked.

"No. I thought—"

"Never mind. I've got one in my purse. Thanks for the kit, by the way," she said.

"Where are we—"

"To talk to Meyersen at the hospital. Before they ship him out. I'll talk. You scribe. And let's not forget to bring Amanda a coffee back with us," Carla said as she squealed out of the back parking lot.

"Holy shit," Mike said, pressing his hand on the upholstery on the car's ceiling to steady himself as Carla maneuvered the car through the heavy morning traffic. "Where did you learn to drive like that?"

"I was in Traffic for three years as a cadet, remember?" Carla said.

"Great. Another fucking Traffic…man," Mike said with a sigh.

"And you're lucky for it. Now, write down any questions you want to ask

CHAPTER THIRTY-SEVEN

Meyersen."

"I thought you said you'd be asking—"

"I am, mostly because your bedside manner stinks these days. But you know the details. Write.".

"Keep your eyes on the road!" Mike said, leaning as their car swerved around the car in front.

"Jesus, Michael," Carla said. "Have you never driven with a traffic cop before?"

* * *

Even with the prepared questions, it didn't take the two detectives long to realize that, not only was Anson Meyersen likely not criminally responsible, he was also highly medicated. The presence of the hospital security officer assigned to Meyersen also didn't help create an environment conducive to a quasi-legal criminal investigation.

"I don't think he had a clue what he was saying," Mike said when he and Carla got back to the car.

"Here," Carla said, tossing him the keys. "You drive."

"What's this? The Big City Traffic Cop can't drive in normal traffic?" Mike said with a laugh.

"No," Carla said as she got into the car. "I want to go over my notes with you before we get back to the station. And you're a horrible passenger."

Mike smiled as he turned the ignition on and drove out of the police-only parking area just beyond the facility's Emerg doors.

"So what I understood from that…gibberish…was that our little fire starter met Lisa on the strip at some undisclosed time and that he's pretty sure that she's dating some guy with a huge scar on his face that may or may not be covered by a beard. Sound familiar?" Carla said, leafing through the steno pad notes.

"Yeah. And it would fit with what her father said," Mike added.

"Which is?"

"That he was pretty sure the guy Lisa was seeing was Malcolm Oakes."

"Am I the only one wondering why he wouldn't drop a dime?" Carla asked.

"Who?"

"The father," Carla said.

"Probably wasn't sure."

"Well, at the very least, it seems we now have corroborating evidence that Malcolm Oakes is in the city."

"I doubt anyone will believe Meyersen."

"We're not looking to build a case here, Michael. We just want to find Oakes. Am I correct?"

"Right," Mike said.

"My next question would be why Oakes was involved with Lisa."

"Or why was she involved with him."

"Point," Carla said. "Maybe she was pursuing him."

"Why?"

"Dunno. From what you said, she seemed to have kept pretty close tabs on everyone from the Juvenile Prostitution days, don't you think?"

"I guess."

"Maybe she just wanted to help," Carla said.

"Help who?"

"You. Help you find Malcolm," Carla said. "Hooker with the heart of gold and all of that."

"So she just had really bad luck?" Mike asked.

"Your guess is as good as mine."

"And you don't think Malcolm Oakes had anything to do with her death?"

"Directly? No," Carla said. "Indirectly, sure. But the point is: he's here. In the city. Now."

"We can get him," Mike said.

"Yes, we can," Carla said.

Chapter Thirty-Eight

"That was likely the longest coffee break on my watch," Amanda said as Mike and Carla strode into the detective office. "And where's my coffee?"

"Busted," Carla said.

"Pardon?" Amanda asked.

"We went to speak to Meyersen," Mike said, taking off his coat and hooking it on the coat rack. "Crazy as a bag of hammers."

"Didn't I just finish saying that we weren't—" Amanda began.

"I don't think we're allowed to say that anymore, Michael," Carla said, following him to the coat rack, where she hung up her own coat with much more care than Mike had his.

"You're right, Amanda," Mike said. "We should have brought back coffees. I could really use one about now."

"So what did he have to say, or should I even bother asking?" Amanda said with a sigh.

"A whole lot of nothing, except that Lisa and Malcolm Oakes were a thing, and they had been for a while," Carla said. "And you're right, Amanda. I don't think we'll be seeing that boy back in town for a long time."

"Well, *I* have some good news," Amanda said. "A couple of pieces of good news, actually."

"Going to share it?" Mike said. "Shit. Why won't this damned computer let me in the first time I put my password in?"

"Maybe because it's the wrong password?" Carla said.

"No. I use the same one every time—"

"People?" Amanda said. "Is this a thing with you two? Like herding cats. I never thought I'd say it, but I miss Ron."

"So what about your news?" Carla said.

"Well, the first part is that Johnstone has pled to manslaughter."

"What??" Mike said, almost jumping out of his seat. "It should have been second-degree murder, at least. He beat that guy to a pulp. That was no accident."

"Yep. And the prosecutor who's been working the case is dead. It would take months to bring another prosecutor up to speed so, in the name of justice—"

"And to save the Crown a few bucks, no doubt," Mike muttered. "What a farce."

"Listen, Crumply Pants, the way that trial was going, we're lucky he pled."

"I beg to disagree."

"Be that as it may," Amanda said. "And, while you two bon vivants were out gallivanting, I was looking over the video of the car going up in flames again and seeing that there's no reason why Lisa Clayton could not have gotten out."

"Except that maybe she was unconscious. Choking someone to the point of unconsciousness is a whole lot different from murdering them," Mike said.

"I'm one step ahead of you, Crumply Pants. After the update about Johnstone, I ran it past the new crown."

"There ain't no flies on you," Carla said.

"He agreed that, at the very least, we've got Hawthorne for manslaughter. If Lisa Clayton was unconscious, Hawthorne should have known that she wouldn't be able to get out of a burning car and that she would die," Amanda said. "With Meyersen going off to Willow Ridge, he's out of the picture, leaving Hawthorne holding the bag."

"Sounds like crim neg to me," Mike said.

"Luckily, you're not the prosecutor. He's willing to proceed. Whether Jordan Hawthorne strangled her to death or left her to burn, the crown is confident that he caused the death of Lisa Clayton."

"Yes!" Carla said.

Mike's cell phone rang.

"Hi, Mom," he said. "Yes, I knew it was you. Call display. What's up?"

"Be gentle with her, Michael," Carla whispered.

"Okay. I'll let everyone here know. You okay? Yeah. I'm good. Okay. I'll see you at O'Leary's later. Because I'll probably be working late. Yeah. If he's picking you up, then have him take you home. Because I'm going to be…I know. But life goes on. No, I haven't seen it. Give me the details. Okay. I'll let everyone know. And Mom? I-I love you. Okay, bye."

Carla and Amanda, who had been watching Mike, looked away once he hung up the phone.

"Funeral's been set," he said. "Thursday at 11 a.m. at St. Francis. Visitation will be at the church from 10 to 11. Reception afterwards in the church gym. The ladies in the C.W.L. make some pretty mean sandwiches."

"I'll let them know at the front desk. They'll call around," Carla said.

"Yeah," Mike said, his voice cracking.

"Where's your mom now, Mike?" Amanda asked once Carla had left the office. "She's not alone, is she?"

"She's at home, but her friend… Francis from the morgue, you know him, the technician…he's going to be taking her to O'Leary's to have a drink with some of their friends."

"Why don't you sign off early tonight? Carla can manage on her own for a couple of hours until the midnight crew comes in. I'll drop you off at O'Leary's. Carla can drive your truck home. I think your mom would want you there."

Mike looked over at the grimy windows. He imagined that he'd be asked to be a pallbearer on Thursday. *I wonder who else will be? If Ron was still here, he'd be another one. Maybe someone from the Crown's Office, and that firm she never got to. So much she never got to.*

"Will you come in and raise a pint for Bridget with us?" Mike asked.

"Well, I don't know about a pint, but I'll certainly have a glass of wine," Amanda said.

Mike began shutting down his computer.

"You know, I saw some packets of sunflower seeds when I was in the corner store the other day," he said.

"And?" Amanda said.

Mike shook his head.

"Fucking Sal."

About the Author

For almost thirty years, Desmond P. Ryan worked as a cop in the back alleys, poorly-lit laneways, and forgotten neighborhoods in Toronto, his hometown. Murder, mayhem, and harms intended to demean, shame, and haunt the victims were all in a day's work.

Whether as a beat cop or a plainclothes detective, Desmond dealt with good people who did bad things and bad people who followed their instincts. And now, as a retired detective, he writes crime fiction.

Desmond now resides in Cabbagetown, a neighborhood in Toronto. He is currently working on the next book in The Mike O'Shea Series, a police procedural series, as well as the second book in the more traditional/cozy A Pint of Trouble Series, both published by Level Best Books.

SOCIAL MEDIA HANDLES:
  @RealDesmond Ryan (Twitter)
  DesmondPRyan (Insta)
  @DesmondPRyan (YouTube)

AUTHOR WEBSITE:

http://realdesmondryan.com/

Also by Desmond P Ryan

Mike O'Shea Series:
  10-33 Assist PC (book one)
  Death Before Coffee (book two)
  Man at the Door (book three)

A Pint of Trouble Series:
  Mary-Margaret and The Case of The Lapsed Parishioner (book one)

Printed in the USA
CPSIA information can be obtained
at www.ICGtesting.com
JSHW020149240524
63322JS00001B/2